Northumbria 1461...

A thick and unyielding midnight fog had descended upon the cabalistic ruins of Mitford Castle, perched like an ancient and forgotten sentry, atop a hill in the dark wilds of Northumbria; the perfect mask for the clandestine and hastily planned gathering of the dwindling Order of the Northern Carmelites. It was a sorry state of affairs that had driven these three descendants of such important Men of God into hiding for so many years; terrified to be discovered for who they really were: the innominate guardians of a terrible secret.

Almost two centuries earlier, their ancestors, the last of the Knights Templar, were disbanded, hunted, tortured and executed by a French King for daring to try to recoup the debts owed to them by the French Royal Family. And what better way to erase your debts than to persecute the very people you owed money to? Almost each and every Templar Knight, branded heroes of their time, were captured and obliterated. But a few remained hidden; the less famous; the forgotten. The ones overlooked.

As the mists rolled through the darkness of Mitford Castle, two of the three men, wrapped in their thick woollen shawls, huddled in the protection of one of the large crumbling walls. They sheltered themselves from the dampening winds, awaiting the arrival of the third and final member of the diminishing Order. The oppressive drizzle and dankness of the Northumbrian winter night worked in their favour; reducing the risk of their shrouded meeting being witnessed by anyone else deranged enough to be out in the wilds in these hypothermic conditions. Yet still they were acutely aware of their vulnerability, and they both felt dangerously exposed.

Over the eerie wailing of the winds through the arches and holes within the derelict structures, the two men suddenly tensed as they heard the faint sound of horse's hooves over sodden ground. They prayed that this was their expected companion and not some sinister foe come to deliver what befell their warrior ancestors and end their quest in an instant.

Both John Croy and Randolph Eastmund held their breaths and tried to melt into the dark shadows as the horse and rider drew close through the moonless gloom, but as the hooded figure dismounted he walked with the unmistakable gait of Bertram Blackwater as he revealed himself to the two cowering Friars.

2

"Blackwater!" greeted John Croy, relieved at the sight of his friend, ally and fellow Friar as he brought with him the security that the other two friars felt they lacked.

"Croy my friend." growled Blackwater in his gruff voice as he approached. "And how is Hulne Priory these days?".

"It is hard times. Yet the Carmelites built my Priory to withstand such torment. I know it will stand forever more." said Croy with authority as he stood to greet his friend.

"And what of Randolph?" asked Blackwater, his eyes searching through the gloom to the other Friar who had remained quiet and shivering against the incessant weather, "What of Brinkburn Priory? Surely you are well rested?"

Eastmund managed only a weak nod, and the three made their way without instruction to the relative shelter of a small dug-out room, deeper within the ruins; perhaps an ancient dungeon, more probably the former kitchens of the time-weary citadel, either way, it was the emplacement of all their secretive meetings: a room of sorts, in as much as it had stone steps descending into it from the grassy mound it inhabited, and four ancient stone walls, but the roof had long since crumbled and was now as open to the elements as any other hole in the ground. There was however a large inglenook fireplace cut into one of the walls, large enough for the three men to shelter under, and dry enough for them to breathe life into a small fire. It was useful to them as there was no sign to passers-by, even in the inclement darkness of midnight, that there was anyone seeking shelter as no fire could be seen from the dirt road that passed close by the ruins and snaked away, following the River Wansbeck, on to what the locals called the Murderer's Path.

Eastmund removed a bag from under his thick brown woollen robe, unpacked some dry kindling and set to task making a small fire.

"What news from the Holy Island?" asked John Croy, his voice echoing from the cold walls as he faced the large bulk of Bertram Blackwater, Friar of Lindisfarne Priory; a man who was as imposing in stature as he was in the way he spoke: like a man who had fought his entire life. A man who snacked and snarled at his own words as they were spoken in a heavily gravelled Irish accent, and who bore devotion and subservience from almost all he encountered.

"Well that is why I have requested this meeting Brothers." rumbled Blackwater in his unmistakably gruff tones, as he settled himself upon a stone bench set against one of the stone walls of the ancient nook. With that, Eastmund looked up from his firelighting, eyes bursting with trepidation.

"We have been discovered?" he whispered through the licking flames and smoke.

"Not exactly." said Blackwater, trying to keep his flighty companion calm, "But the Devil is on his way." he added, finishing with an audible growl.

"What do you mean?" pressed Eastmund, his frail demeanour and outright terror enhanced by Blackwater's comparative mass.

"I have heard tell of a sect," he said, leaning forward and talking with an intensity neither friar had witnessed of their friend before, "A French Order not unlike ours, but whose aim is to remove the last remaining descendants of those of Solomon's Temple in all lands lying from here to Lord God only knows where. Their mission seems to be to wipe away any trace of Templar from the world and recover all that they had taken. They have been spotted in England. And my watchers tell me that these hunters are headed north and have already been spotted somewhere to the south of York." spat Blackwater. Eastmund's eyes were wide with fear as he looked towards Blackwater, who nodded to the smouldering fire which Eastmund had left unattended.

"But they know nothing of us. We have been wise in our shrouding of the Order." stated Croy, only his faith keeping his voice from breaking, but carrying with him a different type of dominant authority. John Croy, Grand Master of the Order of the Northern Carmelites was smaller in stature, kinder in his demeanour, yet possessed an inner strength not even Blackwater could match.

"Perhaps. But I have heard that they are led by Margaret of Anjou." said Blackwater. Both the other's brows furrowed at the sound of her name.

"So the war is finally upon us." said Eastmund gravely as he stoked the licking flames before the fire finally caught and grew to a blaze in seconds. "It was just a matter of time. And if the Wife of the King has the French and the Scots on her side, that is indeed a force to be reckoned with." he said, his voice rebounding from the small confines of the ruins. Eastmund, in comparison to the other two Friars, was a meek mouse of a man: young, fearful and timid. Yet in testing times he had shown he had strength when it was required.

"My greatest fear is that she will attack Alnwick and Bamburgh." said Blackwater, with a wretched look on his wind-battered face. "They want the castles, but I'm sure she has a more sinister plan for those of us she is hunting."

"You really think she knows?" asked Croy, removing a small metal stand and a pot from his bag and handing them to Eastmund.

"I have it on good authority that they have been seeking out and killing Templar descendants in secret as they move through the country." said Blackwater gruffly. "Our Relic is not safe. Certainly not at Hulne." he said, looking straight at John Croy.

"You mean to move it?" asked Croy with a strong tone of incredulity. "That, Bertram, is a fools errand in these uncertain times. And tell us where is safer than Hulne?"

"It would be safer hidden at my Priory." pressed Blackwater.

"Not this again!" said Croy with a sigh as he shook his head. "We strongly disagree." he said, glancing toward Eastmund who nodded in concurrence. "Lindisfarne has been taken before. Its treasure has been taken before, by Barbarians from the sea." He said with a conviction that riled his friend.

"*That* was a long time ago, and we have most certainly learned from our mistakes." uttered Blackwater, curtly. "I am defended on all sides by the tide. If the tide is not there, we can see the attackers coming from miles away. We have more than a warning bell to ring now, Croy. I have doubled my garrison on the island. The Priory is now fortified. What defence do you have at Hulne?" said Blackwater abrasively.

John Croy glared at Bertram Blackwater through the flickering gloom of their inglenook. "You fortified the Priory?" he asked, his voice heavy with uneasy skepticism.

"Yes. It was finished not two months ago. Not only that, I made arrangements for extra hidden areas to be constructed. There are now places in the Priory and surrounding lands that absolutely nobody, save I, know of." said Blackwater.

"Well, you and the workers." added Eastmund.

"Sadly the stonemason and his apprentice did not survive the harsh battering winds that happened to blow them from the walls just as the final stones were laid." said Blackwater, making the holy sign of the cross upon his head and shoulders. The other two frowned at him as he spoke and gesticulated their abhorrence at his actions. "Brothers!" hissed Blackwater, "These steps had to be taken to ensure the safe transit and storage of the Relic." he said, drowning out their protestations.

"Well they died for nothing, Blackwater." said Croy dismissively. "The Relic stays at Hulne. I will speak no more about it." he said as he rose to his feet and instinctively tied his cinture in the customary three knots, signifying poverty, chastity and obedience, as they all had done so many times before, and placed his hood atop his head.

"Sit down Croy!" boomed Blackwater with formidable threat in his voice that shocked the other two Friars into submission. "Listen to me! This is not about whose priory gets to keep our most treasured Relic! It is not about power, here. I do not even want it in my Priory, yet this is what we now must do to stop it falling into evil hands and causing untold damage!

John. Randolph. Brothers. My priory is now a fortress. She sits out in the sea on the Holy Island; unreachable or crossed by a long strait of sludge. Boats are no good with my flaming archers poised at my battlements. One archer has the ability to burn fifty ships. I have twenty archers; trained by the best. They could take out a fleet of boats *and* a charging army before they made it halfway to our walls." spoke Blackwater. "And as for its concealment, there is no better place in the land than the one I have selected." he said. "Lindisfarne is the spiritual home of St. Cuthbert, and a powerfully holy place. Older and more spiritual than Hulne and Brinkburn combined!"

"Maybe we should consider it John." sighed Randolph, weary from the bickering, as they huddled around the flames.

"It is safe at Hulne. It is hidden. None of my priests know of its existence." said Croy, desperately trying to maintain his position as Head of the Order.

"And what of Margaret and her forces?" barked Blackwater. "When they attack Alnwick, and they *will* take the

6

castle, what then of Hulne? She will control you. She will more than likely kill you, but not before she has tortured the answers out of you first, regarding the whereabouts of our Holy Relic. Can you truthfully say you could withstand that torture?"

John Croy began to protest again, yet he had no answer, and he eventually huffed and tutted his way into submission, pulling his shawl around him for warmth as the water for their drink slowly heated above the fire.

"How would we move it?" asked Eastmund.

"By cover of darkness." said Blackwater, quickly. "I will come on a routine visit to Hulne, three days from now. Randolph will arrive the following day. That evening we will retrieve the relic, and I will leave in the early hours of the morning with the relic in my possession. I will request a party of soldiers to escort me back to Lindisfarne but keep their distance from Hulne." said Blackwater.

"Well it seems like you have this all planned out." said Croy, quietly shaking his head. "You have clearly been thinking about this for a while now. But what of the key, the burner and the bell?" he added.

"And there was I thinking you had forgotten..." said Blackwater, the slightest hint of a smile on his worn and wrinkled face as he realised that his plan was coming to fruition in front of the flames.

"We would never forget." replied Croy.

"I figured Randolph here should take the key to Brinkburn. There must be somewhere you could hide such an item from harm, yes?" he asked.

Eastmund nodded. "I know of a place."

"Good. And the burner and the bell stay with you at Hulne. You keep them hidden. So, we split the items between the three priories for extra protection. We talk of this to no one, understand? Not a soul." said Blackwater, in his commanding tone.

"Very well Bertram." Said Croy with a sadness giving weight to his words. "We will move the Reliquary during this time of conflict. But when peace returns to these lands, the Relic comes home to Hulne, the seat of the Northern Carmelites for countless generations." said Croy.

"Of course." said Blackwater, as their tea was finally

ready to drink.

:

A wet and overburdened horse struggled over the rutted and muddied roads that snaked through the damp and interminable forests of Northumbria, pulling behind it a small wooden cart, atop which sat the looming form of Bertram Blackwater in his thick brown hooded robes. The sky was dry and clear, but the ground was sodden, and a frost had formed over the rocks and grasses that lined the dirt road. Blackwater was a brave man of God, but he was anxious as he wound the thirty miles of tracks between the priories of Lindisfarne and Hulne. His mind was unhelpfully pointing out all the vantage points he passed under, all the ambush areas that the Templar Hunters could use to their ill-gotten gains of murder and torture, while his vision played tricks with the shadows cast by the tall evergreen trees of beech, chestnut and pine.

He passed little in the way of traffic on the tracks that day: a few horsemen riding quickly took him by surprise at a bend in the road, but other than that there was little interference with his journey, and as night fell, and the light was all but gone, he saw the familiar sight of Hulne's thick stone walls and large wooden gates, and Bertram Blackwater breathed a relieving breath in the night air as his tension eased.

He was welcomed personally by John Croy a few minutes later as he strode through the gates and was quickly handed some hot soup and bread as he sat at one of the long wooden tables inside the priory. As the coldness of the night drew in, a handful of the younger priests scurried to him, asking how he was and also whether he had any of his famous prayer beads with him. They were quickly shoo'd away by Friar Croy before Blackwater could answer them, and they sat a while in the light of a large fire, discussing the affairs of the church, the wars in general, and of Hulne, with Blackwater suggesting changes Croy should make to improve the defence of the priory, all of which Croy agreed to and then struck from his mind: this was *his* priory, not Blackwater's, he would not be told how to run it, and he would certainly not turn this place of absolute peace into a bastion of war.

The following day, around noon, Randolph Eastmund

arrived from Brinkburn Priory. As a fearful man, he chose to travel alone and to keep off the roads, moving across country, on foot, through woodland and farmland, maintaining a steady pace, and travelling completely unnoticed.

Hulne Priory was a stunningly serene place. Perched on the edge of a small hill, with beautiful views to the south, yet masked by woodland to the north, it was a tranquil place of reflection within the walls of the settlement. Not two miles from the fortress that was Alnwick Castle, the priory had stood for over two hundred years, founded by the Carmelites – a religious group who settled in the area from Europe and North Africa, and who brought with them a secret from the holy lands.

Bertram Blackwater walked the perimeter walls of the Priory deep in thought. There was Croy and Eastmund; the only other remaining members of the secretive Order of the Northern Carmelites who had always used Hulne Priory as their stunning vista of serenity, with their main mission, on the surface, as quiet contemplation and actions to help others. Yet the *Northern* Carmelites, an unknown collection of secretive monks through the ages, never numbering more than twelve, were dedicated to hiding one of the main relics from the reign of the Crusader Knights of the Temple of Solomon, better known as the Knights Templar. This relic was hidden even from the Kings of Europe who had governed the Knights, and absolutely hidden from the Church.

When the Templars were at their height, they spanned the globe, and there were many enemies who wished to imprison, torture, kill and bribe these Warrior Priests, often to discover their secrets and the treasures they had liberated from sacred places the world over. Quite often, in these far reaches of the world, just admitting your affiliation to God, The Pope, Christianity and Catholicism was enough to warrant your death, so the Templars took to, during their initiation processes, denying God, spitting upon the cross, and, as hearsay would have it - worshipping false idols: demons, severed heads, or bizarre religious relics recovered from the Temple of Solomon.

Of course, these notions were indeed just hearsay, but *something* was recovered from that Temple all those years ago, when the Templars first started their crusades, and taken from that holy shrine in the middle east to Europe and used in the bizarre initiation ceremonies for the higher ranking and warrior members of the Templars. Aiding them in their attempts to, on the surface, denounce God and the Catholic Faith for those trying times when they are captured by the enemy and must prove their lack of faith to God.

And, once their reign came to an end in 1312, and the Order was disbanded and almost entirely wiped out, a new secret Order was established to hide this single-most sacred of all the Templar relics, protected from that day forward by the Order of the Northern Carmelites who were housed in secret in the Priory at Hulne, in Northumbria; a far and distant corner of England, where they would remain hidden.

Blackwater was joined by Croy and Eastmund as he walked the walls deep in thought. Was it really time, the first time in 150 years, to move the Reliquary and its accompanying artefacts from the seat of the Order to a tiny priory on a tide-locked island off the coast, even closer to the marauding Scots? It was a very risky move; given who was purportedly on their way to attack any day now.

And yes, if Blackwater were honest with himself, he had a burning desire to have the Relic in his possession. Having obsessed over it since the day he was initiated into the secret Order by Croy's predecessor, more out of pure intrigue than anything darker, when he had laid his eyes on the relic all those years ago, something changed within him and the image he saw had never left him, ever since remaining at the forefront of his mind, and within his dreams. He wanted to spend some time with what he had only glimpsed during a ritual all those years ago, alone, to study it and try to understand its power and its draw to holy men of the cloth, and the warrior monks who discovered it in a distant forgotten corner under the earth.

:

"Blackwater!" hissed Croy through the thick wooden door of Bertram Blackwater's quarters within the walls of Hulne Priory. But before he could even finish the words, the door opened and out stepped a fully clothed Bertram Blackwater, ready to undertake the task in hand in the dead of night.

"I am ready." he said quietly as he brushed past his fellow

Friar and Head of the Order.

"Wait, we need Randolph too." said Croy.

"Then hurry." said Blackwater stopping and waiting to allow Croy to pass him in the cramped space. Rousing Randolph Eastmund took a little longer than it had Blackwater, but soon the three were shuffling along a dark and cold stone corridor, down steps and out into the chilly night air of the cloistered yard.

Croy walked on and lead them across the courtyard and through an arched alleyway that lead through to the rear of the priory. Once out, they hugged the wall making sure they were as hidden as they could be and headed to the northern-most point in the priory boundary walls and into a small stone shelter built against the high perimeter.

It was barely big enough for the three to fit once the small wooden door was closed behind them, extinguishing the moonlight and plunging them into darkness before their guide lit a large candle to bathe the tiny room in an orange glow, and as the two other men looked to Croy wearing expressions of confusion, Croy bent down and revealed a trap door in the stone floor from under a rough, dirty and dust-filled prayer rug, and as Blackwater and Eastmund shared a brief glance to one another, he opened it, and stepped down into darkness. Once all three were down and inside, he used the candle to light a much larger torch that transformed the dark hole into a long light-bathed tunnel. Croy lead them along a narrow and low passageway that seemed to stretch for miles, before he stopped and turned to face his two followers.

"We are now back underneath the priory." whispered Croy. "Follow me closely, these tunnels can be very disorientating."

They walked forward, hunched against the low ceilings, and twisting each and every way, already forgetting their route back, until they followed Croy to a dead end, a wall of stone.

"Are we lost Croy?" hissed Blackwater, the stoop he was forced to make as they hurried through the gloom made his shoulders and back begin to ache.

"Not at all." said Croy giving a small smile in the glow of the flames as he pulled several of the large stones out from the wall revealing yet another chamber beyond. And then, in the torchlight, he pulled out a large golden casket, dulled with age and dust, yet still shining enough to reflect the flickering flames of their light source. And alongside this wondrous casket, he pulled out two smaller wooden chests, which he appeared to take a while to identify in the tight confines of the tiny space, but eventually he handed one wooden box to Blackwater, who turned and handed it to Eastmund. Croy then placed the other back behind the wall, and replaced the stones, one by one, until there was only a wall in front of the three friars. Blackwater then motioned for Croy to slide the large casket towards him, which he did, and the three men began to slowly shuffle their way back through the maze of tunnels: their dangerous mission almost complete.

The casket was heavy and Blackwater was struggling to carry it on his own, especially as he had to maintain his stooped shuffle throughout the subterranean passageways; his lower back not used to such pressures and weight, meaning he was aching, sweating and panting by the time they reached the steps to the trapdoor.

When they climbed the steps and finally made it back through the small opening into the fresh coldness of the tiny room, Croy hissed for them to wait as his breath steamed tendrils of mist in front of his face.

"This is the hard part Brothers." he said, his hushed tones in the darkness amplified by the close proximity of the walls. "We must get the casket out of the priory without being seen by the night watchman. I have a plan. Stay here for a moment, then look to the main gates opposite. Once you see a lit torch by the gates, exit through the rear gate behind you, and follow the walls around to the front. Meanwhile I will relieve the watchman of his duties and send him inside for some soup and extra sleep, and I will take his place – I often do this when I cannot sleep so he will not suspect." said Croy. "When I light the torch, you go."

Then he turned to Blackwater. "Good luck and safe journey Brother." said Croy. "You keep our sacred relic safe and hidden during these times. I do not want to know where it is until this time of unsettling war is over." he said and patted Blackwater on the back, receiving a nod and a pat in return.

"Eastmund, same for the key. You keep it safe, for without it, there can be no relic." said Croy. "And as for the burner and the bell, you know they will remain hidden. No one here knows of the tunnels save I." he said, knowing fine well the importance of his two insignificant looking artefacts, as he left the other two men inside the small room in silent contemplation.

:

The sun's orange glow illuminated the very top of Lindisfarne Priory's north tower as it rose above the Northumbrian horizon and bathed light onto the exposed low-tide sands. The guard glanced at the fiery sky for a moment as the dazzlingly rich orange rays blew fire into the clouds, but as he marvelled at the sheer beauty of the morning, he once again surveyed the landscape in front of him where the light was beginning to paint the distant shores. He spotted movement on the mainland, which focussed his senses and he instinctively reached for a long arrow and his bow.

As he watched, he saw the familiar sign of Friar Blackwater's horse and cart reveal itself, flanked either side by a small group of armed guards making their way slowly towards the priory. The tower guardsman replaced his arrow and laid his bow aside as he returned to his lazy state of sunrise admiration and tooth picking on a warm Northumbrian morning.

The closer Bertram Blackwater got to his priory, the more his uneasiness waned, until, as the cart's wheels hit solid ground again after the wet sand of the causeway, he could finally relax and reward himself for all the hard effort that had gone into making the priory ready for what was to suddenly become its greatest treasure.

He dismissed his exhausted armed guard, thanking them for their loyalty and support, and as they marched wearily through the gates and carried on into the fortified section of the priory they used as their garrison, Blackwater turned his cart right and headed diagonally across the courtyard towards his own private lodgings. Once there, he uncoupled his tired horse from the cart, handed it to one of the attentive young monks, and backed his wooden cart under a covered siding that adjoined his lodgings.

They had trekked through the night and all of the following day to get back to Lindisfarne, and had then had to wait hours for the tides to subside before they could cross. He was beyond tired, yet his excitement, coupled with fear had kept him alert during the long trek back to safety. But he couldn't leave the reliquary unattended, so busied himself cleaning his cart and seeing to nothing in particular, until he felt he could sneak the golden casket into his lodgings without being seen by anyone.

It was proving difficult. There were a lot of people milling around, busying themselves with their early morning tasks; refreshed and alert, and of course the constant questions from three days of his absence meant Blackwater was rarely alone, but eventually, there was a quiet period that allowed him to quickly carry it through his door, covered by a blanket, and he breathed a sigh of relief as he finally had the reliquary to himself, not that he could actually open it, as the key was still sealed within the box now in the possession of Friar Eastmund and safe under the protection of Brinkburn Priory, and the other relics were still lodged within Hulne. But it mattered not; he had the golden casket containing the relic that the Northern Carmelites had protected for so long.

He sat in his sanctum of safety; door firmly bolted, and by the light and warmth of his small fire, he began to polish the golden casket back to all its glorious and dazzling splendour. It took him most of the day, and he missed several of his other duties, shouting through the locked door that he was tired, sick, sleeping, washing and could not come out.

That evening, he remained sat on a rug; his exhaustion leading to delirium, but now with a gleaming casket in front of him once again, after so many years. But this time it was *his*. It was to be interred in *his* priory forevermore. If Croy wanted it back, he would have to take it by force. The secretive Seat of the Northern Carmelites was no longer Hulne Priory, but the Holy Island of Lindisfarne. Times had changed. He now considered himself the Head of the Order. The Grandmaster of the Northern Carmelites – the Protectors of the Templar Relic – and he would hide that which the Templars relied so highly on, and guard it in secret for the rest of his life.

:

It had been dark for hours, and the bell of St. Mary's Church struck thee times. Bertram Blackwater was satisfied that the rest of the inhabitants of the Priory were in their slumber. The

14

only people who should be awake were the Bellringer, who had to remain within the church, and the Tower Guard, who should have their sights directed towards the shoreline of mainland Northumbria, and not over the courtyard of the Priory behind them.

It was a slightly risky move, but Blackwater ruled the Priory with a rod of iron when it came to getting things done and all the inhabitants, the garrison of soldiers included, knew not to question Blackwater's motives on anything, nor did they know what he was up to a lot of the time. His large stature and gruff Irish demeanour made him an imposing figure, and he governed respect wherever he went, and in comparison to the timid Randolph Eastmund, and even John Croy, Blackwater was by far the most feared.

With only his knowledge of his surroundings to light his way, he hurried across the dark courtyard carrying the most secret and important of items that should be known and revered the world over, like a thief in the night, with only the very final stage of his lengthy plan to complete. There was only really one place in the Priory he could use to hide the large relic, and it was somewhere that had been forgotten for nearly 800 years.

Present day Northumberland, United Kingdom...

CHAPTER 1

"Can I see it?"

"See what?"

"The hand."

"You mean *my* hand?" asked Curtis.

"Yeah... sorry... your hand, can I see it?" asked the girl.

Curtis Craxford, owner and curator of Craxford Museum in Northumberland had unwittingly become somewhat of a cult icon amongst conspiracy theorists and student occultists after he publicised and exhibited his experiences in the Jungles of the Amazon Rainforest several years earlier, after discovering what he labelled as a cursed object: a strange blue stone that seemed to control nature and bring forth danger and disaster to its chosen recipient, as well as visions of a demonic white faced woman in black who he seemed to battle with within his own mind, causing the odd effect of fusing his hand closed around the stone itself. But after succeeding in releasing himself from the stone's clutches, with the help of a jungle shaman, he failed to recover it and bring it home; leaving it where it fell, to protect both himself and his friends, so his grand exhibition was left missing it's centrepiece, causing derision and mockery amongst his peers and the press, but wonderment and intrigue from a rather odd and excitable fringe of society.

His story was taken on by believers of the paranormal and the followers of the occult, and they flocked to this small museum from all over the world to see what they utterly believed as truth and the closest to actual proof of the paranormal than they were going to find elsewhere. And every single one of the visitors wanted to meet the man himself: the hero of the day, and the bringer of evidence to the argument for all things unexplained.

Curtis was very selective over who he let inspect his hand after the ordeal in the Jungle, as most of the people who asked were more odd than the happenings he experienced in South America, but this was a very attractive, alternative-looking student in her early 20s with a pierced septum and bright green hair, wearing very short denim shorts that revealed a large Harry Potter tattoo on her left thigh. He figured he'd take a gamble on this one. So, he held out his hand, somewhat gingerly.

The young girl took it in hers and studied it closely. Then

she looked straight at Curtis who suddenly felt his personal space invaded by a strikingly pretty girl who wasn't his fiancee, and he found himself unsure where to look: maintaining eye contact in such close proximity made him feel like he was engaging in something he shouldn't; looking down simply drew his eyes to the young girl's cleavage, and looking up made him seem like he was raising his eyes in hindrance. The young student, however, could see he was slightly uncomfortable, so she let go, just as Naomi, Curtis' fiancee, walked around the corner to see the girl asking questions.

Naomi had rescued Curtis from these conversations at least once a day since the exhibition on the Amazon had made the national headlines almost three years ago, and ticket sales had gone through the stratosphere ever since; they had even been asked to write a book about their experiences; a *guaranteed* best seller.

This permanent exhibition, much like his unfinished book, the working title of which Curtis had called '*That time I got stoned'*, included the entire story of Curtis and Naomi's trip to the Amazon Rainforest on what started out as a bizarre treasure hunt set by an Aristocratic acquaintance of Colonel Percy Fawcett, the man who famously disappeared whist searching for the Lost City of Z back in 1925, and talked of a cursed stone and a 'path of the spider'. Of course, other than a few photographs, a baboon skull and some tribal jewellery, they didn't have a huge amount of evidence to back up their story, causing many critics to deem it to be purely fantasy on the parts of the museum owners to profit on publicity, but the Craxfords had reluctantly managed to gain their rather substantial cult following, meaning that their museum was suddenly frequented by more than their fair share of lunatics, conspiracy theorists, ghost hunters, spiritualists, occultists, hippies, religious fanatics and down-right morons.

And Curtis was a little sick of consistently having to dodge the public in his own museum during opening hours. He had become an unwitting celebrity, much to his embarrassment, and many of the more eccentric patrons asked for him personally to talk about his ordeals and ask him the same questions the other hundreds of eccentrics had asked over the previous weeks and months.

And this day appeared to be no different. In fact, given

that it was a Wednesday, it seemed a lot busier than it should be, with teams of odd people pouring over the large foam-boards of various maps and photographs that lined the walls of the exhibition space, interspersed with glass cabinets of insects and specimens from the Amazon, some of the tribal jewellery and artefacts that the group had collected during their time there. And of course the two centrepieces of the exhibition: an unnervingly identical replica of the accursed stone, and opposite, the pair of beetles that were new to science and named after both Fletcher Grunyard-Jones – the contemporary of Colonel Fawcett and the creator of the elaborate treasure hunt, and Naomi Ashcroft - Curtis' Fiancee.

Curtis had such a full diary these days, from a surprising abundance of press interviews and many other business matters concerning the museum, he was never far from his office down in the basement of the Victorian building, but one errand towards the end of that particular afternoon meant he had to once again, pass through the public sections of the museum during open hours and he braced himself for what was coming.

As he opened a side-door marked 'staff only' and briefly surveyed the room, he spotted a man immediately, who he could tell had been waiting for this opportunity; who was standing by a taxidermy specimen of a Chestnut Eared Aracari, but looking straight at the doorway, and whose eyebrows raised at his sudden arrival. *They always stand there, why do they always stand there?,* thought Curtis to himself as he tried not to meet the middle-aged man's steely gaze and walk around the perimeter of the room. But the man was now walking quickly to cut him off before he could reach the opposite doorway, and it was inevitable that an exchange was to happen. Curtis braced himself.

"Excuse me, Mr. Craxford?" asked the man. He had wiry grey hair pulled back into an impressive pony-tail, wore an olive fishing waistcoat, shorts and large boots, and carried over his shoulder a camera bag, no doubt full of lenses and cleaning cloths; perhaps a comic book and some painted war figures. He seemed just the sort of person that Curtis would avoid at all costs, but this time he'd have to respond.

"Er, yes?" he said, glancing at his watch in an attempt to signify that he was already late for something.

"I wondered if I could have a moment of your time?" He

19

had a very intense stare that both intrigued and intimidated Curtis – he was not like the meek and awkward people who he usually interacted with at the museum.

"I can't really chat at the moment, sir." said Curtis as politely as possible.

"Is there somewhere private we could go? Literally five minutes of your time, that's all I ask." insisted the man, ignoring Curtis' response. It appeared that he had something important to pass on, however Curtis knew this was about the stone, and he knew that what this man thought he had to offer or ask was no where near as important as he thought.

"No. Not really, I'm afraid I'm already late for another meeting. If it is regarding the press or an interview, or some photographs, I'd be happy to do one, but you would have to book it through the museum I'm afraid." said Curtis.

"I'm not from the press." said the man, and he glanced around the room to see who was listening, then gently took Curtis by the arm and ushered him into the corner a few feet away. "I have recently unearthed, quite literally, some information regarding a Northumbrian relic that appears to have had a similar dark past to your stone."

"What?" asked Curtis, his brow furrowed, not only at the unexpected information, but the fact he had been grabbed and physically pushed into a corner by this man.

"I am a detectorist, Mr. Craxford," said the man, with an intensity which had Curtis on edge, although he could have guessed the man's profession a mile off, "and so far in my career I have managed to unearth a a sword, a few coins and belt buckles, the odd bit of shot, but I may have hit the jackpot with this one. It's just a small piece of parchment in a tube, but if my translation is correct, it may be a treasure map to a relic from the Knights Templar."

Curtis' body language changed instantly as he gave him a doubtful look with a raised eyebrow as the man's intensity seemed to drain from the conversation. "You think you've found the Holy Grail?" he added with a slightly sarcastic tone.

"I don't believe it is the holy grail, but I do think it's a significant relic brought back from the Holy Land by the Templar Knights on their sacking of the Temple of Solomon." said the man.

20

"Oh right, you're actually serious." said Curtis, who had little time for the people who had come to him on numerous occasions with fanciful ideas around either treasure maps or cursed objects. Nothing would ever come close to what Curtis had experienced in the jungle, and nothing over the past few years that he had been shown had been proved to be anything but a hoax, a misconception, or simply a lunatic with an overly complex theory surrounding a normal object. And as for items linked to the Knights Templar or the holy grail, he was very sceptical.

"Can I show you?" asked the man.

"Look..." Curtis held out his hand waiting for the man to introduce himself.

"Stuart Cassidy." said the man, a little gruffly from Curtis' dismissive attitude.

"Stuart, I have so many people coming to me with treasure maps and cursed objects they want me to look at I'd be working 24 hours a day if I entertained them all." said Curtis, perhaps exaggerating a little. "What makes you think that this is linked to a Holy Relic and not just a hoax piece of paper buried in the ground?"

"Several things. Please, let me show you." insisted Cassidy, deadly serious and intensely convincing.

Curtis sighed, looked at his watch again just to put the point across that he was venturing very far out of his way on this occasion, and eventually agreed. Secretly, he was a little intrigued, and the meeting he was missing was just a trip to the local Starbucks to order a high-calorie hot chocolate.

"Ok. Fifteen minutes and then I must be going." said Curtis, ushering Stuart Cassidy back through the 'staff-only' door he came through.

When down in his old office replete with oak panelling and walls of books, sat either side of his father's large partner desk – he still didn't consider it his, despite his father having retired from the museum over ten years ago – the desk where he sat as he discovered the parchment written by Fletcher Grunyard-Jones almost three years earlier, he sat back in the chesterfield desk chair and looked at Cassidy, waiting for him to explain what he had.

"So, what's this all about then?" asked Curtis.

"Right, I was out metal detecting in Budle Bay, near

Bamburgh, in a field I have permission to detect on, and found this." he said, taking his camera bag, placing it on the desk and removing a Tupperware container.

This felt eerily familiar to Curtis, who remembered an elderly lady sitting right where Cassidy was, handing him a boxed insect that revealed the parchment that sent him half way around the world to recover something that tried to kill him on several different occasions.

Cassidy lifted the lid, removed some cotton wool, and picked out a tarnished, heavily oxidised and verdigris cylindrical item. He handed it to Curtis.

"This was recovered from about a foot and a half of topsoil. I think it is probably 15th Century looking at the markings. Bronze I think." said Cassidy.

Curtis carefully turned it over in his hands. It looked old. It would sit well in the museum if nothing else, although he doubted this Cassidy fellow would donate it. It was greened with age, which meant it certainly had a high copper content, and carried on its sides a delicate pattern that was hard to make out with its age, but Curtis could see some crosses and patterns that he slightly recognised from the local history section of Craxford Museum, and it did coincide with other items recovered from that era.

"Now, that as a standalone piece is pretty special, you must agree?" said Cassidy, beaming a disarming twinkling smile across the desk at 'the famous Curtis Craxford', who, much to Cassidy's delight, nodded his head enthusiastically as he looked at the artefact.

"But, if you very carefully and gently apply pressure to the top two swirl patterns..." instructed Cassidy. Curtis, as gently as he dared, applied equal pressure on both sides of the purported 500-year-old object, felt a faint click, and to his surprise up popped the lid of the metallic cylinder. This shocked Curtis, and a jolt of excitement shot through his body.

"Oh wow!" said Curtis, now fully engaged and hooked on this man's story.

"You ain't seen nothing yet." said Cassidy. "There's a piece of parchment inside. Do you have any tweezers? And white gloves for handling it ideally?" he asked.

22

"Yes I do." said Curtis, fishing in his desk drawer and selecting the same pair of tweezers he used with Mrs. Robinson's insect donation as a further wave of excitement coursed through his veins, he removed the parchment and laid it on the desk. Donning his white gloves and thinking about how much trouble he got into from his friend Amy when he laminated the other piece of parchment to keep it from being damaged: in hindsight a foolish and excitable move that he should have known better than to have done. "And this was found where?" he asked.

"Budle Bay," said Cassidy as Curtis pulled on his gloves, "Opposite Lindisfarne Island."

As Curtis slowly unfurled the rolled-up parchment, he saw a strange hand written, scrawled note. This was no Lindisfarne Gospel. This looked like a hastily written piece of ripped and smudged parchment; a panic visible even now through the scrawl, as someone hastily recorded their words as quickly as they could. He was a little disappointed that it wasn't another lost gospel and looked confused as he tried to read it as it seemed to be complete nonsense.

"It's written in Middle English." said Cassidy with a chuckle as he saw Curtis' furrowed brow. "Look, before I go any further, the reason I have come to you is that what is contained in this script means I need a financial backer for this project – and it is definitely a project. I need someone who can use their influence to get us into places that are not usually accessible, and someone who can turn this into a legitimate search for a historically important artefact. I need a name behind me. You are by far my first choice. Well you are my only choice really – it's either you or Tony Robinson, and I've heard he's a bit of a dick." said Cassidy.

"Right." said Curtis slowly, mulling the whole thing over in his head. "Firstly," he said eventually, "I've met Tony Robinson a couple of times and I think he's quite nice. He's Baldric for god's sake." Cassidy rolled his eyes. "Secondly, I don't think I can make any decision until we've got this properly translated."

"Ah but I have the translation here. My friend Toby is a qualified ancient language lecturer at Oxford University and he translated it for me quite easily – though I only sent him snippets at a time and jumbled the sentences around to keep it all a secret." said Cassidy.

"Right then Mr. Bond." Said Curtis jokily. "Well can I see

23

it?"

"Will you be my backer?" asked Cassidy, trying to retain a level of control in this negotiation.

"I will if I like what I read." said Curtis. Cassidy seemed to hesitate, fighting a small internal battle in his own mind as he weighed up the pros and cons of showing Curtis whatever the translation was. Curtis could see Cassidy was reluctant. "Look, if this is what you say it is Stuart, I think there's no doubt that I will back you, as long as I can be physically involved in the process, out in the field. This needs to be a joint effort of both Stuart Cassidy and The Craxford Museum. Your name will be the one used, not mine, but whatever *we* find, it is to be displayed in the Museum - not sold to rich collectors, ok?"

Cassidy thought about this for a moment. "I thought you'd say as much, agreed." he said, finally.

"Good. Now show me this bloody translation." said Curtis, smiling.

Cassidy handed him a handwritten piece of A4 paper, and Curtis began to read aloud:

The day is the twelfth of July in the year of our lord Fourteen hundred and Sixty Two.
These are quite probably the last words of Bertram Blackwater – Friar of Lindisfarne, Master of the Secret Order of the Northern Carmelites – Silent Protectors of the Templar's most powerful relic.

Word has reached me of the execution of Friar John Croy of Hulne – Keeper of the Burner and the Bell, and Grand Master of the Order of the Northern Carmelites, together with Friar Randolph Eastmund of Brinkburn – Keeper of the Key. I wouldn't believe such word, but as I write, the enemy are forming on the eastern shores of the mainland waiting to take my Priory too. I fear this is the end of the Order.

I pray to St. Cuthbert to protect me from what is about to happen – as he has protected us from the darkness. I pray to St. Cuthbert that he keep the Burner, the Bell and the Key safely hidden from the unknowing enemy as I know he will the golden casket and what therein lies forever at the Holy Island of Lindisfarne.

I wish not to die at the hands of the French Hunters but I fear that not even my faith can protect me from their relentless attack.

May this parchment find its way into the hands of the next Grand Master who will one day look to the enemy shores as I do now and not see death but peace and enlightenment, yet in short-sightedness, he may espy something different. Or may St. Cuthbert aid me in my attempt at escape, save the enemy discover my secrets and all is lost.

Curtis looked at the parchment and then up at Cassidy, who wore an intensely expectant look on his face: a face framed in grey stubble.

"This is a remarkably similar situation to what I found myself in three years ago." said Curtis across the desk, still looking at the parchment with a desire and a reluctance. "I was sat at this very desk, wearing these gloves, holding these tweezers. You were an old woman, called Mrs. Robinson, but you had identical hair." he said as Cassidy rolled his eyes. "The other parchment was, if anything, even more deranged and cryptic, but this comes a close second."

"And you acted upon that one." said Cassidy. "I think this is genuine, too."

"Have we verified any of the names on the parchment?" asked Curtis. "Do we know if a Bertram Blackwater *was* the Friar at Lindisfarne in 1462?"

"I haven't had much luck yet, but if this is indeed the 15th Century, there were a small collection of people inhabiting the Priory, usually sent from Durham, but there is little in the way of records. And this was around the time of the Wars of the Roses, so a lot of castles and Priories were fought over, ransacked, burned, looted. Records were lost. The Castles in Northumberland changed hands multiple times." Said Cassidy, clearly knowledgable on his British history.

"The Wars of the Roses? That was pretty much exactly like Game of Thrones wasn't it?" said Curtis.

"Erm, without the Dragons I suppose." said Cassidy. "When this guy talks about other Friars being executed, French Hunters and the enemy massing on the shores, I'm fairly sure that he's talking about the Lancastrian Armies." he said. "They were aided by the French."

"But what the hell has this got to do with the Knights Templar?" asked Curtis. "Surely the Templars were finished by then? I thought they were all killed in the 1300s."

"Well, yes, but some will have survived. They spanned the globe. He talks about this secret Order of the Northern Carmelites." said Cassidy.

"Where have I heard that name before?" asked Curtis with a furrowed brow, more to himself than Cassidy, as he looked around the office for inspiration, finding none.

"I've done my research: the Carmelites were a Catholic Order from the Crusader States originally and rumoured to be involved with the Templars. They spread throughout Europe and the Middle East, and, here's the exciting bit, they built Hulne Priory in Alnwick, mentioned in that parchment." he said, sitting back and smiling to Curtis.

Curtis' eyebrows raised at this information. It was all starting to come together and make sense, but what if Cassidy had just invented all this and written the parchment himself just to get some funding and fame? He seemed legitimate. Curtis sighed a large sigh. "What sort of funding are we talking about here?" he asked.

"Not much to be honest. It's more the access you'd be able to wangle with your contacts and position." said Cassidy. "I just need the museum to cover my costs really; you know, travel, bills and stuff. Plus, you may want to get yourself a metal detector if we're going to be serious about this."

"Is this your full-time job?" asked Curtis, a little alarmed.

"No, I'm a freelance photographer." said Cassidy. "I spend my weekends shooting weddings or promo shoots for people. It pays the bills usually. Just. But my passion lies in archaeology." Curtis paused for a moment, mulling everything over in his mind.

"Ok, look, I think this is worthy of pursuing, quietly at first though." said Curtis. Cassidy nodded. "Where do you want to go with it?"

"I think we need to visit Lindisfarne, Hulne and Brinkburn

Priories. Do a bit of digging, metaphorical at first!" said Cassidy holding up his hands, pre-empting Curtis' objections to attempting to dig up world heritage sites. "But, if we can convince the powers that be at these three sites, maybe they'll let us do some non-invasive detecting."

"I know Lindisfarne and Brinkburn are both owned by English Heritage. They are notoriously difficult to deal with when it comes to this sort of thing." said Curtis. "But I do have a couple of contacts in the organisation, so all is not lost there. Hulne Park, and the Priory, is owned by Alnwick Castle, and I think both are owned privately by the Duke of Northumberland, and, again, they can be a tricky bunch to deal with when it comes to granting access for research purposes." he said. "Don't get me wrong, they're a lovely bunch who run the estate, and they love a bit of Harry Potter which is a bonus, but this would be asking a lot of their world-renowned hospitality."

"But you like a challenge, right?" asked Cassidy, the glint back in his piercing blue eyes.

"I do." said Curtis. "Look, give me a few days to get a few things sorted here at the museum, and I'll make a few calls. Meanwhile, there's no harm in having a visit to Lindisfarne Priory, as simple tourists, to have a little look. What are your plans on Friday?" he asked Cassidy.

"Nothing fixed." he said with a smile.

"Right." said Curtis, flicking open the lid of his MacBook and accessing the internet. "Let's check the tide times for the crossing." he said as he tapped and clicked away opposite a very happy looking Stuart Cassidy. "Ok, great. The Causeway is open from 9am until about 3pm. Fancy a look around? I'll drive us up. I like the drive up there, it's nice." he added, always keen to stretch one of his vehicles legs.

"Sounds great." said Cassidy. "Now, will I meet you here at the museum?"

"Yes. Meet me in the car park at eight. We'll be up there for about half past nine. No tools, ok? We're just looking." said Curtis, offering his hand to his new partner in this hunt for unknown treasures.

"Great. Listen, can you keep this just between us for the foreseeable future? I'd appreciate it if you didn't go telling *anyone* what we're doing here or what I've uncovered, ok?" pressed

Cassidy, to which Curtis agreed.

CHAPTER 2

"You're doing what?" asked Naomi, laughing as she sat at the kitchen table in their charmingly eccentric house named the Old Rectory that evening. "Trying to find the Holy Grail?"

"Kind of, yeah." said Curtis, himself a little incredulous and suspicious of the meeting he had had earlier that day.

"Are you Dan Brown now?" she asked, sarcastically.

"Do you mean Robert Langdon?" asked Curtis.

"No, the guy who wrote the Da Vinci Code." said Naomi.

"Do you mean am I an author or am I the character he wrote about who searched for the Holy Grail?" asked Curtis.

"Yeah." said Naomi. Curtis simply shook his head at his fiancée.

"You're an idiot." he said, taking a large gulp of his coffee.

"Sorry, so you're going with your new friend to Holy Island on Friday to search for the Holy Grail?" she asked him.

"Yes, essentially." said Curtis through gritted teeth.

"Well I hope you find it. I bet no one's thought to look there, behind the curtains, in a heavily visited, world renowned tourist attraction." said Naomi.

"I can't help but think you're not taking me seriously." said Curtis.

"I very rarely do, darling." said Naomi, as she kissed him on the forehead and left the room.

Curtis made himself another strong coffee from the machine built into his kitchen units and he made his way up to his home office, or 'The Insect Room' as he liked to call it. As he opened the door he was met with all the familiar sights that he found so relaxing: there were the countless framed butterflies, beetles and spiders that adorned the walls, all individually framed, some set in multiple arrangements. There was his wall of books, a tall glass cabinet of interesting items that he'd found on his travels around the world – from a huge Whale Vertebrae to a Horseshoe Crab, a Spinosaur Tooth to a zipped purse made from a Toad, even the beak from a worryingly large Humbolt Squid, each with individual memories that he savoured as he looked at them. He had his desk set in the window so he could enjoy the view over the rolling south-Northumbrian hills which stretched all the way south towards Hadrian's Wall.

He fired up his iMac and opened up the Safari app. He googled the Carmelites, St. Cuthbert and Lindisfarne. He learned little about the history of the area that he didn't already know, but Cassidy was correct in what he said regarding the Carmelites and Hulne. He tried googling Northumbrian Templar Relics but drew a blank save a few oddities relating to a computer game.

He sat back in his chair and looked out of the window across the fields. *Was he about to be embroiled in a flight of fancy? Was he about to repeat the horrors of a few years ago? Or was he about to be part of an amazing discovery? It could quite easily be any of the three.*

He began to absent-mindedly turn over an ammonite fossil in his hands that had been sat on his desk as he thought about what possibilities may be found in this glorious county of England, right on his doorstep. He knew it was a county of intrigue, of magic, of stunning beauty, and of a rich and turbulent history, but could the famous Grail really be here? He doubted that very much. But the idea of finding a relic from the times of the Templar Knights is certainly a possibility, although he couldn't imagine how such a thing could remain undiscovered for so many years. And if there were other relics hidden at the other priories, this could prove to be an exciting project indeed.

This was, essentially, what Curtis lived for: aside from his eye-watering car collection, getting down and dirty, out in the field; discovering and obtaining amazing artefacts from every strange nook and corner of the world was the passion that kept him fizzing with happiness and excitement on an almost constant basis, and this newest lead had so much potential, he could hardly keep himself calm and grounded. He was an obsessive; when he became enthused about something it consumed him. He threw himself fully into his passions and very little could stand in his way, as he burned with a blue flame of excitement, and he had already offered himself to this new cause with a careless impetuosity that he knew could carry him into situations he may live to regret.

He was fidgety, and hyperactive as his head became a cocktail shaker of emotions and possibilities, all amalgamating as he allowed his mind to wander into the realms of potential discovery. He imagined a dazzling golden and gem-encrusted relic becoming the famous icon of the Craxford Museum; no longer famed for its missing cursed stone only sparking enthusiasm from the strange, but for a historically important religious artefact that drew crowds from every corner of the world.

The criticism he had received regarding the story of the stone had been savage: from peers in the museum trade, the press, and simply the opinions of the 'keyboard warriors' who had taken to social media in their droves to viciously attack he and Naomi personally regarding what they believed to be a pack of lies surrounding the incident in the jungle. The accusations bordered on the obscene, with Curtis being branded a liar; an impostor of the museum trade, only in it for fame and fortune, willing to sell his soul to the devil for the sale of a few extra tickets. He had been hounded by the press: paparazzi snaps of him climbing out of one of his sports cars, with bitter headlines linking his vast wealth to fraudulent claims of discovery and webs of lies surrounding his exploits in the rainforest of Brazil. One newspaper even accused him of faking his own wealth and reporting that both he and the Craxford Museum were in huge amounts of debt.

It had been a tough few years for Curtis and Naomi, yet the museum itself had seen an upturn in visitors and seemed to be thriving in its niche. But this new lead could turn that niche into something huge. And Curtis was about to throw himself head-first into another fanciful project. And he couldn't wait.

Friday morning arrived, and with it a pleasant blue sky and the promise of high temperatures. Curtis, always the true petrolhead, had decided to take his Alfa Romeo 4c Spider for the journey and as he pulled up in the museum's car park to see Cassidy stood by his rather battered and rusting silver VW Golf, he saw him eyeing his mode of transport for the day with a certain degree of repulsion.

"Travelling in style, are we?" said Cassidy as Curtis slowed to a stop.

"Yes, I thought this would be the best use of the entire budget." he said, opening the front of the Alfa so Cassidy could store his bag. "How else are we to get to these places?"

"Well you said yourself: keep a low profile and act like normal tourists. We're off to a great start." said Cassidy as they both chuckled before Curtis fired the Alfa into life again with a loud bark. "Does your boyfriend get to drive it too?' he added as they pulled away, the exhaust note echoing off the outer walls of the museum and drowning out the jibes coming from the passenger seat.

To Curtis, it was a wonderful drive up through the length of Northumberland, which took them the best part of an hour, and they both enjoyed passing the interesting landmarks and sharing knowledge and stories about various places as they passed by, and as they reached the famous causeway that granted them access to the island, the tide had receded just enough for the raised road to be uncovered, save a few salt-water puddles at the far side. Then it was a quick drive through the dunes and into the public carpark where they parked up, stretched their legs, and set off on foot.

"It's not what I would call comfortable." Said Cassidy as he stretched his back after sitting in the tight and hard bucket seats of the sports car.

"It's a driver's car." Said Curtis. "It's not supposed to be comfortable."

Both men walked slowly through the small village, taking their time through the balmy sea air on their way to the priory, and once there, they took in their surroundings. It really was a beautifully powerful place, especially on such a glorious morning. The columns of sandstone pointed skyward connected by tall arches and low ruinous walls. It was an impressive structure, even in its crumbling state, and both Curtis and Stuart commented on how imposing and majestic it would have been back in its glory days of old.

"The moment you see a large golden box you be sure to shout for me." said Curtis as he and Cassidy seemed to head in different directions through the priory.

"What are we even looking for?" asked Cassidy.

"Clues..." said Curtis in a theatrical tone. "If this was a Dan Brown novel, we'd be interpreting symbols."

"Do you see any symbols?" shouted Cassidy as they grew further apart within the structure.

"Nope." said Curtis. "But I do see a pub over there." he added, shielding his eyes from the rays of sunshine and looking across a stretch of grass towards a white-washed building.

"Look, let's go to the visitor centre and see if they have

any records of a Friar Blackwater." said Cassidy, joining Curtis as he looked towards the village.

"Who's that a statue of?" asked Curtis, walking off in the opposite direction towards a tall, modern-looking metal statue. He read the plaque. "It's Saint Cuthbert! It's who Blackwater did a lot of praying to while he was writing his panicked note. Apparently, this was the guy who was going to protect the golden relic from beyond the grave." he said as Cassidy arrived next to him and they both looked up at the face of the statue. "He's not that imposing, is he?"

"I doubt he was eight-foot-tall back in the day either." said Cassidy.

"Or green." added Curtis.

A short while later they both headed over to the visitor's centre after trying to interpret any symbolism or markings on the statue, before reading the plaque once more and realising the statue was installed in the year 2000 to mark the millennium.

"Do you know if there was a Friar Blackwater resident in the priory in the 1400s?" asked Cassidy to the lady in the visitor's centre once they had made their way there from the priory.

"Erm, I'm not sure sir." said the lady "I haven't heard mention of a Blackwater, but then there weren't that many records from that period regarding specific Friars. They came and went as they pleased, it seemed. You should check the Durham records." she said.

"Do you know if there was a link here between Brinkburn Priory and Hulne Priory at that time?" asked Cassidy in his intense and pressing manner, practically ignoring the first answer the woman gave.

"Well, given that they were all active priories at that time period then I suppose they were linked in that way." Said the woman. "Why?"

"Just interested." said Cassidy, nonchalantly. Curtis rolled his eyes in the background as he flicked through a photographic coffee-table book featuring Lindisfarne landmarks. "One last question," added Cassidy, "Did the French attack Lindisfarne in the 1400s?"

"The French?" asked the Woman with a degree of perplexity. "No, I don't think so, no." said the woman.

"Well aren't we doing well!" said Curtis as Cassidy came

to join him at the books.

"Well we've found a link to St. Cuthbert." said Cassidy. "At least that bit was accurate."

"So, it says here that eight-foot green Cuthbert was Bishop of Lindisfarne in 684ad." said Curtis, reading from another glossy book where he just happened to be reading that very subject. "But there have been four 'Saints' at Lindisfarne. Saint Aidan seemed to be the founder and the bringer of Christianity to Northumbria. So why not pray to him? What's so special about old Cuthby?" asked Curtis, looking to Cassidy, who shrugged. "And what about Eadfrith and Eadberht, other than their hard-to-pronounce names?"

"Should we go to the pub?" asked Cassidy, adding an abrupt change to the conversation that excited his comrade.

"Yep." replied Curtis quickly, closing the book and placing it back on the shelf.

They walked across the grass to the Crown & Anchor pub and ordered an early lunch to satiate their rumbling stomachs. They talked briefly about what they had discovered so far, but that was a remarkably short conversation. They agreed that there was going to have to be a whole lot more work involved, and possibly a good chunk of luck, before they were going to solve this thing and find the potentially world-altering relic of a forgotten era.

Their large fish and chip lunches, washed down with a local ale, two in Cassidy's case, made their energy levels drop, and they decided enough was enough on the Holy Island of Lindisfarne, and they were to head back south to the museum, but not before a stop off at Hulne Park in Alnwick, where Hulne Priory stood majestically amongst woodland and rolling hills, for a little more fact-finding.

There were no cars allowed into the private estate of the Duke of Northumberland, so they decided that a stroll through the footpaths of Hulne Park was the perfect way to work off the large lunch. After parking the Italian roadster in the town, and what turned out to be a lengthy walk, they found themselves at a high wall, with a large wooden arched doorway, flanked by two small towers: This was the impressive entrance to the ruins of Hulne Priory.

"It's locked." said Curtis, trying to get through.

"It houses the Duke of Northumberland's private shooting lodge." said Cassidy. "But a public footpath does go through it. Come on, follow me." he added.

They followed the perimeter wall around to the other side of the priory, where they found a much smaller wooden door that, when the catch was lifted, granted them access inside.

"No Picnics." said Curtis, wagging his finger at Stuart as he read a small plaque nailed to the door. "Doesn't say anything about not searching for Templar relics, so I think we're ok."

Cassidy shook his head. He wasn't sure how much more of Curtis' over-enthusiastic humour he could take. He was a man of some wit, but in small doses, whereas this Craxford chap was relentless and beginning to border on tedium, like an excitable child.

Once inside they were met with a veritable Garden of Eden on such a beautiful day. From the well-kept lawns to the creeper-covered pillars of ruined stone, the low-hanging trees to the statues of ancient Carmelite Monks praying to the walls. It truly was a beautiful place of tranquillity and reflection: an English equivalent of the overgrown temples of Angkor Wat.

"Well," said Curtis as he took it all in. "It appears, Master Baggins, that we have arrived in Rivendell." he said, as Tolkein's Elven stronghold sprang into his mind immediately. He placed a hand upon Cassidy's shoulder, "Now you can finish your book." he said, before walking away. Cassidy looked at him blankly.

"So, let me get it right," said Curtis, once Cassidy had caught him up, as he looked again at the translation he had in his pocket, "Friar Croy of Hulne, Keeper of the burner and the bell and Grand Master of the Order." he said. "I still don't really know what we're looking for."

"Anything to corroborate this parchment I guess." said Cassidy.

They began to walk slowly around the grounds, trying to take in as much as possible, without really discovering anything.

"Aha!" shouted Curtis eventually. "Look at this!" Cassidy hurried over.

"What? What have you found?" he asked.

"Laothoe Populi." said Curtis. Cassidy's brow furrowed as he looked at a large moth clinging to a recessed piece of stone shelf.

"A butterfly..." asked Cassidy, with a tone that did not indicate enthusiasm.

"A Poplar Hawkmoth." corrected Curtis. "Isn't she beautiful?"

"Nope." said Cassidy, walking away towards another part of the priory they hadn't visited. This didn't disconcert Curtis, he was used to hatred and indifference towards insects, but to him it was an enthralling encounter with one of Europe's largest moths, and a beautiful, natural piece of pure art.

"I can't see anything here." said Cassidy. "There are no plaques or information boards. I wasn't expecting any to be honest, but it would have been nice to read 'Here lies Friar Croy, A 15th Century keeper of a burner and a bell belonging to the Knights Templar." he said.

"Well that would have been nice." said Curtis.

"I think we need to do some old-school research mate. We need to get to look at old ledgers and records." said Cassidy.

"Well, we've at least had a look and familiarised ourselves with two of the locations." said Curtis. "It's all helpful. Time was not wasted here."

Cassidy agreed, and they made their way back to the town of Alnwick and headed south down the A1. Curtis dropped Cassidy back at his car in the museum car park and drove back the scenic route along the country roads to his home, The Old Rectory. As he pulled through the wrought iron gates, and followed the gravel drive through an ivy-covered archway, and through to the barn-like garage, he stored the Alfa Romeo inside the barn alongside his and Naomi's car and motorbike collection, locked up the barn and made his way to his front door – keen to see Naomi and tell her all about the things they hadn't discovered.

CHAPTER 3

"So, your new best friend; Mr. Ponytail," said Naomi, "He still thinks the Holy Grail is just around the corner?"

"We both do – well not the Holy Grail, but an item of treasure belonging to the Knights Templar." said Curtis, unable to mask his childlike fervour.

"So you keep saying." said Naomi. "Are you any further forward?" she asked.

"Well we've managed to at least prove that Saint Cuthbert was involved with Holy Island." said Curtis.

"Curtis, everyone knows that Saint Cuthbert was involved with Holy Island." said Naomi, a degree of frustration building in her voice.

"Well exactly, there's a massive green eight-foot statue dedicated to him in the middle of the Priory." said Curtis. Naomi shook her head.

"What else have you discovered?" she asked.

"Nothing yet." said Curtis, looking away. "We're both doing research, ok? Stuart is looking into anything to do with the Knights Templar in the area, and I'm trying to find out if there are any records that mention either of the three Friars that are mentioned in the parchment. We're meeting up in a week to discuss our findings."

"Oooh, how exciting!" said Naomi in mock piety. "Meanwhile, we have another exhibition to plan, and we haven't decided on what the topic is yet. And *you* still haven't cast your vote." she said.

"I haven't." said Curtis. "But the more I look into this thing with Stuart, the more I think this could be the next exhibition."

"Curtis, you haven't found anything apart from a piece of paper that, for all you know, could have been written in 1993." said Naomi. "It's not a basis for an exhibition."

"Naomi, we don't have to have the exhibition planned for another three months." said Curtis. "Give me a couple of weeks."

Naomi fixed him with a stare that said *You're wasting your time.* Curtis replied by blowing her a kiss. She followed that with what she liked to call a 'one fingered salute'.

Curtis headed upstairs to his home-office and prepared to

spend some time researching the three Friars. He figured he'd start with the internet, then, if he couldn't find what he was looking for, begin to call in some favours from his contacts.

As he sat at his desk, a steaming cup of coffee sitting in front of his keyboard so the evaporating vapours went straight up his nose meaning he lost none of the caffeine hit, he brought his iMac to life with a tap of a random button of his keyboard. He sighed, not really knowing where to start, but the moment he double clicked the Safari icon, and the familiar colourful Google logo appeared, he simply typed in the first name on his list; Friar Bertram Blackwater.

The first few entries were relating to the Dorset town of Blackwater, and its Friars over the years, none of which bore the same name as the town. Next were more obscure entries relating to the word *'Blackfriars'*, but still nothing of interest. He got excited for a moment when the name Bertram Blackwater appeared on his screen, but when he clicked the link, it took him to a boat; a 36-foot Blackwater Seastorm named 'Bertram' currently for sale for £80,000. With a tut, he skimmed through the first few pages of google before returning to the search box, a little irritated and devoid.

Frustrated, he deleted that name, and tried the second name on his list; Friar John Croy. But apart from a Scottish footballer from the late 70s, there was, again, no record of a John Croy from 15th Century Northumbria.

"Ah, howay man! Give me something!" said Curtis to his screen. He decided to attempt the third and final name on the list, without holding out much hope; Friar Randolph Eastmund. Again, nothing came back of note.

Curtis sat back in his chair and rubbed the back of his neck as he looked out over the fields outside The Old Rectory. The weather was glorious, but he was irked that he couldn't find anything out. He really wanted to bring some successful research to the table with Stuart Cassidy, who seemed like a font of local knowledge. But annoyingly, he was going to have to dig deeper.

The next step for Curtis was to send a message to his friend, Kim Ardnach, who worked in the local records office. She often helped with research projects for the museum, and likewise, the museum often furnished her with historical information if they uncovered anything new or interesting. He composed an email that outlined what he was after, and the names of the three Friars that were mentioned in the parchment, as well as the three priories they were supposedly affiliated with, without giving away what he and Cassidy had stumbled upon.

Once sent, there wasn't much more Curtis could do until he had heard back from Kim, so he decided to drive through to the Museum, and search through the archives there to see what he could uncover about the Templars in the area. He was in an excitable mood, intoxicated with the thoughts of what may be around the corner. He hadn't felt this alive since the beginnings of his adventures in the Amazon that had nearly cost him his life.

When he opened the locked key cupboard that offered him all his motoring possibilities, which would have made an exotic car dealer blush, his eyes stopped on the oldest looking key hanging on the hooks. A smile spread across his face as if remembering an old friend. He selected the key of choice with vigour, kissed Naomi goodbye, and headed out to the barn attached to the house. He opened the large white wooden doors and disappeared inside like an excited schoolboy.

A few moments later the sound of a 3-litre engine preceded the sight of Curtis driving his beloved 1956 Mercedes Gullwing out onto the red gravel of his driveway, out of his gates and away towards the museum. He didn't often choose to drive what was by far and away the most expensive part of his car collection, but when he did, he was never disappointed.

Sat in the tartan covered seat, holding the large cream steering wheel, and looking down the silver bonnet with its rises and falls, he made his way through the Northumbrian countryside towards the city, savouring every moment with this special piece of motoring history.

When he reached the museum he drove the classic Mercedes around the back of the buildings, down a wide and gentle ramp, and through an open large shutter door, opened especially for him by the warehouse foreman on Curtis' request, and he brought the car to a stop inside the museum's storage facility. Once the engine had been extinguished, he started the rather laborious process of getting out of the car. Firstly, he pulled the door handle and began the theatrical opening of the 'gullwing' door as it rose from the car upwards and came to a rest pointing towards the ceiling. He then had to hinge the steering wheel downwards allowing him to lift himself up and out of the car. It was never a graceful exit, but Curtis couldn't care less. He was still high on a rush of motoring adrenaline; driving though the centre of the city in that car always attracted attention – be it beeps from other cars, pointing and photography from the public, or just a simple smile from people as he passed them by.

As the museum's main storage facilities were firmly closed to the public, he didn't need to close the gullwing door, so he left it up and walked towards a doorway that eventually lead to his office.

But he passed his office door and carried on towards the research areas that connected the museum to the University. There were laboratories and libraries, computer facilities and endless racks and drawers of specimens and items, full of busy people in their *zone,* conducting their own research.

He entered the library and headed over to an empty computer booth. He sat opposite two students who he nodded warmly to as he selected the search box that scanned the database of all the logged information held within the buildings, but received nothing in return, so concentrated solely on the screen. He simply typed 'Templar' and pressed the enter key. Several entries came up, mostly books held within the shelves of the vast library, but there was an entry right at the end that apparently was an artefact held down in the vaults, surprisingly not far from where Curtis had parked his car. All the entry said on the database was *'Inscription believed to be Templar in origin'.*

He noted down the location code and set off once again, through the corridors of the museum, towards the storage area. He dodged a few employees that he knew would ask him questions or give him tasks to do by faking a telephone call, and he managed to make it back to his car without interruption. He passed by the classic silver arrow, stroking it as he went, and on towards location 488b, not far beyond. He found it shortly after, and selected the wooden box, a little larger than a shoe box, and carried it over to the packing table.

After a vigorous bout of prizing from the crowbar on the table, the lid opened, and Curtis read the paper packing note inside.

"Small section of carved stone tablet, believed to be

Templar in origin, found at Hartburn Grotto, January 1983 by F. Wilson."

Curtis, after an initial excitement, sighed a little. This, despite being quite exquisite, didn't really help him in the slightest. There were a few marks, a square cross and letters carved on the stone. Nothing made any sense; there were no full words, and certainly nothing that linked Holy Island, Bertram Blackwater or templar treasures.

"It's too early isn't it?" said Curtis to himself. "Blackwater came 100 years after the Templars. Back upstairs I go!" he shouted to an empty warehouse.

Curtis reattached the lid, replaced the item in the correct location and went back to the computer station in the library.

This time he typed 'Bertram Blackwater' into the search box and hit the enter button. To his delight, it returned a single entry which he clicked on instantly. It displayed an item location number together with the words '15th C Tapestry recovered from Lindisfarne'.

"Holy shhh...Island!" said Curtis, noticing the Librarian watching him with a furrowed brow, yet he smiled to himself, an excitement growing from within. The two students who were still sat opposite were viewing Curtis as if he were an intruder from a mental asylum, but he simply winked at them, jumped from his desk and practically sprinted out of the library and back again to the storage facilities in the bowels of his museum, looking for the unique location number and the item of interest.

Once found, he carried it over to the packing table and once again spent time prizing the top off the specifically built wooden crate that stored an apparent tapestry recovered from Lindisfarne.

As the top came off, Curtis could see a rolled-up piece of fabric, roughly thirty centimetres long. He carefully picked it out, unrolled it on the table and tried to take in what he saw: there was certainly a lot going on, despite its faded appearance: a central panel dominated of an image of a monk-type figure who seemed to be addressing a crowd with what looked like a castle or indeed a fortified priory behind him. There not only religious figures, but also soldiers within the crowds. Bordering the delicate panel was a border of various words that Curtis couldn't really make out, but towards the bottom of the tapestry there was the unmistakable name of 'Bertram Blackwater'.

"Yes!" shouted Curtis at the top of his lungs as he banged the desk hard with the palm of his hand, causing the warehouseman, Mick, to poke his head out of his office, banana in hand. Curtis sent him an abashed and slightly apologetic wave, and slowly and carefully wrapped the tapestry up again, placed it inside the crate, carried it over to his Mercedes Benz, and placed it into the boot, making sure he wasn't being watched. He shut the boot, took out his phone, sent a quick text, then left the museum and returned towards the country roads that took him back to his home.

The drive home was, if anything, even better than the drive in for Curtis. The Mercedes, despite being over sixty years old, still packed a punch, and Curtis always enjoyed opening up the car's ample power on one particular stretch of 'B-road' that was arrow straight for well over a mile.

"Still got it Old Man." he said as he slowed for the corner at the end of the straight; intoxicated by the rush of adrenaline, sounds, smells, and the feel of the car he was driving, and he grinned the grin of a small child.

Curtis often took a moment to reflect on just how lucky and privileged he was: inheriting his family's vast wealth carried with it more than its fair share of headaches, but it also allowed him to indulge his passions to an extent only a tiny percentage of the world had ever experienced, yet he always carried with him an internal guilt; a grinding in the pit of his stomach as he thought about those less fortunate. There he was, driving around in a piece of metal with a value that could exceed a million pounds, in one of the poorest areas of the country, whilst there were a record number of food banks and children living in poverty.

And five years ago, after one of his gut-wrenching conversations with his father regarding his spending habits, when his feelings of guilt became overwhelming to him, he had decided that the museum would hold charity events whenever possible to support as many local, national and international causes that he could, focusing on homelessness and poverty in the North-East area before anything else. Yet the further down the charitable rabbit hole he went, the worse the situation appeared to be, so he took it upon himself to donate, support and volunteer at local charity events whenever his time was free enough to do so, and it was these acts that allowed him to justify within himself his motoring and travelling exorbitances.

Both he and the Craxford Museum Foundation had raised more money than he had ever spent, and as he piloted his classic Mercedes, or his Alfa, or indeed any of his other cars and motorbikes, he thanked his lucky stars and appreciated all that he had. It was his ancestors, and their shrewd business acumen, who made it all possible.

That evening, Stuart Cassidy rang the doorbell of the Old Rectory and Curtis eagerly opened the door like a six year old seeing his best friend for the first time in at least a day.

"So this is how the other half live is it?" said Cassidy, looking into the house over Curtis' shoulder. "Quite the crib isn't it?"

"Well it certainly keeps the rain off the antiques, most of the time." said Curtis, shaking Cassidy by the hand, patting him on the shoulder and inviting him in.

"Museum curation is a hidden goldmine is it?" asked Stuart as they walked into the large and cavernous kitchen.

"Alas, no, this house is one of those that gets passed down the generations." said Curtis, who removed two bottles of Doom Bar Ale from the fridge, removed the tops, handed one to Cassidy and then clinked the bottles together before taking a long drink.

"Your kitchen is bigger than my house, including the garden. That's a nice beer." said Cassidy.

"One of my favourites." said Curtis, ignoring the slightly awkward tension between them as Cassidy took in the eccentricities of The Old Rectory.

"Why am I here then?" asked Cassidy, "Other than to drink your ale stash?"

"I've found Bertram Blackwater." said Curtis, with a raised eyebrow.

"What do you mean '*found him*'?" asked Cassidy through narrowed eyes.

"In a 15th century tapestry." said Curtis. "Stored in my museum's vaults." Cassidy's eyes narrowed even further.

"Can I see it?" he asked.

"It's on my desk next door." said Curtis. "Come on."

CHAPTER 4

"So the parchment is legitimate." said Cassidy quietly to himself as he perused the tapestry depicting Friar Blackwater.

"It appears so." said Curtis.

"This is great!" said Cassidy, beaming at Curtis.

"What's all this though?" said Curtis, pointing at the writing around the edge.

"It's middle english again." said Cassidy. "I'll have to translate it when I get home."

"Oh really? Can't you translate it here?" asked Curtis. Cassidy shook his head.

"I need my books for this." he said. "Can I take the tapestry with me tonight?"

"Sadly not, I'm afraid. I can't let it out of my sight really, it being 500 years old and part of the museum archives. But, I've done a very high resolution scan on it and have it here for you." he said, handing Cassidy a small white memory stick. "It's quite a big file, but you should have no problems seeing every single thread and whatever was living within them, in high detail should you want to." Cassidy took the memory stick but seemed a little disappointed. "I'm sorry I can't lend you the original, but you understand why, right? I shouldn't even have taken it out the museum to be honest."

"Yeah, sure, it's a piece of historical importance. I get it." said Cassidy.

"Thanks mate." said Curtis. "But the scan is, if anything, better."

The two men wandered through to Curtis' sitting room which was far bigger than the kitchen, and caused Cassidy to swear out loud as he walked in. This took Naomi by surprise, who was sitting on one of the sofas, reading a book.

"Hi." said Naomi. "You must be Stuart." she said, standing up and shaking his hand.

"Hello." said Stuart, blatantly looking Naomi up and down as she stood in front of him.

"Good. You've met." said Curtis, ushering Cassidy over to another part of the room where they sat in two armchairs where they talked and finished their beers.

"So, what's the story here, Curtis?" asked Stuart. "How are

you a multi-millionaire? Ok, so your house is inherited, but that can't just be it?"

"My family have been very successful in the past, certainly in the Victorian era, in various industries like ship building and others, and all have invested their money well.As a family we own quite a lot of shares and businesses. We've also been very lucky." said Curtis.

"Well, I can't say I'm not jealous." said Stuart. "But you're a canny lad, so I'll let you off." he said, draining his bottle of beer. "I'm going to have to go, though, I can't stay. I was just passing on my way home, and I've got some errands to run. I'll translate this when I get home." said Cassidy patting his inside pocket that contained the USB stick. "Will you be at the museum tomorrow?"

"I can be." said Curtis. "I've got some meetings in the morning but I'll be available after lunch."

"I'll have a translation for you tomorrow afternoon then."

"I really feel like we're on to something you know." said Curtis as they made their way towards the front door.

"Let's see if it turns up any clues." said Cassidy as he left the Old Rectory. "Nice car." he added, as he passed the 1950s Mercedes still parked by the front door. "How many have you got for Christ's sake?"

"A few, they are my hobby, as you know, and I'm lucky enough to be able to indulge myself."

"Clearly!" said Cassidy, as he turned and headed to his own car. "Amazing what you can afford when you don't have to pay a mortgage isn't it?"

Naomi appeared behind Curtis as he waved Cassidy off through slightly gritted teeth, and closed the door. She looked at him with a sly glance. "What have you and your boyfriend been up to then? Found the Ark of the Covenant yet?"

Curtis rolled his eyes. "I found a tapestry." he said. "In the museum archives. That may help us with information about a 15th Century Monk."

"Oooh!" said Emily. "Exciting."

Curtis suddenly laughed. "Are you jealous?"

"What? No!" said Naomi.

"You are! You're jealous!"

"What? Of you and Steven Segall? Please." said Naomi.

"Oh my god! Why?" said Curtis. "Why are you jealous?" Naomi held his gaze.

"...because I want to go on another adventure with you!" said Naomi eventually. "You're getting all enthusiastic and excited and I'm not part of it!"

"Then be part of it." he said, matter-of-factly.

"I think I should let you have your 'bromance'." she said.

"It's not a bromance, it's work." said Curtis. "And you can be part of it whenever you want."

"No, it's fine, really." said Naomi. "Have your fun, just don't shut me out. Besides, I'm not that taken with Mr. 1970s Willie Nelson anyway. The thought of going on day trips with him leaves me a little bit nauseous."

"What's wrong with him? I think he's fine!" said Curtis, a little taken a back with his fiancees hostility towards his new friend, and instantly feeling slightly defensive.

"Did you see the way he looked at me? It's just a vibe I got. He didn't really want to talk to me. I just don't think he likes women." said Naomi.

"You think he's gay?" asked Curtis.

"Noooo, that is *not* what I'm saying!" said Naomi, holding her hands up. "I think he feels threatened by women. I don't think you're in any danger, darling!" she said. Curtis shook his head at Naomi.

"Jealous..." he uttered as he walked away back to his study.

"Knob head." replied Naomi in similar utterances.

Later that evening, as Curtis was idly surfing the internet on his MacBook in front of a rather tedious episode of a hospital based documentary that Naomi was fully engulfed in, his phone vibrated in his pocket and upon viewing, it was a text message from Stuart Cassidy:

"You will not believe what this tapestry is telling us! Speak tomorrow. S."

A jolt of excitement coursed through Curtis' body once more and he sent an immediate response back to his friend:

"Come on then. Let's have a preview. I can't wait until tomorrow."

He placed his phone on the arm of the sofa with a grin, caught Naomi's glances, and changed his expression to that of a naughty child pretending nothing is happening. Her eyes narrowed with an accusatory glance, but then a moment on the television took her attention.

A few moments later, Curtis' phone once again buzzed with a notification of another text message:

"Not fully translated yet, but is basically about Friar Blackwater and his allegiance to St. Cuthbert. We've definitely found him."

Curtis read the message. "Get in!" he said.

"What?" enquired Naomi.

"Just a message from the woman-hater." said Curtis. Naomi simply shook her head.

"Tell me all tomorrow! Can't wait to see if we can solve this."

Replied Curtis, before pouring himself a large single malt from a Scottish Island and sitting back down for the evening, eager for the following day and the possibilities they may uncover.

The following morning, Curtis woke with a spring in his step and a knot of excitement in his stomach. He was due to meet Cassidy later that day, at the museum, and he set off early to make sure he had everything ready for their revealing meeting, leaving Naomi to make her own way into work shortly after. They very rarely shared a car journey into work, knowing that they would inevitably have to venture out from the museum during the day for various meetings and errands. They found it was just easier to both take their own cars, despite the carbon footprint they were leaving. Plus, they were both red-blooded petrolheads and really rather poor passengers.

He pulled his Alfa Romeo to a stop in the car park of the Craxford Museum shortly before eight thirty, and to his shock, saw Cassidy standing with his back against the wall of the museum; bag sitting on the ground next to him. Their meeting wasn't scheduled until after one.

"Stuart? Everything ok?" asked Curtis as he approached the grand front facade of the victorian stone-built building.

"I couldn't wait until this afternoon mate." he said. "There's too much to discuss."

"Wow." said Curtis once he had read the translation, two warm cups of coffee filling the office with the aromatic smells of an Ecuadorian plantation as they sat either side of the desk in Curtis' office. "Well that's definitely the proof we were after."

"I know." said Cassidy. "And who'd have thought that the answers were here, in *this* museum the whole time?"

"Well you say that but we are the local museum to the area in question so we would expect to house most of the artefacts from around here." said Curtis. "But you're right, it's still amazing."

"Well, I guess." said Cassidy. "So what do you think? It's definitely legit right?"

"Oh absolutely." said Curtis. "It's definitely 15th Century. I didn't knock it up in front of the telly last week, I promise, it's been in our vaults for over a hundred years."

"So we know that Blackwater was a Friar of Lindisfarne, and he spoke of St. Cuthbert both in my parchment and your tapestry." said Cassidy, instantly assigning ownership to both artefacts, which put Curtis slightly on edge. "I think there's irrefutable proof that my parchment is as legitimate as your tapestry." said Cassidy as Curtis nodded along to what he was saying.

"I need to read through this again." said Curtis, taking the translation and reading aloud. "Friar Bertram Blackwater of the Holy Island of Lindisfarne, the Priory, and the Church of St. Mary the Virgin. Spiritual successor of St. Cuthbert, St. Aidan, St. Eadfrith and St. Eadberht, servant of God, and Guardian of the North."

Curtis looked up at Cassidy. "Guardian of the North?" Cassidy shrugged.

"Perhaps it's a nod to the Northern Carmelites." said Cassidy. Curtis continued.

"Friar Blackwater delivers a blessing to the pilgrims of St. Cuthbert and his Island Guard in the grounds of Lindisfarne

Priory." finished Curtis, placing the translation back onto his desk and glancing back at the Tapestry that was also unfolded next to him.

"It doesn't exactly tell us anything about a secret Templar treasure though, does it." said Curtis.

"It doesn't, but it does confirm that Blackwater was a Friar, at Lindisfarne, in the 15th Century, and that he obviously bangs on about St. Cuthbert all the bloody time." said Cassidy. "Its what we call a 'golden ticket': it legitimises our whole project."

"I suppose it does. But where do we go from here?" asked Curtis.

"We go and look for clues." said Cassidy. "But proper clues. We need to start back on Holy Island."

"What about the other Friars mentioned in that parchment?" asked Curtis. "Did you get anywhere with them?"

"That was a tough research session!" said Cassidy. "I had to delve deep into the internet to find anything, but eventually I managed to get confirmation of a Friar Eastmund at Brinkburn, and the dates matched up so that was good enough for me. If two of them are authenticated I'm pretty sure that Friar Croy of Hulne is a real person too."

"Great!" said Curtis. "So what are we looking for?" he added, lost as to the next step of this journey.

"Well therein lies the question." said Cassidy. "We're looking for a hidden clue that reveals the location of a Templar artefact."

"You make it sound so simple." said Curtis sitting back in his chair and scratching the back of his head. "We need a little more of a plan than that, surely?"

"Right, look," said Cassidy, sitting forward, almost leaning over the desk towards Curtis. "What *do* we know?" he asked, counting on his fingers, "we know that Friar Blackwater apparently hid a Templar relic somewhere at Lindisfarne Priory. We know that there were two other Friars, erm, Eastmund and Croy, who were keepers of the burner and the bell, whatever they are, and the key, which I imagine grants us access to the relic. I'm still not sure what the burner and the bell have to do with anything but I'm sure that will become apparent when we find them."

"That's a bold claim given that this parchment was written in the 15th Century." said Curtis. "The odds are severely stacked against us in actually locating physical artefacts."

"So, my question to you is, have you heard about the Templar relic that *was* discovered at Lindisfarne?" asked Cassidy.

"What? No!" said Curtis, suddenly expecting some new information.

"Exactly!" said Cassidy. Curtis cottoned on to what Cassidy meant.

"Oh. Right. I see."

"Curtis I'm sure it's still there, somewhere, hidden." said Cassidy. "If we find it, it would be one of the greatest discoveries of the century."

"Yeah, I thought that about the stone I found in the Amazon but the general consensus there was that I made it all up to try to financially benefit from a superstitious story." said Curtis.

"But what evidence did you bring back with you? An injured hand and some photographs of a rock." said Cassidy. "And for the record I totally believe your story! I have had strange experiences. I know that there are things in this world that cannot be explained, and I know that there are a shed-load of things that are covered up, just look at chemtrails, nine eleven, Roswell, the stuff they find in places like Antarctica for god's sake! But that is a story for another time, right now we have to get to the bottom of this mystery."

"Maybe we should go to Lindisfarne Priory again then." said Curtis, keen to steer Cassidy away from a rant about conspiracy theories.

"Yes that's exactly what we have to do." said Cassidy. "We have to get into the mind of a 15th Century monk who wanted to hide a big box for millennia."

Curtis' eyes narrowed as he stared into the middle distance while he tried to recall something in his mind.

"What is it?" asked Cassidy.

"I remember reading somewhere about a pilgrimage to St. Cuthbert where people walk across the sands at low tide to the priory from the mainland. Seemed like a bunch of god-bothering hippy claptrap to me, but maybe we should do it. Get a bit *method* about it all."

"I like that idea." said Cassidy. "He seemed obsessed with St. Cuthbert, so I guess it's fitting."

"Right, lets give it a go, see what we can find." said Curtis.

"When can we start?"

"I can spare a day this week." said Curtis.

"Great. Let's do Thursday, if we can." said Cassidy, rising from the desk and popping his shoulder bag on.

"Ok, I'll check the tide times and get back to you on a time." said Curtis. "Hopefully we can get this thing licked."

CHAPTER 5

Curtis and Stuart stood on the mainland of the Northumbrian Coast, at Beal, in the very spot where the parchment was discovered by Cassidy, looking out towards the Holy Island of Lindisfarne, with the arenaceous straits between them and the ancient Priory.

It was a bright but blustery day, and as the wind buffeted the two men, they set off directly towards the island.

"So this is called the 'Pilgrim's Crossing' right?" asked Curtis.

"Yeah, you see those wooden poles?" asked Cassidy, pointing his hiking stick towards a line of marker posts standing about 10 feet high and roughly 30 feet apart, stretching away in front of them.

"I do." said Curtis. "They're hard to miss."

"Well, until the road was built in the 1950's, this was the route the pilgrims took." said Cassidy. "It's 3 miles. Should take us a couple of hours at the most, as it can be slow going. But people have walked this route for thirteen hundred years."

That statistic impressed Curtis, and he soaked in the atmosphere of the primal coastline as they left the solid ground of the rocky beach and began to walk onto the wet sands, following the route of the ancient marker posts.

"You know, there is another thing about this place that I've been researching," said Curtis as they walked side by side, maintaining a steady pace. "There are these things called 'St. Cuthbert's Beads' that can be found on the sand here at low tide. They're actually fossils, of something called Crinoids, which are like a sea anemone type thing. Anyway, they look like beads with a star-shaped hole in the middle, and were originally strung together by the ancient monks to make Rosary Beads." he said. "I'd like, if nothing else today, to find at least one of those."

"Well, let's hope we find a whole lot more than that." said Cassidy.

They were making good progress, and were more than two thirds of the way across. Curtis had been spending a lot of time staring at his feet, seeking out anything that he thought looked like a round bead or coin, but so far he had not found any fossils.

He was not only getting a little frustrated, as Curtis always did in these situations, but he was also getting a bit of a stiff neck.

They were almost at the rocky shores of the island, and the familiar sight of the ruined priory was just beginning to come into the fore. Less than one hundred yards from the grass and rock of Lindisfarne, Curtis stopped dead and dropped to his knees.

"Oops! You alright?" asked Cassidy, hurrying over and offering to help Curtis up.

"I found one!" he shouted, a little loud for Cassidy was now leaning over with his head close to Curtis'.

As he stood up he rubbed the sand off and held it up on the palm of his hand for them both to study. It was roughly the size of a five pence piece, only thicker, and of a brownish sandstone colour. There was, indeed, a perfect star shaped centre hole, now filled with ancient sediment, and surrounded by fossilised lines spreading out to the edges.

"What a beautiful little thing." said Curtis.

"I kind of want one too." said Cassidy.

"I'm sure we'll find more." said Curtis, quickly pocketing his find and searching the ground in front of him.

They ambled about for a further ten minutes and Curtis managed to find one other, but it was a third of the size of the first one, and Cassidy refused it.

"Right come on, we need to do some detective work, not play on the beach." said Cassidy, eventually, and Curtis could detect a hint of frustration in his voice. But he had his bead, so he was happy to carry on to the priory and search for more clues that he secretly knew were going to be virtually impossible to find.

When they made it into the interior of the ruins, and had gulped down some water from their packs, they began to walk the perimeter walls, looking for any markings to see whether they could be interpreted or linked to the parchment or the tapestry, which Curtis had on his iPad in ultra high resolution.

"This is a long shot mind, given the state of the place." Said Curtis as they walked, more to himself than Cassidy, as he came to the sudden realisation of the condition the wind-beaten and ancient ruins they were in.

They scrutinized as much of the stonework, both on the interior and the exterior of the ruins, as they could for what felt like hours and hours. They looked closely at every hollow, every dirt floor they could find, and tried to imagine where they would attempt to hide what was probably a very large metal chest. There were a few marks here and there on the sandstone, and some inscriptions that Curtis photographed meticulously, but none felt like they were clues to hidden Templar treasures.

After making the mistake, once again, of eating too much lunch, washed down, on Curtis' insistence, with a pint of ale each, their initial excitement waned as the wind picked up and blew a cold air through their bodies as they resumed their search.

"What about over there?" asked Curtis, pointing along the coast line towards the other stand-out structure on the island of Lindisfarne: The Castle that was built on the highest hill on the small island.

"Nah, that didn't come along until the middle of the 16th Century. They built the fort when the Priory fell into ruin, and used most of the stone from here to build that." he said, pointing with his head.

"And they didn't uncover any golden caskets you think?" asked Curtis.

"I think we'd all have heard about it." said Cassidy.

"Damn it."said Curtis, huffing as a gust of wind blew him slightly off balance.

"I think we're flogging a dead horse here mate." Said Cassidy eventually.

"Yeah I think you're right." Said Curtis. "There's nothing here. And to be honest, if there is, they're not making it easy for us." he said, dejectedly.

"I think we should head back to the museum and have a proper debrief over a coffee and that tapestry, the actual one I mean, and see if we've missed anything. If the monks were anything like the Templars they claim to be descended from, there should be subtle symbology and iconography that spill secrets to eyes trained to see them. I'm not ready to admit defeat quite yet." Said Cassidy, patting Curtis on the back.

"You've been watching too much Discovery Channel." said Curtis as he looked out over the sandy straits and noticed that the tide was making its way back towards the shoreline. "We need to head off anyway if we're planning on going back the way we came." He said, pointing with his head towards the water.

"Ooh, crikey, yes." said Cassidy, knowing too well how easy it was to get stranded on this tide-locked island.

Towards the end of their fairly arduous walk back into a strong headwind that sand-blasted their exposed skin as they went, they were caught by another couple of pilgrims who were making the journey back to the mainland: two men, both of whom seemed to be dressed entirely wrong for the task in hand. Where Curtis and Stuart were dressed in walking attire and waterproofs, these chaps sported chinos, shirts and jumpers.

They began to make small talk as they went, about how tough this journey must have been for barefoot monks wearing their robes with this whistling wind blowing underneath them.

"So what brings you here today?" asked one of the walkers in a rather upper class accent, oozing with privilege, a private education, and most probably a right leaning voting habit.

"We're researching something on the island." Said Curtis.

"Oh right!" said the walker, a tall balding man wearing a bright red scarf under a long black overcoat. "What are you researching?"

"It's highly confidential!" said Cassidy, a little wild and hysterical before Curtis had the chance to open his mouth again.

"Understood." Said the walker, holding his hands up in mock surrender immediately.

"What about you?" asked Curtis, trying to steer the conversation down a different path. "Why are you here today?"

"Oh, we walk the Pilgrim's Path every year. It's a bit of a tradition of ours; walking over the sands, touring the priory, fish and chips in the Crown and Anchor, a walk up to the castle and then, if the tide allows, we have a quick pop over to St. Cuthbert's Island, and then head back to the mainland." Said the walker, happily.

Curtis stopped dead. And Cassidy was almost identical in his own reaction. They both stood and looked at the man, who carried on a little with his companion, before turning and looking back at the two researchers. "What?" asked the man.

Curtis shot Cassidy a glance, looked back at the tide slithering its way across the sands towards them, and then turned to the man in the red scarf.

"St. Cuthbert's Island?" he pressed.

"Yeah, you know! Where he lived out his days as a

recluse." Said the man.

Again, Curtis and Cassidy shared a glance. "Where is this island" asked Cassidy. "I can't believe I've never heard of it."

"Neither can I, it's plastered all over the visitor's centre!" said the man, chuckling to his friend.

"Did he have a house on the island?" asked Curtis.

"Well, after a fashion." said the man. "It's a rather small dwelling; more of a hovel I'd say."

"Where is it?" asked Cassidy, again.

"It's just over there!" said the man, pointing back over the sands, now submerged in a few inches of salt water, towards the Priory. And sure enough, cut off from the main island already by the ripping tide, was a tiny island, no more than a grassy hillock, marked with a wooden cross atop its small crest, looking even more isolated and desolate than Lindisfarne itself.

"Interesting." Said Curtis to Cassidy, as they looked back towards the island; frustratingly now cut off until the tide, once again would recede, the following day at the earliest. It was so unassuming and insignificant that both Curtis and Stuart Cassidy had dismissed it as purely a mound of grass-topped sand on the landscape and no more. They had both seen the wooden cross many times and never given it a moment's thought, assuming it was simply a decorative beacon of christianity.

"Anyway, we should be getting back, Stuart." Said Curtis as they motioned onwards towards the shores of Mainland Northumberland. The two other men continued to walk with them, as they talked about the St. Cuthbert's Beads that Curtis had found, and how both the other walkers had tins and tins of them back home, but both Curtis' and Stuart's minds were awash with possibilities on learning the facts handed to them by the two unassuming people that had happened upon by chance.

When they reached Curtis' car, the Alfa Romeo he so coveted, they waved goodbye to their saviour in the red scarf who had possibly just told them the golden nugget of information they were so desperately searching for, and quickly slipped into the bucket seats of the sports car. They both sat there, staring out the windscreen over to the island for a moment, before Cassidy broke the silence.

"So, St. Cuthbert's Island, eh?" he said.

"Yeah." said Curtis. "Who knew?"

"Well Old Mr. Red Scarf for one. And by the sounds of it, everyone other than us." said Cassidy.

"So St. Cuthbert lived like Gollum for the last years of his life, in a hole in the ground, just off Lindisfarne." said Curtis. "It makes perfect sense that the obsessive monk would hide his hoard in his hero's hovel!"

"It's got to be, hasn't it?" said Cassidy, an excitement in his voice causing it to falter.

"Hang on!" said Curtis suddenly, fishing around in his bag for a copy of the translation from Cassidy's parchment. "Hang on..." he repeated as he read a section of the copy. He tapped the paper in apparent triumph and looked at his friend.

"What is it?" asked Cassidy.

"I always thought this section had a hidden meaning, and now it all makes sense!" said Curtis, and he began to read: "May this parchment find its way into the hands of the next Grand Master who will one day look to the enemy shores as I do now and not see death but peace and enlightenment, yet in short-sightedness, may he espy something different." he read. "I thought initially he meant that to be short-sighted, or closed-minded, you would fail to find enlightenment, but if you actually think that through, he was standing on the shores of the priory looking back to the Northumbrian coast. Yet in short-sightedness, may he espy something different; looking in the foreground of that view, there sits St. Cuthbert's Island! Don't look to the shores, look in the foreground and see something different, a Templar relic for example!"

"It has to be buried there." said Cassidy in full agreement. "Shall we come back tomorrow?"

"We shall." said Curtis, as the engine barked into life and he reversed the car out of the parking space, leaving the sight of Lindisfarne behind them.

CHAPTER 6

"You're going back again tomorrow?" asked Naomi, incredulously.

"Yes, we've discovered a lead. We think we may be really on to something." said Curtis.

"Is this the Holy Grail thing again? Which is conveniently close to home?" asked Naomi.

"Will you stop with the sarcasm, please?" said Curtis. "I'm doing this for the museum, you know!"

"No you're not!" said Naomi, "You're playing Indiana Craxford and the Templars of Doom with your new boyfriend."

"That was quite good, actually, darling. Well done." he said, clinking his wine glass with hers, and kissing her on the cheek. "Now, my little pun queen, are we calling in a takeaway?" he asked.

"What did you have for lunch?" she asked her fiancee. Curtis clearly did not want to answer that line of questioning.

"...Fish and Chips and a pint." said Curtis.

"Then we're having something healthy then. You're getting a bit porky you know."

"How very dare you?" said Curtis. "I am an Adonis. This body is a temple."

"It's not darling. But I still love you." said Naomi.

The following morning, Curtis made himself a large bacon sandwich to counteract the quorn and halloumi salad he had been forced to eat the night before, and afterwards he set off once again with Stuart Cassidy in the passenger seat of his Alfa Romeo, northwards past Alnwick, past Belford, past Bamburgh, and on to the Holy Island of Lindisfarne.

They decided that walking the Pilgrim's Crossing was unnecessary and time consuming, so they drove across the causeway that lay uncovered by the tides.

"This car does not like salt water." said Curtis, avoiding the surface puddles wherever possible. Stuart rolled his eyes as he looked out the window as they went.

"Should we go to the visitor's centre first? See what we can find out about St. Cuthbert's Island before we go plodging over to it?" suggested Cassidy.

"I suppose we should, although I don't think we missed any sections on where a hoard of Templar treasure is buried last time we were in." said Curtis as they walked down the street to the visitor centre after parking up in the public car park.

As they entered, they began to browse the posters and information boards with a specific location in mind.

"Stewart!" hissed Curtis in a loud whisper across the room, which attracted the attention of the lady working behind the desk.

"Oh hello you two." she said, remembering them from the last time they were in the building. "What can we do for you this time?"

"Hello my darling." said Curtis, approaching the desk and leaning on to it in a mock-letch. "We are seeking information on St. Cuthbert's Island." he said with a smile.

"Ok." said the lady. "Well, when Cuthbert retired from his work touring the country as a missionary and healer, he became a bit of a recluse and opted for a life of quiet contemplation. And that involved cutting himself off from the world. So he set up home on a tiny island that spent a lot of the time cut off from the main island on a daily basis, so it was pretty perfect for him." she said.

"What was his dwelling like?" asked Curtis.

"Well, I mean, pretty bloody awful compared to modern standards." said the lady, laughing loudly. "It was a glorified hole in the ground. He built a few walls and a roof for shelter, but, you know, this was the 670's." said the lady.

"Yeah, I hear you," said Curtis, "Wifi was slow." Cassidy looked towards his friend as if he had just put forward an argument for the support of the Hitler Youth.

"It would have had a fire pit and possibly a stone seat. He would have slept on straw or maybe even just the bare earth. He opted for a very simple life." said the Lady, totally ignoring Curtis' attempts at comedy.

"What is left of the structure?" asked Cassidy.

"Not much really. Some of the walls are left but that's

about it." she said. "You can go and see for yourself. The tide is out, so you still have a while before it is cut off."

"Thank you my dear. I think we've heard enough. We need to go see it." said Curtis.

"What are you chaps up to?" she asked with a tone that suggested suspicion.

"Nothing really, just doing a little research." said Cassidy.

"Well good luck with whatever you are researching." said the Lady. "Be sure to tell us your findings."

"We certainly will!" said Curtis as they exited the building.

"Not..." said Cassidy quietly, once they were out of earshot.

They made their way through the streets of the village until they reached the priory, through the grounds of which they walked, and found themselves on the shoreline, looking out over the water towards the mainland; between which lay the small hillock, topped with a wooden cross, that was St. Cuthbert's Island.

The tide was at its furthest out to sea, allowing access to the island via a rocky and precarious walk. Avoiding the rock pools and fronds of slippery seaweed, the two men made a bee-line for the island with haste.

"Ooh look!" said Curtis, stopping at one of the first rock pools they reached.

"What? What?" asked Cassidy, hurrying over to Curtis, who was now bent double with his hands under the water. What he brought out only interested one of the two men. Instead of a piece of Templar treasure that Cassidy was somehow expecting, Curtis picked out a Star Fish.

"This is a Brittle Star." he said. "*Ophiura Ophiura* I think."

"Astonishing, come on." said Cassidy, walking away. Curtis frowned at him, gently replaced the animal back in the rock pool, and continued to tiptoe his way over the large boulders towards the island.

They had now left the rocks of the shoreline and made their way, briefly, onto the flats of the sand before they would have to negotiate more rocks on the lead up to the island. But before those rocks, Curtis once again stopped and called Cassidy back.

"What is it this time? You found me a shell?" asked Cassidy in a taunting tone that Curtis whole-heartedly ignored.

"Almost." said Curtis, brushing the sand off something small and holding it out to Cassidy. "I've found you a bead."

"Ah! Thanks." he said, visibly smiling as he took the round fossil from Curtis.

"And look, there's another one." said Curtis, walking a few feet and picking up another of the St. Cuthbert's Beads. Even Cassidy began to look around him where they stood. "And another!" said Curtis.

They spent nearly half an hour looking for and collecting these beads, and by the end, both men had found a handful of big, and quite a few small, Crinoid fossils.

"Well it looks like we found the best hunting grounds for these beads, rather fittingly right next to his reclusive island." said Curtis.

"Yeah, speaking of which, we need to get a wriggle on and get onto that island. There don't seem to be many tourists here today, and none have bothered to walk across to the island so we should be able to work undisturbed." said Cassidy.

"What exactly are we looking for here?" asked Curtis, who was still convinced that whatever was buried by Blackwater, if anything, *must* have been discovered already.

"Who knows, mate." said Cassidy. "Anything. Keep your eyes peeled. Anything that seems out of place or not a natural occurrence, tell me."

"Will do." said Curtis as they left the tide line behind them; their feet hitting grass once more. They walked along a small ridge with a great view of the mainland of Northumberland, and the Castle of Bamburgh in the distance to the south through the afternoon haze.

"You know, there's a place somewhere round here you can stand and, on a clear day, you can see five castles." said Cassidy.

"Really? What, Bamburgh, Dunstanburgh...?" said Curtis, counting on his fingers.

"Warkworth, Alnwick, and Lindisfarne." said Cassidy.

"Not many places in the country can boast that." said Curtis.

"We've got more castles than anyone else, thats why. 70 in total I think." said Cassidy.

"That's too many, isn't it? Just greedy." said Curtis.

"We had a turbulent past." said Cassidy.

The further along the ridge they walked, the closer to the small ruined dwelling they came, which seemed to sit at the end of the small island, on a promontory of grass-topped rock, overlooking a deep channel of water where the tide had not drained from, and in which there were several seals playing.

"Look! Grey Seals." said Curtis. "One, two, three, four, five, six, seven, eight of them."

"Can we focus, please?" said Cassidy without turning to Curtis.

"I. Like. Wildlife." said Curtis in retort, through gritted teeth.

"And I. Like. Treasure." said Stuart. Curtis nodded.

"Touché."

"It's not much of a dwelling, is it." said Curtis as they surveyed the small-hole-with-walls. "What do you think it looked like one thousand three hundred years ago?"

"I mean just put a roof on it and you're pretty much there." said Cassidy.

"Right, so, what can we see?" asked Curtis, sitting down in the middle of the hole and viewing his surroundings, like a child about to attend a school assembly.

"Nothing immediate, but then that's expected." said Cassidy. "Let's keep on looking, sometimes it's the smallest thing."

But they looked at every square inch of the remaining stone structure, and nothing gave any clues as to a buried secret. They had spent a while inching their way around the walls, looking at every blemish, every nick that each rock contained, but nothing really looked like it could point towards a cache, nor did they look at all like they were put there by anyone but nature herself.

After what seemed like hours, Curtis stood up and stretched his back. And a sudden realisation hit him. The tide had come in quick, and they were minutes away from being cut off on the island.

"Stuart? By my calculations we have about fifteen minutes before we're stranded on this island." Said Curtis, a hint of panic in his voice that Cassidy hadn't experienced before. "And I don't mean *this* island, I mean Lindisfarne."

At this, Stuart stood up and looked out to sea, and then back to the main island, and the priory. "Christ. We better go. We may have to run to the car at this rate."

"I'm not running." Said Curtis.

"You might have to, unless your Ferrari is good at wading through ankle-deep water?" said Cassidy, hoisting his pack onto his back and hurrying off along the grassy hillock.

"Right, a, it's not a Ferrari," said Curtis, as he followed closely behind, "b, I wouldn't risk it anyway, and c, we have enough time. Have faith in my expert tidal predictions."

The car park was out of view of the tide and the causeway, but when they returned, they noticed that theirs was the last car left in the entire sprawling car park. They hurriedly stored their packs and jumped into the blood-red sports car. Curtis had already started the engine and was moving backwards as Cassidy closed his door, and the rear wheels spun a little as Curtis accelerated out of the gravelled car park and onto the access road through the dunes.

When they made it to a section of road that granted a view of the water, at speed, a little over a minute later, they could see the tide was almost at the causeway, and to Curtis' horror, had crossed the causeway at its lowest point; the point closest to the banks of Holy Island. He pushed on along the winding road that hugged the edges of the dunes, and to his slight relief he watched as a four-by-four began to cross the causeway, and they realised that the water was less than an inch deep at most. But they still had half a mile to cover before they reached the causeway so Curtis maintained his high-speed driving.

Cassidy remained unusually quiet as they blasted around the corners and accelerated hard on the straight sections with impressive power and, at least to Curtis' ears, a raucous cacophony of pure Italian music, until they finally made it to the start of the concrete road that linked the island to the mainland. Curtis slowed to a crawl and edged his way through the water, as it lapped at the tyres of the low-slung sports car, eager not to splash salt water up and into the workings of the engine.

"I'm going to have to get this professionally cleaned when I get back. The salt will eat through it."

"Just concentrate on driving straight." Said Cassidy.

They made it through the shallow waters and onto the dry causeway, and after a quick sprint along the deserted straight road, Curtis wearing a huge grin as Cassidy searched for something he could grab hold of, they were back on dry land and winding their way through the Northumbrian countryside. The mood in the car on the way home was a little subdued, as they once again returned from the Holy Island of Lindisfarne entirely empty handed, and with more questions than answers on the location of any loot.

As they made their way back south, Curtis suddenly broke the silence with a statement that neither of them had really considered for a while: "Of course, we've not looked in the third location yet."

"Brinkburn?" asked Cassidy. "That's true, we haven't."

"We still have a few hours of sunlight. Fancy a detour?" asked Curtis. "I really want to find *something* today."

"Yeah why not." said Cassidy.

"Friar Eastmund, the Keeper of the Key." said Curtis as he indicated to leave the A1 and cut across country towards Rothbury. "There's evidence of his existence, so I reckon there's a key hidden somewhere in Brinkburn Priory. At least I bloody hope so."

"A key that unlocks something we can't find." said Cassidy.

"I'm convinced that a chest is buried under St. Cuthbert's house, on that little island." said Curtis. "It ticks all the boxes and makes perfect sense. Literally no one, other than the person who read your parchment would know of its existence, especially if Blackwater suffered the same fate as the other two friars and failed to pass on his secret."

"But we can't just turn up and dig a large exploratory hole in a world heritage site." said Cassidy with frustration ebbing at his words.

"No..." agreed Curtis, although Stuart Cassidy detected the slightest hint of doubt in his voice. "You do have a metal detector though. That's non-invasive and would tell us if there was anything metallic buried under the surface." he said with a wry smile.

Half an hour later, both Curtis and Stuart were walking down the track from Brinkburn's public car park, down through the woods, to the beautifully tranquil and picturesque priory nestled in woodland with a river trickling past it's green lawns. There were a few tourists bustling around the entrance, together with what looked like a young couple being shown the wedding area and what it would be like on their big day by looking through large portfolios of photographs.

"Good afternoon chaps." Said a man suddenly from a little red hut, in an effusive voice that caught them both unawares.

"Ah, hello." Said Curtis, turning to the man.

"Ah the Heritage Mafia." Said Cassidy under his breath as they approached.

"Two please." Asked Cutis, ignoring Cassidy. The Craxford Museum paid their dues and they entered the church first. It was a stunningly impressive interior to the large and powerful religious building – with its chasm-like height and vaulted ceilings, its stained glass windows and beautifully tiled floors. This church would have looked more at home in the centre of a city, yet it was hidden in woodland in the middle of Northumberland. Both men stopped and took in their surroundings. Cassidy spoke first.

"It's far too late." He said.

"For what?" asked Curtis, checking his wrist-watch.

"For a key from the fifteenth century to be hidden here." said Cassidy. "This church is clearly nineteenth century, look." He said, pointing at things that Curtis didn't recognise as being newer in age.

"So, what, this didn't exist at the time of Friar Eastmund? But it did! We did research and he was a real person based here."

"No, it existed, just in a different form. It probably became abandoned during the dissolution of the monasteries, and was then rebuilt sometime in the Victorian era." Said Cassidy.

"Oh bollocks!" Said Curtis. "Foiled again by Henry the bloody Eighth."

"No, not necessarily. There will be plenty of original features. It looks like it's been restored fairly sympathetically to the medieval original." Said Cassidy, walking to a table and picking up a guidebook, before walking further into the large church, totally ignoring the £3.50 price tag attached. Curtis followed in tow, still taking in the architecture.

"The acoustics are amazing in here." Said Curtis, and he let out a loud "Lah!" to really put his point across, his voice rebounding off the walls and causing a few other visitors to turn and look at him.

"It says here that the manor house next door was also built around the old monks buildings from as late as the 1500s so there are possibilities there, I guess." Said Cassidy. "Let's just spend time looking for a while. There are inscriptions everywhere, so we need to really *look*."

"It's like going from the sublime to the ridiculous." Said Curtis, thinking back to the rather barren rocks that made up the ruins of St Cuthbert's house on Lindisfarne.

"So if you were a fifteenth century monk who had to hide a very important key in a hurry, where would you hide it?" asked Cassidy.

"Under the floor?" suggested Curtis.

"I doubt he'd have had time. If the Lancastrian army suddenly attacked and executed him, he'd have had no time at all." Said Cassidy.

"Unless he'd previously hidden it before the attacks." Said Curtis.

"Well, let's hope." Said Cassidy. "Perhaps they had planned for such an event. It sounded like Blackwater's parchment had the artefacts split between these three places, and hopefully all were well hidden before the other friars were executed."

They began their search, firstly together, but then splitting off and searching different sections of the priory individually to cover a greater area in a quicker time.

Curtis headed towards what he decided was the oldest looking section of the walls; in one of the transepts off the main nave of the building. He disregarded the tiled floors and concentrated on the stonework of the walls, trying to cover every inch as closely as he could. He found that there were several marks that could be interpreted as 'key shaped', but they could also equally be interpreted as 'snake shaped' or 'arrow shaped'; as they were, in fact, just marks on the stones. There were words and

67

writings on the walls too, and Curtis struggled with the translations of a few of them, but he thought it unlikely that there would be, chiselled into the walls, a literal description of a hidden key. But nowhere did they see any reference to a Friar Randolph Eastmund.

After a while, he sighed and stretched his back, and walked over to where Cassidy was hunched over looking at a section of text on what looked to be a headstone set into the floor.

"Anything?" asked Curtis.

"Nothing concrete, if you excuse the pun." Said Cassidy.

"Perhaps we may have more luck in the house?" suggested Curtis.

"I dunno, that was almost fully rebuilt." Said Cassidy, visibly frustrated.

"Are there no secret hermit's grottos or Gollum caves around here? There was a Templar slab recovered from a grotto not that far from here that's in my museum's vaults." said Curtis.

"That's the bugger with secret things," said Cassidy, "They're secret."

"Well, perhaps we would be better off having a little explore of the grounds." Said Curtis. "A lot of churches like this had secret tunnels and escape routes. In fact, I could bring up a topographical map on this app I've got that shows any caves and things in the area. Hang on."

They sat at a pew near the large organ, and both watched Curtis' phone as a map began to slowly load in front of them. Curtis dragged his finger around the screen until the section of map covering Brinkburn was displayed.

"Right, see these dots and topography lines?" said Curtis.

"I know how to read a map thanks." Said Cassidy, "this 'aint my first rodeo."

"Yeah ok, well, according to this there aren't any visible caves, but if you follow the river in either direction you can see a few, dotted here and there, and there are loads of caves in the area if you zoom out a bit. Look at Cragside! There are hundreds."

"Maybe you're on the right track then." Said Cassidy. "Let's go have a look down by the river."

They made their way out of the priory and headed towards the water. Brinkburn sat on a curve of the River Coquet, with crenelated walls running down to meet the waters edge in places, and natural cliffs in others, no more than ten to fifteen feet high, but certainly high enough to contain crevices and caves within them.

At first they stood at the walls, looking over to the water below, but there was no real way of getting down to the water's edge. So they walked the battlements until the walls were replaced by trees and estate fencing.

"There's a gate over there." Said Cassidy, walking off.

"It says 'private' though." Said Curtis.

"Where?" asked Cassidy, deliberately blocking the sign with his back, and looking around him as he tried to unlatch the gate. It wasn't locked but it wouldn't move, due to years of foliage growth around the base.

"Well at least we can say this gate isn't used much." Said Cassidy. "That's a good sign." He said as he simply climbed over it. Curtis glanced back over the well-kept lawns, to the priory and house beyond, but couldn't see anyone watching, so followed quickly. He felt like he was back at school, clambering over something he shouldn't and trespassing into some dilapidated and dangerous building to take photographs or mess around with his friends, as kids were known to do the world over. But he was now worryingly close to forty, and Cassidy even older than that, and for some reason he was sure he wouldn't be let off with a clip around the ear by the authorities, yet still he pressed on through the woodland, following the sound of running water, and the footsteps of Stuart Cassidy; the antagonist, the assailant, the raider.

After a brief trek through some thick woodland they found themselves by the river once again, and clambered down a steep bank.

"It's getting dark, and I need my wellies if this is going to work." Said Curtis as they stood on a rock a few feet into the river Coquet.

"Well, look, we can walk around the bend here and at least see if there are any visible openings in the rocks." Said Cassidy, keen to press on and find something to keep the dream alive.

Curtis agreed, and they carried on, hugging the rock face as they balanced on the larger rocks within the river, trying to find a dry section for a foot. The river was luckily very low, as there hadn't been much rain over the past few weeks, so what would be more of a torrent for the majority of the year, was currently a placid trickle in comparison.

The going was getting a little hairy and they were running out of dry rocks to use. Cassidy stopped at the end of a larger rock and tried to look ahead to see where his path could progress, just as he heard a very loud splash behind him, turning to see Curtis sitting in the river, face full of rage, and building up to an almighty bout of swearing.

After Cassidy had finished laughing, and Curtis had taken a badly needed breath after a tirade of language that could make a docker blush, he stood up, realising that the stream was only ankle deep where he was, he decided that, as his shoes and trousers were already soaked, wading through the stream was a good way of seeing further sections of the cliffs. And as he waded, his expression changed.

"Stuart!" said Curtis. "Stuart, there's an opening!"

CHAPTER 7

"I just don't think it's appropriate to be driving around in a hairdresser's car with no trousers on." Said Cassidy, staring out of the side window, arms folded across his chest.

"It's not a hairdresser's car, it is a mid-engined Italian thoroughbred sports car for enthusiasts such as myself, and I don't want to get the seat all wet with river juice. You're just lucky I've still got my underpants on." Said Curtis.

"Jesus Christ." Said Cassidy.

"Anyway, it's all worked out for the best. If I hadn't fallen and wet my bum, I wouldn't have spotted the cave entrance, and we would have been driving home all forlorn. Instead, I'm driving, minus my trousers, granted, but with a plan forming in my mind."

"Which is?" asked Cassidy, still refusing to look at Curtis.

"I have fly fishing rights on the Coquet, right, so we dress in our fishing gear with waders, I imagine you have them, yes?" he asked, knowing that Cassidy favoured a fishing waistcoat on these outings.

"Nope. Fishing is for old men who hate their families." Said Cassidy.

"Then you can borrow my spare pair." Said Curtis, ignoring the sarcasm and too excitable for any resistance to his rapidly forming plan. "We then will park outside of the Brinkburn land, gain access to the river upstream, and wade our way down to the cave. I'm afraid we will need to carry rods and a fishing bag each to look authentic, but we can use them to carry our tools and even your metal detector if it'll fit, then we won't get harassed by anyone, and if we do, I have a licence to present granting us permission to be there."

"Then we get into the cave and have a good look." Said Cassidy. "I don't hate that plan."

"Then," said Curtis, "we visit St. Cuthbert's Island again, this time with your detector, and see what results we get back."

"By this time next week, we could potentially have two of

71

the three artefacts we're searching for, although I'm not sure what a burner or a bell have to do with any of this to be honest." Said Cassidy. "Perhaps they're solid gold and encrusted with precious gemstones."

"I really don't want to get my hopes up, but I'm finding it hard not to imagine us returning home with real treasure." said Curtis.

"It might not be literal treasure, you know that right?" said Cassidy, finally turning to Curtis. "The Templars were shrewd businessmen as well as battle-hard warriors. The items we may recover could be the deeds to a vast wealth of land and property long passed on, or even just notes on their banking system. Historically huge, powerful things in their time, but not necessarily shiny and gold or indeed anything like a cursed stone." he added. "It wasn't all flaming torches, hooded robes and rituals in basements you know."

"Well, as the current custodian of Craxford Museum, I would welcome any of what you've just listed, I mean even the original parchment, which we can tie to the museum's tapestry is a hugely significant find. We could almost make an exhibition out of just that, but I'd really like to think that there is some sort of old-school treasure." said Curtis.

"Blackwater did speak of a golden casket." said Cassidy.

"Yeah, he also spoke about being protected from a 'darkness'." said Curtis with some apprehension, before indicating and pulling out to overtake a slower moving vehicle, suddenly thrusting them back into their seats with the acceleration and drowning out any reply Cassidy could give as they tore through the Northumbrian landscape.

"So you found a cave, but didn't bother going in it?" asked Naomi, later that evening, incredulity rife in her tone.

"It was getting dark and I had wet trousers." Said Curtis.

"Well I guess that's as good an excuse as any." Replied Naomi, chuckling.

"I still think we're on to something." Said Curtis.

"Even though you've found bugger all?" asked Naomi.

"We found an entrance in a place where we predicted an entrance may be!" said Curtis.

"But surely someone else will have also found that

sometime in the last five hundred years?" argued Naomi. "It only took you half an hour."

"Possibly," agreed Curtis, "But the entrance is low on the rock, it's practically a crawl space, so probably submerged the majority of the time due to higher river levels, we won't get into it if it rains before we go back. It's also totally invisible from the Priory side, and the other side is thick woodland and then national park. It's a natural looking fissure so unless a person floundering and splashing in the river was particularly nosey, perhaps it's just gone unnoticed. Why not take a look and put our minds at rest?"

"Absolutely darling, you go and have a look." Said Naomi, before kissing him on the head.

That evening, whist Naomi was watching a show about competing drag queens, Curtis was idly surfing the internet on his MacBook whilst enjoying a beer. After his weekly check to see what concept cars and rumours had been unveiled by various automotive manufacturers, and a brief read of his natural history and scientific newsletters he had emailed to him from all corners of the world, he decided to redirect his efforts to researching a little more into the origins of the Knights Templar.

"Ah, look, Naomi." said Curtis suddenly, after browsing a particular web page, "Remember when we drove past Gisors Castle in Normandy? It was the year we went to LeMans?"

Naomi glanced over to him with her brow furrowed. "I'm not sure I do remember."

"Well it turns out that it was the place the last Grand Master of the Templars, Jacques de Molay, was imprisoned at the end of the Templar reign, *and* crucially where the hoards of Templar treasure is rumoured to be buried." said Curtis.

"So, hang on," said Naomi, pausing the television and processing what Curtis had just said, "the Grand Master was imprisoned there, so someone else, the French I assume, had taken control of that castle, and control of him. Yet they never found any treasure there?" she asked.

"Maybe they hid it really well." said Curtis with doubt in his tone. Naomi looked at him with raised eyebrows and her head cocked to one side as her dark hair fell over her shoulders, framing her face in the low light of the evening. Curtis was truly in love with her. "Fair point." he added and turned back to his computer as his mobile phone pinged signalling that he had received a text message.

It was from Stuart Cassidy. Curtis opened it and read aloud the two-word text.

"Larmenius Charter."

"What?" asked Naomi, her attention once again drawn from the television programme she was watching.

"A text from Stuart." said Curtis. "It just says *Larmenius Charter*. What does that mean?"

"I don't know, darling, he's a strange man. I imagine he plays a lot of dungeons and dragons, perhaps it's from that." said Naomi.

"I doubt it." said Curtis.

"Well, perhaps it's what he calls his winky." said Naomi. Curtis chuckled.

"Well I was going to google it, but now I don't want to." he said.

"Go on, I'm intrigued." said Naomi, pausing the television once again and turning to face Curtis on the sofa, sitting cross legged beside him as he clicked on his laptop's mouse.

Curtis typed the words into the search box, pressed enter with a flourishing gesture, and began to read.

"Ok, so the Larmenius Charter is supposedly a 14th Century manuscript... written in Latin... blah, blah, blah." said Curtis as he read. "Oh wow. It talks of the continuation of the Templar order following on from when they were disbanded... transfer of leadership... twenty two subsequent Grand Masters... well into the 19th Century... now housed with the Freemasons in London... oh, believed to be a forgery." said Curtis, a little dejectedly at reading the last section.

"Well, there you go then." said Naomi, turning and resuming her programme. Curtis took his phone and replied to Cassidy.

"Thought to be a fake. What's the significance?"

The ellipsis appeared on Curtis' phone almost immediately as Cassidy typed his reply. Once again it was short and sweet.

"Look at the Grand Masters. Link the dates."

Curtis once again began to search for a full and literal translation of the cyphered Latin text and eventually he found a list of the twenty or so listed Grand Masters. He scrolled down to the name that was listed for the time of Blackwater's parchment; the middle of the 1400s, and the name at first meant nothing to him: Johannes Croyus. But then the sudden realisation hit him like a lightning bolt as he sat up straight, inadvertently knocking over his bottle of beer as his body jolted stiff.

"Oh Christ!" he said loudly, causing his fiancée to jump at the sudden flurry of excitement, as lager began to fan out across the wooden floor of their sitting room.

"What? What is it?" she asked.

"Johannes Croyus!" He shouted. "John Croy! He wasn't just the Grand Master of the Northern Carmelites, he was the Grand Master of the Knights Templar!"

Following the revelations of the previous night, the two men had agreed to bring forward their search of the cave at Brinkburn to the following day where they met up, full of excitement and adrenaline, to take the plunge to see if the small cave held any secrets. This time Curtis decided to take his Land Rover, partly because Cassidy clearly didn't share his passion for cars, and partly because they were due to get horrifically dirty. Of course, in true Curtis fashion, this was no ordinary Land Rover, but a modified Defender with an engine developing nearly 500 horse power.

"We happy we've got everything?" asked Cassidy as they drove away from Morpeth and along the A697 towards Brinkburn.

"Yep. Waders, rods, and fishing bags containing collapsible shovels, torches, pliers, chisels, and hard hats." Said Curtis.

"Wow! Hard hats and chisels? You planning on doing some tunnelling?" asked Cassidy. "I've brought my detector, rope, head torches, and a spare pair of trousers for you." he added, smiling.

"I'm sorry about removing my trousers in your presence."

Said Curtis. "It won't happen again."

"It's fine, I just wasn't expecting it." Said Cassidy.

"Wait until you find out what I've had to do to keep our secret about today." Said Curtis quietly and quickly as he looked out of his side window and tried to cover up his own sentence with a coughing fit.

"What do you mean?" asked Cassidy in a monotone brimming with apprehension and the beginnings of anger.

"Well, after looking at the map of the local area, there are no real places to park up that aren't private farms, road side passing places, or entrances into fields that we can't really block for hours. Apart from one place; a holiday cottage. So I had to book the cottage." Said Curtis.

"Well that's ok. It's a little extravagant just to use as a parking space but I can see why you've done it to avoid any suspicion." Said Cassidy. "How much has it set us back?"

"Well here's the thing, they had a special offer for a single night, lover's retreat for only £50 per night, so I had to convince them we are a couple who just wanted to get away and grab some fishing time alone together." Said Curtis. Cassidy remained quiet, looking straight ahead, stoney faced. "What?" laughed Curtis.

"That's ridiculous." Said Cassidy, through gritted teeth and clearly uncomfortable.

"It's our ticket in." said Curtis. "But we have to convince Beverley that we are a couple when we arrive."

"You can piss off." Said Cassidy. "I'm not pretending to be gay for anything."

"You don't have to pretend to do anything, gay people are just the same as straight people, only generally more stylish." Said Curtis.

"Well that's bollocks." Said Cassidy.

"Oh come on Stuart, we don't live in the nineteen eighties anymore." Said Curtis in an overly camp voice, placing his hand on Stuart's knee very briefly before it was swatted away with force by Cassidy.

When they pulled up outside Thornyhaugh Cottage, Cassidy was still huffing and puffing about the situation as a whole.

"Look, I'll do all the talking, you just mince around at the back of the car pretending to look at something in the boot." Said

Curtis, laughing at his own joke, and receiving a barrage of angry swearing from his friend.

CHAPTER 8

A little over twenty minutes later, after pretending to unpack an overnight bag, they were both walking off down the track towards the river, fly rods in hand, and full-length waders buckled up to their shoulders. Cassidy refused to hold hands on Curtis' taunting request, knowing full well, and hugely enjoying, how uncomfortable Cassidy was with the situation.

"I feel like a berk." Said Cassidy eventually as they walked the dusty track along the side of a field.

"Yep. But you may soon be a berk with an ancient key that unlocks a Templar casket." Said Curtis, as they climbed a wooden stile, and crossed another field towards some woodland.

Once through, and after battling trees with their fly rods, they suddenly found themselves at the water's edge; an excitement growing ever larger inside both men.

"Right, so we wade down-stream until we reach the priory walls." Said Cassidy.

"Yes, and for God's sake try not to fall in this time." Said Curtis, receiving a look from Cassidy who knew full well that it was Curtis, not he, who failed to stay on their feet at their last attempt.

Walking along the dirt banks, and wading through some sections was fairly easy going as the water was so unusually low, but it still took them the best part of an hour before the priory's river walls came into view. As the two fishermen approached, they could make out a couple of tourists leaning over the walls and looking into the river, not far from where the opening was, although it was totally invisible from their side of the river.

"Right, we're going to have to wait for Nosey McNebface and his mate to leave before we go any further, so let's pretend to start setting up our rods and wait." Said Curtis.

"Right. You do realise I haven't a clue how to set up a rod." Said Cassidy. "It's not going to look convincing."

"Just copy me." Said Curtis, sitting on a rock and beginning to connect various sections of cane rod to each other. One of the men moved off, but the other remained, almost fixated on what Curtis and Stuart were doing, until a shout of "Nigel!" from an unknown female voice seemed to rouse him from his voyeuristic rubbernecking and he too moved away and out of sight.

"Right." Said Cassidy, throwing two thirds of a fly rod to one side and making his way quickly down river and across the water to the opening in the rocks. Curtis followed after retrieving his spare rod, quickly collapsing it down, and safely stowing it, along with his other rod, on a natural shelf of rock not far from the opening, and well out of sight of any prying eyes.

Cassidy was already on his knees peering into the small dark hole as Curtis reached him, and after fitting a head torch, and handing another to Curtis, he began to make his way inside. Curtis was a little frustrated that Cassidy would be the first to possibly discover a Templar artefact, but he was also sensible enough to realise that the agreement allowed him to display whatever they found in *his* museum, and take the academic credit amongst his peers.

The dark opening was like that of a gaping mouth, spewing mud that was thick and uninviting at its entrance; on the inside of a natural bend in the river, the water graced the rock with little force, concentrating its eroding efforts instead on the deeper channel on the opposite banks as the water made its way towards the coast.

Curtis could hear muffled talking from Cassidy in front of him as they began to slowly push their way inside, but couldn't make out any words as he slithered along on his belly following the bottom of Cassidy's waders ahead of him. But just as Curtis was beginning to feel the beginnings of a claustrophobic event in the horrifically tight confines of the tunnel, Cassidy suddenly stood up, turned around and began to pull Curtis into a small cavern by his arms. This annoyed Curtis, as he was perfectly capable of moving on his own, but as he stood up, the excitement overcame his frustrations, and he began to look around the small cave that appeared to be the perfect makeshift storage area for secret treasures.

It was high enough to stand up in, even for him to carry someone on his shoulders, smelled of damp mould and river sludge, and within seconds their feet were disappearing into the cloying mud of the cave floor. The bare rock walls of the interior had many shelves chiselled into them by ancient hands; these were no natural occurrences, and sure enough, it took them only a few seconds before both their head torches came to a stop in exactly the same place, at exactly the same time, where they both illuminated a small wooden box, sat high up on one of these hollowed out sections of rock; high enough to evade any rising waters that would have entered the cave, and blending into the brown stone of the rock, hidden in the shade of the chiselled hole.

"Holy crap." Said Cassidy slowly, as Curtis exhaled with a smile.

Cassidy rushed forward as quickly as he could through the gloop, but he couldn't reach the high shelf, so Curtis offered his hands in a cradle for Cassidy to climb onto for a bunk. This time, he was able to reach easily and as he landed back on the wet clay-like silt with a deep splodge, he was carrying an ancient-looking wooden box in his arms; it was small; no bigger than a shoe box, made of plain dark wood banded in black metal, and held closed with an equally dark metal clasp and pin. Both men looked at each other and began to laugh in triumph.

"No lock." said Cassidy with suspicion once both men had calmed from their frenzied and hysterical mirth.

"Let's get it back to the cottage before opening it, just in case anything falls out." Said Curtis. "We'd never find it again in this mud."

"Ok, I'll shuffle out backwards and you can hand it to me." Said Cassidy, before having a good look around him to make sure they hadn't missed anything in the small cavern. As far as they both could see, there were no other items hidden in the recesses of the small, cramped space that sucked at their feet like tar pits, so they began the task of extricating themselves before they got truly stuck.

Once out, and considerably muddier than they were when they arrived, Cassidy transferred all of his equipment from his fishing bag over to Curtis', safely stowed the box in the empty bag, almost the perfect size for the chest, and slung it over his shoulder. They then began excitedly wading back up the stream towards their self-catering cottage. The entire way back both men took increasingly more elaborate guesses at what this key could potentially unlock.

Once out of the river, and a little cleaner after washing

most of the mud from their waders and clothing, they made their way back up the dirt track towards Thornyhaugh Cottage, and after removing all their fishing attire, chucking it all into the back of the Land Rover, and cleaning themselves up a little more at the kitchen sink, they both made their way into the small living area where the ancient wooden box was sitting atop a towel on the small pine table.

Placing his cup of tea well out of spilling distance of the box, Curtis studied it intently from all sides, taking in every mark, every dent, every detail. He reached forward to remove the metal pin that held the clasp in place.

"Wait!" said Cassidy, holding up his hands. Curtis stopped and pulled his hands back as if from a coiled snake.

"What?" he said.

"I'm just thinking, the Templars were well known for their booby traps." Said Cassidy. "This box could well be rigged with some kind of defence mechanism. I should have thought about this, sorry, don't touch it."

"Is it Templar though?" said Curtis. "This was hidden by Friar Eastmund a century later."

"But we now know that Eastmund is linked to John Croy, or Johannes Croyus to give him his proper title, who is absolutely linked to the Templars, even if it is a couple of hundred years later. Whatever is inside this box; we think it's a key, unlocks another box that is very much Templar in origin, so we think that the key within this box is also Templar, and therefore this box could also be Templar." Said Cassidy.

"You said 'Templar' a *lot* there." Said Curtis. "You've convinced me. So what do we do now?"

"We can still open it, but I suggest we open it facing away from us, just in case anything happens. Maybe we could use a pole or something to open it with." Said Cassidy. Curtis looked at him like he was mad. "Look, I've heard about Templar boxes that have spring-mounted blades built into the lids, and I've heard of one that gutted the person who opened it without deactivating it first." Curtis' eyes narrowed.

"Wasn't that on Indiana Jones?" he said.

"No, this was very real." Said Cassidy, seriously.

"So how do we deactivate it then?" asked Curtis, shaking his head at Cassidy.

"Well I'm not sure we can as we're not Templars so don't know the secret ways they did things, but if we do what I suggested and open it facing the other way, at a distance, we can hopefully safely get to the contents inside." Said Cassidy. "It may just be a box, but I'd rather be safe than sorry."

"Why don't we take it to the museum and x-ray it?" said Curtis suddenly. "I'd hate to have to take you home armless or with a large wound to your stomach, no matter how much I want to get into it."

"Perhaps that's a good idea to be on the safe side." Said Cassidy. "Can we do it now though? I don't think I can wait any longer. Have you got 24 hour access?"

"Pretty much." Said Curtis. "I mean, it's part of the university, not the museum, but it's kept on museum property and we're granted access to it whenever we need to x-ray anything. I don't think we could waltz in during a lecture and remove whatever artefact they were currently scanning, but by the time we get back there, when most, if not all students have gone home, we should be able to access it, and I have had all the relevant training to use the machine." Said Curtis.

"Well let's go." Said Cassidy, standing up and carefully carrying the box towards the door.

"But what are we going to tell Beverley?" asked Curtis.

"Tell her we've had a lover's tiff and I've left you." Said Cassidy. "I could punch you in the face outside if it would sell the story a little better?"

"I don't think that's necessary." Said Curtis, washing their mugs in the sink. "I'll call her in the morning and pay over the phone." He said as they took their final possessions, including their latest acquisition, placed it in the back of the car, locked the cottage door and posted the key back through the letter box, before driving away up the drive and onto the road that would take them back to Newcastle.

When they finally walked through the doors of the university, and Curtis used his special key fob to gain access to the museum corridors, it was almost deserted, save for cleaning staff and the odd over-enthusiastic student who was still glued to a computer monitor. Cassidy was carrying the small box, with the towel draped over it to hide it from prying eyes as they walked down the stark and clinically lit corridors.

"You know you're probably going to have to pay for that tea towel you've stolen." Said Curtis.

"Erm, she's got your card details mate." Said Cassidy. "And remember, you're funding this project."

"Yeah, I wasn't expecting to be paying off B&B owners with theft-related hush-money." Said Curtis.

"She'll probably not notice one missing tea towel. There was a pile of about ten in the cupboard." Said Cassidy. "You're not Indiana Jones, despite what you may think."

They finally came to a stop outside a white door with another card entry system, and Curtis granted them access with a flamboyant swoosh of his card against the reader.

The room was as polar opposite to the old Victorian museum as any room could be, with a harshly lit and distinctly medical feel to it, as the strip lights cast a blue-white and very uniformed light over everything in the room, including a large white piece of machinery with 'Siemens Luminos' written on one side of it, and a large yellow sign stating 'Caution – X-Ray Radiation' stuck to the other side.

"You, erm, you know how to use these then?" asked Cassidy, tentatively.

"I do." Said Curtis, walking over to the machine and pressing various buttons before taking the box from Cassidy and placing it carefully on the platform. "I'll take an image from above and from the side so we really know what we're dealing with."

A little while later, once Cassidy had come back into the room, insisting he waited in the corridor while Curtis carried out the x-rays, they glanced at the screen of the digital machine that revealed the inner contents of the ancient wooden box.

"And there she is." Said Cassidy, quietly, as he saw, in a dazzling white against the dark background, the unmistakable shape of a large iron key.

"I love it when a hypothesis is proved right." Said Curtis, smiling. "Makes one feel rather Darwinian, wouldn't you say?"

"There does look like some sort of metal mechanism built into the box though." Said Cassidy, ignoring Curtis. "We're going to have to be careful, that looks like a sprung spike to me. Can you see here," he said, pointing at the screen, "that, there, appears to be a small linkage to the clasp that runs to the right corner of the box? Look. There." He said, tapping the screen. "I think that if we can somehow press that as we open the box, it will disable the spring release here." he said, pointing to another section of the x-ray.

"That seems fairly high-tech for the twelfth century Stuart." Said Curtis.

"This could be fifteenth century, remember, but it could have been made as a tribute to Templar technology as I've seen these contraptions before on boxes that belonged to the Templar Order." Said Cassidy. "They were very protective of their secrets and didn't want them falling into the wrong hands."

"But surely after so many years the mechanism would have seized?" asked Curtis. "These are metal moving parts kept in a wet environment. They'll have rusted to dust by now."

"Not by the looks of things. Let's not risk it." Said Cassidy.

"I'm almost more excited about having the box on display than the key." Said Curtis, already thinking about how he would be exhibiting it at the museum.

"Is it safe to go to the box now?" asked Cassidy.

"I shouldn't think so, looking at these images." Said Curtis.

"I meant with the radiation." Said Cassidy.

"Oh right, yes, all safe and powered down." said Curtis.

"Right." Said Cassidy, moving over to the box. "So, theoretically there should be a way of disabling the... yes, look!" Curtis joined him, peering over his shoulder. "There's a small section of wood that moves and must disengage the spike when pressed." He pressed it and there was an audible click. "And look at the little round hole here," he said, pointing, "That must be where the spike comes out of."

"It's remarkably subtle." Said Curtis. "And advanced for it's time. I kind of want to see what it does." He added. Cassidy shared a look with him, before releasing the safety catch once more. There was another audible click as the internal spring re-engaged.

"I'm facing the box away from us, and I'm opening it very slowly." Said Cassidy.

"Wait, let me set up my iPhone over there and record what

happens." Said Curtis, jumping up and propping his phone up against a pile of folders on a desk opposite them, framing it so that the box almost filled the screen. "Right." He said, pressing the record button. "Whenever you're ready."

"You're not going to live stream it or anything are you?" asked Cassidy.

"No, it's all for the project archives, that's all." said Curtis. Cassidy seemed to ease a little.

There was a noise, as Stuart slowly opened the lid of the box after carefully sliding out the metal pin and lifting the latch, which sounded like Curtis' old air rifle he used to play with as a child being fired. Both men looked at each other, then slowly moved around to the far side of the box. There was no protruding metal spike. There was nothing.

"Looks like we have a dud mechanism." Said Cassidy.

"We heard something though." Said Curtis. "It sounded relatively powerful. We need to be careful. It might be like a firework; never go back to an opened Templar box."

"Hang on! Holy hell!" said Cassidy suddenly, running over to the far wall of the room and bending down. "I think I've found it!"

Curtis joined him and saw a dark metal spike protruding six inches from the wall. He stood open mouthed, shaking his head. Cassidy was laughing out loud.

"So that has travelled, what, fifteen feet, faster than we could see it, and stuck fast in a solid wall?" he said. "I guess the mechanism is still functioning then!"

Curtis still couldn't quite speak, amazed at the power from such an ancient device. It appeared to be a primitive bolt gun; and a very effective one. He touched the metal spike and tried to pull it out of the wall, but it seemed stuck fast. With a little bit of bending and coaxing it eventually came free and Curtis could then see that the bolt had travelled at least an inch into the plaster and left a sizeable hole. It was almost black, thin and cylindrical in shape, but with an elongated bladed point to it with backward grooves cut on one side, much like a primitive fishing spear, and unnecessarily sharpened to a very thin, needle-like tip.

"This is incredible." said Curtis quietly.

"And that's just the box." said Cassidy.

"Actually I'm still recording!" said Curtis. "The phone

should have caught the moment it shot out, so I may be able to slow the frames down for us to see it."

"Later." said Cassidy. "Look."

Stuart Cassidy reached into the open chest and removed an even odder looking box. This was around eight inches long and a couple of inches high and wide, and it appeared to be made of a marble-like stone. It was pale in colour, with no real lid to speak of. In fact, it looked like it didn't open at all, instead every square inch of it was covered in symbols and markings that even Curtis found utterly bewildering.

"Let me see that." said Curtis, taking the object. "What *are* you?" he said, turning it over in his hands. He gently shook it, and could hear the key that they had seen on the x-rays rattling around inside it. "It reminds me a little of a prayer box, but this is different. I have no idea what those symbols are for a start. Definitely not Egyptian, not Tibetan, I don't think they're Indian. Certainly not English or Celtic symbols. I'm flummoxed with that one. And how do you open it? It feels solid."

"I think we need to be careful with it." said Cassidy. "Given the fact that we've just shot one of your walls by mistake."

"Well I suppose we haven't got a need for the key yet." said Curtis. "Given that we haven't found the golden casket, so we don't need to get into it. Look, this is *huge*; a massive win for our project. We've proved the theory. We predicted there would be an ancient key, in a specific area, and we found it. We've also predicted that there is a box containing a Templar artefact which I now absolutely believe is buried in the dirt beneath St. Cuthbert's House, and there is also a burner and a bell hidden somewhere at Hulne Priory or the surrounding area that has some significance to all of this. Maybe it's time to go public with this. We should tell the Heritage. They'll probably get a dig organised."

"Woah...I don't think we should go public yet. Let's just hold our horses on that front." said Cassidy. "I think this calls for celebration, but let's just keep it to ourselves at the minute, otherwise it'll get out, what if the press get hold of it? We'll have other people trying to find the other items before we get the chance." he said, a little panic in his voice. "It'll become a race for the prize."

"Yeah ok." conceded Curtis. "Come on, let's get something to eat, I'm starving. Why don't we head back to my house with these boxes, crack open a beer, and do some symbol research?"

CHAPTER 9

Once their stomachs were full of pizza, on Cassidy's request and to which Curtis put up no resistance whatsoever; bottles of Spanish lager in their hands, they sat down at the kitchen table of the Old Rectory, and began looking up symbols that may match what was carved onto the small stone box they had found. Even Naomi was sat with them, looking at the strange box that had suddenly turned their project from a joke into a very real treasure hunt.

"Why don't I send some pictures to Amy?" asked Naomi. "She's an international expert on Ancient Egypt." she added, to Cassidy.

"I really don't think these are Egyptian, but I guess she may be able to shed some light on it." said Curtis.

"I thought we were keeping this a secret until we're further on." said Cassidy boring his eyes into Curtis to press home the point.

"Well, yeah, but Amy doesn't count." said Curtis. "She was the other member of the Amazon project that nearly killed us a few years back, and a great friend of ours. She's helped with many of our projects, and she's far more experienced in treasure hunting than we will ever be. She'd not talk of it to anyone else."

"I still think the less people we involve in this project the better, both privately and business-wise." said Cassidy shaking his head.

"She's very pretty." said Curtis. "And single."

"Right, let's Skype Amy then." said Cassidy without pausing.

Laughing, Curtis minimised the internet window of his MacBook that was sitting on the table with them, and selected the FaceTime application. He clicked on Amy's contact details and within a few seconds the computer was playing a ringtone through its speakers. A few seconds after that there was another tone, and Amy's face suddenly appeared on the screen.

"Hi guys!" she said excitedly. "What's up?"

"Hey hun." Said Naomi. "We're not interrupting are we?"

"No, not at all." said Amy through the computer. "Was just settling down to watch Invisible Cities on the Discovery Channel."

"That's a great show!" said Cassidy suddenly. "I love their computer modelling." Curtis shot Cassidy a look one would give someone who turned up to a funeral in a clown costume.

"Amy, this is Stuart Cassidy." said Curtis. "Stuart, Amy." he said in an introductory tone. Cassidy waved at the screen awkwardly and Amy smiled and waved back. Amy was Naomi's best friend from university, and an archaeologist, spending a large chunk of her time in foreign countries on international digs, uncovering amazing finds and making a lucrative career from it, and was the third member of their team who trekked into the Amazon rainforest in search of unknown treasures, from which they very nearly didn't return.

"Hi Stuart. What's this all about then guys?" she asked.

"Well, Stuart came to me with something he'd discovered, and he and I have been working on a theory over the past month, and today, that theory became a reality as we found what we were looking for." said Curtis with a smile.

"Right!" said Amy enthusiastically. "No, sorry, you'll have to elaborate." she said, still none the wiser about the situation.

"Ok, in a nutshell, Stuart found an old parchment whilst metal detecting the shores of Northumberland near Holy Island. This is a fifteenth century manuscript we're talking about, that speaks of a religious order who were basically descendants of the Knights Templar. They have hidden a Templar artefact that we believe to be legit. They split it amongst three Priories, so hid the artefact on Lidisfarne, the key to the box at Brinkburn Priory, and what we know as a 'burner' and a 'bell' at Hulne Priory in Alnwick." said Curtis. "Today, Stuart and I found the key in a box, in a cave, at Brinkburn. When we opened the box there was a classic Templar booby trap that fired a bolt across the room and would have easily killed one of us had we opened the box in the usual way. Luckily, Stuart here foresaw that trap and took the relevant precautions." Curtis took a much needed breath after gabbling at high speed into his computer.

"So," said Amy, slowly, processing all that information, "you've found a key in a box that opens another box that you haven't found yet, that you think contains a Templar artefact?"

"Correct." said Curtis. "Only the key is also in a box, a stone box, within the other box."

"Christ, that's a lot of boxes." said Amy.

"And one of which, the main one, we believe to be a golden casket." said Curtis.

"Like the Ark of the Covenant?" asked Amy, looking a little sceptical, one of her eyebrows raised.

"Why does everyone...we don't know what it is Amy, at this point." said Curtis. "The Templars recovered religious artefacts from all over the world."

"So, this is all very interesting and exciting." said Amy, sitting back in her arm chair. "What do you want from me?"

"Well..." said Curtis

"I'm reluctant to get involved with another one of your treasure hunts, Curtis, if I'm honest." said Amy, quickly.

"I know, don't worry, I'm not going to take you up the Amazon again." said Curtis with a comedy wink, in full innuendo mode. "Look, we found this box that contains a big old key, inside the other box and it's covered in inscriptions that none of us can make out. I don't think it's Egyptian, or Tibetan, or Celtic. I just wanted to see if you could make it out." he said, and held it up to the tiny webcam that was integrated into the screen of the Mac.

He could see Amy squinting slightly at her screen, and she pushed her small, frameless glasses up her nose and concentrated on the symbols in front of her. "My initial impressions, at a glance, would be full-on TK Maxx." she said.

"What?" asked Cassidy.

"I think its rubbish." said Amy. "Modern tourist-tat from North Africa, probably. Those inscriptions don't mean anything."

"But it came from a Templar-designed chest that had clearly been stored in a cave for millennia." objected Cassidy at the effrontery of this woman's dismissive attitude.

"As I said, it's just an initial impression based on what I can see on a webcam. I mean, as far as I'm aware those symbols and inscriptions are utter gibberish. I think you've been played." said Amy, as Cassidy huffed and puffed whilst shaking his head and folding his arms in protest, refusing to look at the screen, much to Naomi's silent mirth.

"I don't think so, Amy." said Curtis. "Look at this here."

he said, holding up the initial parchment that was still sitting on the table. "This is a legitimate fifteenth century parchment by a Friar who was based at Lindisfarne Priory during the Wars of the Roses, and has been verified by another tapestry that we have had stored at the museum for over a hundred years, that speaks of these three items being stored at the three Priories, and through field research by myself and Stuart we predicted its location and then subsequently found the item in a hidden cave. To me that can't be a hoax, certainly not in the time that TK Maxx has been around."

"Yeah, I didn't mean that it was actually bought in TK Maxx, Curtis, that's just an expression we archaeologists use if something is a modern reproduction for the tourist market." Said Amy. "The sort of things you see for sale in places like TK Maxx, but perhaps you're right chaps, perhaps it is the real deal, but as I said, I've never seen any of those inscriptions before and to me they are just random decorative shapes that don't mean anything."

"Right." Said Curtis, a little down-hearted.

"So, what do you think is at Lindisfarne, then?" asked Amy. "Is there any clue from your parchment or tapestry that speaks of what it could possibly be?"

"Hello Amy," said Cassidy, suddenly, "this Friar, called Blackwater, called himself a Master of the Order of the Northern Carmelites..." he said, changing his attitude almost immediately.

"Hang on!" said Amy. "The Carmelites?"

"The Northern Carmelites." Corrected Cassidy.

"I've never heard of the Northern Carmelites, but the Carmelites were a religious order that came from the..."

"Yeah, we know about the Carmelites, I've done all the research into them." Interrupted Cassidy, waving his hand and talking over Amy as she tried to offer her knowledge to the group. "They built Hulne Priory in Alnwick, which is the location of one of these supposed hidden items, so there is definitely a link there, as well as a link to the Templars which I'll explain in a moment, but he also talks of a golden casket buried at Lindisfarne. He also speaks of being protected from a darkness." Amy remained stony-faced.

"Well that sounds ominously fitting for you Curtis." She said eventually. "Why do you seem to attract cursed objects?" she asked.

"I don't!" he protested.

"You do! I've spent my whole life discovering treasures, and it's always you who manages to find the ones that have threatening auras, and seem to want to wipe out humanity." Said Amy.

"The stone is a given, right, that *was* cursed. But surely that was a one off? No one else has found a provably cursed object, have they?" said Curtis. "This friar may be talking about a different type of darkness, the scrawlings are all a bit vague."

"Can you even prove your stone was cursed?" asked Cassidy. There was a sound of a sharp intake of breath through pursed lips coming through the computer speakers as Amy relished in the fact that she knew Cassidy had overstepped the mark with that comment.

"What? Yes! It nearly killed us!" said Curtis.

"Can any of it be proven, though? Scientifically?" asked Cassidy. This riled Curtis, and he could feel himself losing his cool. He took a deep breath and shrugged.

"I know what happened, these two know what happened. I don't need to prove anything to anyone." He said.

"I'm just saying…" started Cassidy.

"Stuart," interrupted Amy, "how are you going to dig up a golden casket from a protected heritage site exactly? You won't personally get permission, I promise you that."

"We haven't crossed that particular bridge yet." He said, reluctantly. "But if we can prove that the other things exist, then *perhaps*, you never know, we may get permission."

"You won't." said Amy in a way that put that matter to bed. Curtis and Naomi shared a look that spoke a thousand words as to the clashing of personalities between Stuart and Amy.

"Do you know," said Curtis, "If a kid was there digging in the dirt and sand of St. Cuthbert's Island and plonking bits of turf into his bucket and carrying it off into the sea, no one would bat an eyelid."

"Well he should be parented properly for a start, but you know as well as I do about the rules and red tape surrounding this kind of work, especially if there is a known artefact there. It'll take months of planning, meetings, bloody risk assessments. You know what they're like, Curtis, you've had dealings with them before." Said Amy.

"Well, we'll worry about that side of things." Said Cassidy, dismissing Amy's concerns with a wave of his hand.

"So this box you've found in another box," said Amy, a little irked with this man's outdated way of speaking to women, and apparent in her tone as she spoke, "The one that's *not* from TK Maxx. You said it has a key inside that unlocks a golden casket, according to the parchment you conveniently found on a beach, but you haven't found the casket yet, *that's* buried under Lindisfarne Priory. What does this key look like? I could probably tell you immediately if the key is modern." Said Amy.

"And therein lies the difficulty." Said Curtis taking a sip from his bottle of beer. "We can't seem to get into the box." Amy frowned at the computer screen.

"So, how do you know there's a key inside?" she asked.

"We performed an x-ray of the larger box, which showed up the booby-trap mechanism, and as well as that, we could clearly see a large key inside this smaller box, but as far as we're concerned, we can't open it." Said Curtis.

"So that one could be booby-trapped too." Said Amy. "Did you work out how to bypass the mechanism that fired the dart on the bigger box?"

"Yes," said Cassidy, "there was a small area that, when depressed, disengaged the spring."

"So we were really mean to it and said it had no friends and looked fat." said Curtis. All three looked at Curtis without a reaction. He realised the poor quality of his joke, and waved them on to continue the conversation.

"So is there not something on this smaller box that can do that job? Disengaging a spring that is, not whatever Curtis was talking about." asked Amy.

"We haven't been able to find one." Said Cassidy as he once again picked the stone box up and began to try to press random parts of it. He then held it at eye level and began to study every inch of it.

"Well perhaps there isn't a lock and, if the box is indeed stone, or marble or even clay, maybe it was designed to be broken to gain access to the key?" suggested Amy.

"Do *not* smash that box." Said Curtis to Cassidy, who didn't look like he had any intention of smashing it at all, as he was still studying it closely.

"It's certainly not out of the ordinary." Said Amy.

"I've found something." Said Cassidy, suddenly.

"What?" asked Curtis, Naomi and Amy all in unison.

"There appears to be a small slot in the stonework that blends into the symbols if you're not directly looking at it." Said Cassidy. Curtis was next to take a look, and then he held it up to the webcam for Amy to see, before handing it to Naomi.

"So it looks like we need another key." Said Naomi to the group. "Could there have been another key hidden in the larger box? Either tiny, or very skinny."

At this question, both Curtis and Cassidy locked eyes and came to the same realisation at the exact same time. "The dart." Said Curtis. "It's got to be the dart." He fished it from the plastic tub he had placed it in for safe keeping and passed it to Stuart.

"Thanks. Hang on, why are you giving it to me?" asked Cassidy.

"It might be booby-trapped again." Said Curtis, "quick Naomi, give Stuart the box!"

Naomi handed Cassidy the small, pale coloured box, and Cassidy reluctantly held the projectile in his other hand, eyeing both items wearily: He seemed reluctant.

"At least see if it fits." Said Curtis.

"Which wall would you like me to aim it at?" asked Cassidy.

"Aim it at the third shelf from the top of those shelves." Said Curtis, pointing towards a cabinet of glasses.

"That's very specific." said Cassidy.

"I want new wine glasses and Naomi won't let me buy any." he said.

Cassidy placed the small box on the kitchen table and walked around so he was standing on the far side of the box. He leaned across as Naomi walked to the back door and opened it, and even Curtis began to back away from the kitchen into the corridor. Amy was still watching the whole thing from Curtis' computer screen, eyes wide in apprehension. Cassidy held the bolt from the other box in his fingers, pointing it back towards himself, and he fumbled for the tiny slot that went unnoticed the first time he looked at it.

"Found it." He said, a hint of panic in his voice. "Here goes nothing."

94

As he slowly and awkwardly inserted the sharpened projectile into the slot, and standing as far away from the box as his arm span would allow, his face contorted with the expectation of something terrible about to happen, there was a quiet 'click' and the top panel of the stone box flipped open, releasing a small puff of dust, and revealing an ornate old iron key and absolutely no hidden traps.

Instantly there were sighs of relief from everyone in the vicinity, even Amy who was safely miles away, watching the excitement unfold through the internet connection, let out a mollifying breath of ease as a man she'd only just met, and didn't really like, went unscathed from the ordeal.

"Pussy." Said Curtis with a quiet laugh as they all sat back down and Cassidy drew breath.

"So, we now have a key for a box that we can't find, and another box that fires projectiles from within it, that protected the other box from being opened by wrong'uns." Said Amy, summing up over the internet connection. "And by the looks of it, the key does look old. It's not repro."

"Definitely not." Said Stuart.

"So you need to find and dig up a golden casket, possibly the Ark of the Covenant, from Lindisfarne, and find, what was it, a bell at some other priory?" asked Amy.

"A burner and a bell. It's as simple as that." Said Curtis.

"Which are you going to attempt to negotiate first?" asked Amy.

"Lindisfarne." Said Cassidy. Curtis shrugged his approval.

"Good luck with that one then!" shouted Amy, stifling a laugh. "Let me know when you've managed to get permission for that dig, I'll speak in, what, two years time?"

"Yes, love you, bye." Said Curtis quickly, shutting the conversation down with the click of his mouse.

"Curtis!" said Naomi, appalled at his manners with her best friend and slapping him hard on the arm.

"We don't need that kind of negativity." He said.

"I'm going to ring her back." Said Naomi, as she went to leave the room, removing her mobile phone from her back pocket as she went. Cassidy waited until the kitchen door had closed behind her, before whipping around and talking in hushed tones to Curtis, leaning across the table.

"Right, I have a plan." Said Cassidy. "We go back to Holy Island, this time I'll bring my detector in my pack. I've got one with a short handle for easy packing and subtle use, it'll fit in a rucksack. That island with the little house on it isn't really that busy, especially if we aim to go on…" said Cassidy, selecting an app from his phone and tapping away, before continuing. "…Thursday, when it's forecast to piss it down all day. Pack your waterproofs, but only if they're dark colours, I don't want to attract any unwanted attention if we're going to just do some exploratory stuff, you know what those Nazi's are like."

"Is there even a rule for using a metal detector if we're not actually digging?" asked Curtis.

"We might actually dig though…" said Stuart with a wry smile.

"That's a dangerous game." Said Curtis, wincing at the thought of the repercussions.

"No harm in bringing a folding shovel, just in case." Said Stuart. "One of us would have to keep vigilant and make sure that we could easily fill in anything we dug."

"Stuart I'm not sure I'm happy about this." Said Curtis slowly as he sat back and took another swig from his bottle. "We could get in a lot of trouble, and I am the owner of our local heritage museum. If we get caught, that's my career and your hobby done for. The stakes are too high, mate. It's a prison sentence."

"So we don't get caught." Said Cassidy. "I'm going to ask you to contact whoever your most influential friend is regarding Lindisfarne and ask if you and I can detect along the beach of the Pilgrim's Way. That passes right by the island. All we do is stray a little too far in land, and if we do find anything, we just shift its discovery position by a hundred yards, and no one is the wiser."

Curtis exhaled as an internal battle raged in his mind between his hunger for discovery and his hesitation with morality.

"That's *so* risky." Said Curtis, wide eyed as he stared into the middle distance.

"Only if we're stupid, and I'd like to think that neither you nor I are *that* stupid." he said.

"You do have your moments, Stuart." replied Curtis, quietly, still processing the radical fundamentals of the suggestion.

"It's foolproof unless we are foolish, therefore, we must not be foolish." he said. Curtis mulled it all over in his head. It was an idea that could actually work, but also a very risky one that could end so badly, he could end his entire family history in a heartbeat. *But then, what great discoveries are ever without their associated risks?*

"Ok." said Curtis, eventually. "We go on Thursday, we take your things in a backpack, but we only start by using your detector, and only when there are zero people visible anywhere, understand? And in no circumstances other than a direct hit, does the shovel come out of your pack, deal? We are non-invasive unless the unthinkable happens and we literally strike gold." He said. "And, for the record, if we get rumbled I *will* be running away, into the sea if necessary, and *will* deny any affiliation or knowledge of you as a person."

"Sounds reasonable." said Cassidy. "You're probably faster than me anyway, I've got a gammy knee."

Curtis shook his head and exhaled, astounded at what he had just agreed to. And after a moment of silence, he spoke. "I'll call Freda and see if she can 'ok' us for a quick detect across the sands."

"Brilliant." replied Cassidy. "Can you get me Amy's number too?" Curtis frowned at his new friend.

"Absolutely not."

CHAPTER 10

The following day, Curtis woke very early and found himself immediately awake, knowing within a few seconds that there was no chance he would return to slumber, as his mind was instantly busy with thoughts of monumental discoveries and the potential marketing promise. He looked over to see Naomi still beautifully asleep, with an open mouth full of her own hair, so he got up and ventured downstairs.

The morning was still in its infancy, and the light had only just broken across the fields of Northumberland stretching away through the southern windows of the Old Rectory. Instinctively, and in full autopilot, Curtis made his way immediately to the coffee machine and fired it up before selecting his favourite mug from the cupboard, collecting the milk from the fridge on his route back to the machine, and made himself a deliciously strong coffee.

As he sat in one of the leather arm chairs nestled into a nook of the kitchen, sipping at his drink, his mind wandered back and forth between archaeology and law-braking, as his shoulder devil and his conscience fought an epic battle, fuelled by fresh caffeine.

"This is ridiculous." said Curtis quietly to himself as he stood and emptied his mug of its contents before heading to the locked key box containing all the keys to the Craxford car collection. When things got on top of Curtis, he would either sit in the shower for hours on end, or go for a drive, and, thanks to the enormous family wealth bequeathed to him, he had a considerable and constantly changing plethora of motors to choose from. He considered his classic Mercedes, but it had recently had a run out and he never liked to tempt fate too much with what he liked to call his 'pension fund', not that he really needed one of those. He considered, also, the Alfa Romeo, but his eye instead stopped on another rather inconspicuous and mainstream looking key, which he, after a quick glance out the window to check the weather, took from the box, closed and locked it with the master key, and ventured to his cavernous barn of a garage.

As the gates began to close behind him, the silence of the

Northumbrian morning was broken by the throaty bark of a twenty-year-old Renault's exhaust pipes as a flash of yellow tore through the sleepy village and out into the Northumberland National Park.

The wind whipped at Curtis' neck and he slightly regretted not wrapping up a little more before he headed out in a car that possessed no roof, but his burning hot passion for motoring carried him through the sweeping bends as the Renault Spider reached optimum temperature, allowing him to pop the heater on.

Another impulse buy, the Renault Spider resembled a supercar, yet was powered by no more than an engine from a hatchback, and was another car that Naomi referred to as a 'plastic crisis car'. But it was a car that Curtis had lusted after in his early adulthood, and when one of the rare examples came up for sale, he made the decision to snap it up. It wasn't particularly expensive or powerful, nor was it well made, yet, when driven with purpose and vigour, it made him feel extremely alive.

Curtis speared his way through the crisp Northumbrian air as his mental cobwebs were expunged, as he passed landmarks that sparked happy memories from throughout his life. He crossed a small bridge, underneath which he had sat and crammed for his A Level exams for a few days, meaning his results were a huge disappointment to his father; he passed the house his cousins grew up in and where he spent many a happy summer playing in the garden and surrounding woodland; he passed the end of a road along which he used to walk with his Grandfather who would point out all the different birds and trees, and then test him on the walk back; a test he always scored highly on; and he passed the large metal gates to a country estate that he trespassed onto with Naomi to officially propose his hand in marriage inside one of their many Victorian follies. This was *his* journey; his circuit, and the route he always took when he needed to distract himself from the pressures of real life.

But that morning there was no distraction from the dilemma his mind was awash with: was he really going to give his blessings, or be actively involved, in illegally digging on a world heritage site? It seemed preposterous. In any other circumstance he knew there would be no question; a blanket 'no', however, this man who had crashed into his life with a huge impact not two weeks earlier seemed highly persuasive, and the stones they had over-turned had rewarded them with so much already. This was going to be a moral minefield, and he knew the easy way out was to simply walk away. But the currents were too strong, and they pulled him back towards the dangerous and the irresponsible.

He felt his telephone buzz in his pocket, so he quickly pulled his car to a stop on the side of a deserted tree-lined road and answered it: "Hello darling" he said.

"Where are you?" asked a sleepy sounding Naomi.

"Erm, Netherwitton." said Curtis.

"What?" she asked, shocked at the answer. "I meant where in the house. Why are you in Netherwitton?"

"Couldn't sleep so took the Spider for a run out." he said, "I didn't want to wake you."

"Ok, when are you coming back?" she asked.

"I'll not be long; I'll make bacon sandwiches when I get in." he said.

"Ok, drive carefully." she said through a yawn.

"No chance." he said as he ended the call, built the revs high, and quickly released the clutch to engage power and catapult himself up the road with a childish squeal of tyres and exhaust noise. He decided, knowing the road very well and the fact that it was so early in the morning that the roads would be practically empty of motorists, to drive hard all the way home, and within a whisker over fifteen minutes, he was slowly crossing the gravel of the Old Rectory's driveway, teeth chattering but extremely content.

When he entered the kitchen, Naomi was sat at the table with a cup of tea. He crossed the room and kissed her. "Morning." he said.

"Morning. So what's the matter?" asked Naomi, "What's caused the sudden insomnia and spontaneous road trip this time?"

"Nothing in particular," lied Curtis, "Just thinking about this whole Templar relic thing, really."

"Please don't get obsessed with it, Curtis, you know what you're like, it will consume you, and you'll probably be left disappointed. And as for trying to dig things up, you know it's wrong. You won't do it will you?" said Naomi. "And you still have other duties to attend to at the museum, remember, like your meeting with Mr. Brampton in an hour and a half?"

Curtis frowned again as he took his iPhone from his pocket and selected his appointments app. "Ah, yes, regarding the Fijian war clubs." he said, replacing his phone and heading off to get ready. "I hadn't forgotten." he added, lying once again.

A few days later, and four 17th Century Fijian Vounicao stronger, the Craxford Museum was once again bustling with patrons looking on in awe at the various exhibits throughout the cavernous building as Curtis strolled through the corridors, his mind once again on the potential treasures buried in his county, or more accurately just off the coast of his county.

He was hurrying to his office, excited to make a phone call to Stuart Cassidy regarding some news he'd just received via a text message from a friend. They were due to meet the following morning and carry out a day of secret exploratory experiments, hopefully shrouded by the poor Northumbrian weather conditions forecast for the foreseeable days to come. As Curtis walked he glanced out of one of the large stone windows that wrapped the Victorian leviathan of a building, and could see the weather front already streaking across the sky, bringing with it a diesel gloom that for once he welcomed with child-like excitement.

Once inside his office he hurried to his desk and took a seat in his father's button-back chair, picked up the telephone handset and typed out Cassidy's number. After five rings, Stuart answered: "Hello buddy." he said.

"Stuart, hi." said Curtis, "Good news."

"You've heard back from your friend?" he pre-empted.

"I have, and we have been granted permission to detect along the pilgrim's trail, but only in the sand, and all digs must be left as found, filled in and returned to normal." he said.

"Fine, as that's really kind of irrelevant anyway." said Cassidy.

"Well, yes, I suppose it is." said Curtis. "It also carries another caveat."

"What?"

"We must present any items we find to English Heritage, and they will decide where the items will end up, be that at Craxford Museum or the Heritage Centre on the island, or indeed anywhere else the Heritage feel it would be best presented."

"Right..." said Cassidy, slowly; a hint of worry in his voice.

"Look, depending on what we actually find, we can cross that bridge when we come to it, and the Museum has the best chance of actually retaining the items anyway, as I've rarely lost in a bidding war for items of local significance, and we are recognised globally, especially if I personally discover things, as for some reason the press seem to think I'm Lara Croft, after our little escapades in the Amazon." said Curtis. Cassidy snorted his disapproval, yet that was the main reason he chose Curtis as a partner in this tomb raid.

"All I ask is that you don't wear the outfit." Said Cassidy.

"I'd look brilliant. Anyway, what I suggest," continued Curtis, "is we try to find this chest, but let's do a little detecting on the sands too, just in case anyone is watching, and if we do find anything, we don't have to present it immediately. We can spend time first, looking into it all, and essentially gathering the rest of the pieces of this puzzle."

"So you want to do some detecting on the sands too, even though we pretty much know the chest is buried on the island?" asked Cassidy.

"Stuart, we shouldn't be doing this at all, but I want a concrete reason to be there, and if that means spending a couple of extra hours covering our arses in terms of why we're there with a dirty great metal detector in hand, it makes sense to actually detect on the area that we've been given permission to detect on." said Curtis. "Besides, we might find more stuff, you never know."

"Ok, whatever you want." said Stuart, clearly not in agreement to be wasting time detecting in other areas. "Does your friend know we're going tomorrow?"

"No, I suggested it would be at least a month before we got ourselves sorted, which should buy us some time if we do find anything tomorrow and allow us to properly examine it."

"Right, so should I meet you there? Tide times are in our favour, and mean we can make safe crossing until 9am, and then as long as we leave before 9pm we're good for the whole day." said Cassidy.

"Yes, I've noticed that, the Gods are smiling upon us it seems. And we should retain enough light until that time in the evening so we can work right through." said Curtis.

"No boozy lunches this time, I'm bringing sandwiches and a flask of tea. I want to find this chest if it's there." said Cassidy.

"I agree," said Curtis, "though to be honest I'm bringing coffee, I'll need plenty of that."

"So, I'm aiming to be there for no later than 7am." said Cassidy.

"Crikey, ok, it *is* going to be a long day." said Curtis. "But nevertheless, I will meet you in the carpark there at 7 sharp." said Curtis.

"Ok, and don't bring the Ferrari, come in the Jeep, we don't want to attract any unwanted attention." said Cassidy.

"It's an Alfa Romeo." said Curtis. "And a Land Rover."

"Whatever, just blend in." said Cassidy in a frustrated tone.

"Fine." said Curtis. "I'll see you in the morning." And with that he hung up the telephone and wandered out from his office, back into the throng of public, and on through the Hadrian's Wall exhibit, the Ancient Egypt room, the invertebrate room full of his favourite insects, and finally halting at the cafe, where he selected a sandwich, two packets of crisps, a bottle of Fanta, and headed out into the car park, where he proceeded to drive home and prepare for the long day to come.

Curtis' alarm sounded at the ungodly hour of 5am, when the night was still very much in control, and he hauled himself out of bed with a groan. Dressing as silently as he could so as not to wake Naomi, he pulled on his jeans and a t-shirt, and made his way downstairs. He made himself a large flask of coffee, pouring himself the leftovers for immediate consumption, collected his pack, and jumped in the car.

Rumbling through Northumberland in his Land Rover, as the saturation began to wash into the fields and woodland from the dawn sun, Curtis had a burning excitement in his stomach. Just *what* would they unearth? The ideas crashing and colliding within Curtis' thoughts were all-consuming and caused Curtis to drive faster and faster in his impatience to arrive and begin their hunt.

The damp emerald hues of the mainland were replaced with the sandy straits of the causeway as Curtis headed for the island of Lindisfarne nearly an hour after he set off from his home, and as he pulled into the almost deserted public car park, Stuart Cassidy was already sitting on the lip of his open boot, sipping at his steaming cup of tea, large backpack propped against the bumper of the car.

"Morning." Said Curtis, failing to muster much enthusiasm as the dampness attacked him as he stepped down from his car.

"Ready?" asked Cassidy.

"I guess so." He replied.

"I've brought two detectors to look more authentic." Said Cassidy. "Have you ever used one?"

"Yes, on several occasions." Said Curtis. "I once found a Penny from 1890. That was my greatest and only find."

"Astonishing." Said Cassidy, sarcastically. "Shame it wasn't a 1933 one."

"Why?" asked Curtis.

"Well, surely you know that the 1933 penny is the rarest in existence?" said Cassidy, as they walked through the streets of the village.

"I was unaware of that. Why?" said Curtis.

"They only made seven of them." Said Cassidy.

"Seven thousand?"

"No seven."

"Seven! Really?" asked Curtis. "Why only seven?"

"They were never supposed to be circulated, but seven made it out into the system. I believe that two are still unaccounted for, making them worth about seventy thousand pounds each."

"Seventy grand for a penny? Not bad." Said Curtis. "What's the best thing you've found then, other than the obvious?"

"Well, aside from what I found over there," said Cassidy, pointing vaguely in the direction of the mainland where he dug up the parchment, "I've unearthed a lot of Roman artefacts; a sword, coins, a belt buckle, and a small metal horse ornament, as well as a few later coins. Nothing, other than the sword are of any real significance." He added. "But I was detecting in the same field as my friend Cliff, who dug up a bronze age gold chalice, which later sold for nearly three hundred grand. Which was both annoying and exciting I suppose."

104

"Bloody hell, did he get to keep the money?" asked Curtis.

"Yes, well he split it with the landowner, which is the general practice." Said Cassidy.

"Interesting." Said Curtis, and they both fell silent as they walked on towards St. Cuthbert's Island.

"So are we starting by detecting on the sand? Or are we heading straight to the island?" asked Cassidy.

"I'd say see who is about, and if it's quiet head straight for the island, and I'll keep watch while you detect." Said Curtis.

But as they approached there were a few people milling around the general area, as well as a couple of dog walkers, so they made the decision to detect along the sands, whilst keeping an eye out for the people dispersing.

"I reckon we've only got about an hour or two before the tide comes in and covers all this so let's at least make a start and see what happens." Said Cassidy looking out to sea.

"It was supposed to utterly piss down with rain today." Said Curtis, removing his iPhone and checking the weather app. "It now says rain from 10am."

"Well at least that will drive people away I guess." Said Cassidy. "Come on! Let's get to work."

They started by walking backwards and forwards on the beach area not far from the island, and occasionally got a rewarding beep from the machines that generally delivered bottle tops, ring pulls, a spoon and the odd modern coin. Curtis was extremely excited when he uncovered a small necklace with a cross attached until Stuart pointed out that it was stamped '*made in China*', and other than that, all they found was a large quantity of rusted fishing tackle.

But it was a while before the rain started to batter them, much to their delight and as the tide prevented them from detecting any further on the vanishing sands, they retreated to St. Cuthbert's Island, where they sat, shrouded from the shore by an ancient wall, and began what they were there to do.

Curtis stood, like a sentinel, watching out for any signs of movement, whist trying to remain invisible, yet also keep an eye on what Stuart was doing with his metal detector. He was on his knees, slowly and methodically moving the detector over every inch of grass and dirt on the island, headphones covering his ears,

105

and in deep concentration.

Nothing was happening quickly, and after an hour, Curtis decided to pour himself a hot coffee to try to warm himself up. But as he took his first sip, Cassidy stopped dead in his tracks.

"I've got a result Curtis." he said. "There's something here. It's quite deep, but it's registering as metal and it's quite big."

"Oh Christ! Right, let me check if the coast is clear." replied Curtis excitedly. "The coast is wet, but clear. You dig, I'll keep a look out." he said, still incredulous to the words he just spoke, as he poked his head over the wall and scanned in all directions like a bedraggled meerkat surveying a hazy grey seascape.

The rain was growing in intensity with every minute, and soon the space that Stuart Cassidy was working in was becoming a quagmire of thick mud and sludge. But he dug, using his folding shovel, as quickly, yet as carefully as he could, making sure that any of the soil he dug out was kept at close quarters in case a rapid refilling of the hole was required.

It was heavy going, as the clay-like mud was almost solid, packed tight from millennia of footsteps. Cassidy paused and picked up his detector once more and listened in through the headphones. He nodded to himself and carried on digging, until eventually his shovel hit an object. Cassidy's head darted up and he met Curtis' gaze. He began to dig with his fingers, trying to remove the cloying mud from around the object he had found. Slowly, something began to materialise in the ground as more of the surrounding mud was removed. There, before them in the rain, sat the top of a metal box.

It was hard to see in the late afternoon gloom. The rain had abated, but it had left its mark upon the sky, darkening the landscape in all directions, and as Cassidy excavated around the chest using a trowel and his hands, they both quickly realised that this was certainly not what they were expecting to find.

"Well that's wrong." Said Curtis, looking at what Cassidy had uncovered.

"This is relatively modern." Said Cassidy. "Probably First World War."

Cassidy lifted the shoe-box sized tin from the ground and wiped it clean with an old towel he had in his sodden pack. "Looks like someone's lunch box."

"Can we get it open?" asked Curtis, excitement growing once again, even though it wasn't what either of them was expecting to find.

Cassidy tried the latch of the tin, but it snapped under gentle pressure, so he fished in his pack once more and pulled out a large survival knife with a bright orange handle.

"Bloody hell, were you planning on catching a seal for our tea? Why have you brought a machete?" asked Curtis.

"It's just my knife, comes in very handy." Said Cassidy.

"Yeah, if dinosaurs still roamed the place!" said Curtis. "That's an offensive weapon, man! That's another thing we can add to our list of felonies."

Cassidy ignored him and began trying to prize the lid off by using his knife as a lever. He seemed to be struggling with it, but eventually the lid began to move slightly, and after a few further prods, it hinged open as both men peered over into the rusted box.

It was an anti-climax. There were some soggy pieces of paper, the writing on which was now totally illegible, and as Cassidy fished around inside, fell apart around his fingers. He did pull out an old black and white photo portrait of a woman, but again, it was so badly water damaged, it was hard to make out any discernible features.

"Is this someone's love box?" asked Curtis.

"Well, it's a box of papers and photos." Said Cassidy, throwing it down next to his pack, followed by a small bout of swearing.

"Let's have the rest of our sandwiches." Said Curtis, dejectedly. "Do you want a coffee?"

"No, I've got tea." Said Cassidy, equally forlorn.

"Let's have a break."

After they finished off their sandwiches and the contents of their flasks, the rain began to pour once again, dampening their spirits even further.

"I'll go and get a rock to put in its place, then we can fill the hole back in." said Curtis.

"What, we're keeping it?" asked Cassidy. "It's practically worthless."

"Yes, but it's a find, and we can present it to the Heritage, should we need to justify our being here." Said Curtis. "If word gets out we found anything, this could throw them off the trail for a while." Cassidy nodded in agreement. "I can't believe I've just said that." added Curtis, shaking his head in disbelief at his own words.

"I guess I'll carry on then," Said Cassidy, picking up his detector once more and resuming his hands-and-knees scanning of the areas within and surrounding St. Cuthbert's House.

It was cold and tedious work for both men; Curtis kept watch as the wind blew the heavy rain directly into his face; now numb with cold and worsened by the incessant saline picked up from the crashing waves beyond the sands and causing his throat to ache and his teeth to chatter. Meanwhile Cassidy continued the scan of the area, the rain running down his face and into any exposed areas of clothing, but roughly half an hour later, Cassidy once again called over to Curtis to say that he had generated another result from below ground.

"Please Christ let this be it," said Cassidy as he set the detector to one side and grabbed his trowel once more. It was well into the evening, and both men had lost track of the time, and again failed to notice the inbound tide creeping its unstoppable way up the sands towards their small island: too engrossed in their search for treasures. Curtis paid the occasional glance to the shore and the footpath that lead back to the priory for signs of life, but the moment he was satisfied they were alone, his attention darted back to Stuart Cassidy and the careful excavation of dirt that could lead to a history-altering discovery.

This time, he had to dig deeper into the wet mud, and after what felt like an eternity, when he finally struck the top of the object he had detected, the light was beginning to fade from the dull evening sky. Their eyes met as he hit solid material, and he began to pull the mud away with his hands to try to reveal its size.

"Is it even metal?" asked Curtis, peering over Cassidy's shoulder at what was being excavated.

"No." said Cassidy. "This is a wooden trunk."

"Oh for god's sake!" shouted Curtis. "Has your machine just picked up its metal fastenings?"

"Potentially, yes, but it's old!" Said Cassidy. "I think we've found what we're looking for mate. The casket could be inside! It makes sense. It's unlikely they'd just bury a golden casket in the earth, unprotected."

"You think?" asked Curtis, the fire rekindling within his stomach.

"Can't say for sure, but we've just located an old buried chest. In any situation it's a huge win!" said Cassidy, continuing to dig around the dirty chest.

"This is actually happening!" said Curtis. "Well done mate. Right, you keep digging it out, I'll go and find some big stones to put in its place when we fill the hole back in. We need this place to look exactly as we left it. No hollows, no signs of an excavation." he said, as he stood up and exited the foundations of the ruins and made his way up onto the top of the island. He stopped dead in his tracks. "Oh shit!"

"What is it? Is someone coming?" asked Cassidy from beside the half-excavated chest.

"Not exactly." replied Curtis. "It appears we've lost track of time a little, Stuart!"

"What do you mean?" replied Cassidy.

"The tide's in mate. We're stranded." said Curtis as the once distant waves were now crashing all around him.

"We're cut off?" asked Cassidy, standing up and joining Curtis.

"So it would seem." he said with a manic chuckle as Cassidy stood beside him and looked at the body of water that now stood between St. Cuthbert's Island and the main island. It looked deep, and cold: an abyss of blackness.

"Christ." said Cassidy. Curtis took out his iPhone and looked up the tide table on the website.

"Causeway doesn't open again until 5am." said Curtis. "So we'll be looking at five thirty for us to get back onto the main island."

"Great. Bloody great." said Cassidy, throwing his trowel down onto the ground in anger. "So not only are we soaked to the skin, freezing and covered in crap, we now have to sit for..." he glanced at his watch, "...seven hours, in the dark, with no food, waiting for the bloody tide to go out!"

"Relax." said Curtis. "I have snacks. And whisky." he added, trying to keep Cassidy's spirits up. "Come on, let's get it out of the ground, then we can try to have a look at what we're dealing with. At least no one is going to creep up on us."

109

They both knelt down and tried to dig around the wooden chest. It was a considerable size, and it took them a while to uncover it from the surrounding soil, and by the time they both manhandled the chest out of the hole and onto the grass beside it, they had lost the majority of the light, and they were struggling to see what they were dealing with, but they knew they were on to something too exciting to comprehend.

"This is stupid." said Curtis eventually. "It could be another booby-trapped chest, and we can't see the thing properly. I want to get it back to the museum and scan it before we go any further. The last thing you or I need right now is a large bolt to the face."

"I agree." said Cassidy eventually. "We need to fill this hole in too."

"Right," said Curtis, trying to blow some heat into his hands, "Let's get to work on that." he said, as he picked up Cassidy's folding shovel and began to fill in the large hole. "We need some rocks."

CHAPTER 11

"Christ it's cold." whispered Curtis as he and Cassidy sat huddled in the ruins of St. Cuthbert's house; trying their best to shelter from the coastal winds that battered the small island in the dead of night. They had done a good job at filling the hole, and unless one looked closely and was very familiar with the lie of the land to the nearest inch, nothing appeared any different or out of place. They had spent as long as their energy would allow stamping down the mud to make it look compacted and as it was, but eventually exhaustion had got the better of them.

The rain had not abated, and it was pitch black given the lack of artificial lighting on the island, and both men were beginning to feel numb and lethargic with the cold, despite it being summer. Curtis glanced at his watch every ten minutes, willing the night to pass quicker than time would allow.

"I'm going to have to do some squats or something." said Cassidy eventually.

"What?" asked Curtis. "Is that the hypothermia talking?"

"It will be soon if we don't warm up." he said, standing up and beginning to slowly run on the spot. "Come on, get up, I need you to be able to function if we're going to get this chest open."

Curtis shook his head but stood up and began to perform slow star jumps in his soggy and heavy waterproofs. This surprisingly made him feel better as his body began to slowly warm up. "Three hours, that's all, just three hours to go before we can get back to my Landy with it's beautiful heater." he said to himself.

"I wish you'd thought to bring the key." said Cassidy. "At least we could have had a good look to see what we're dealing with."

"Booby traps, Stuart." said Curtis. "It all needs scanning before we go anywhere near it, or one of us could end up dead. That's if the cold doesn't get one of us first. Or the ghost of St. Cuthbert."

When the sun finally rose in the sky enough to shed an eerie greenish light on the landscape, Cassidy and Curtis were both ready to leave Lindisfarne the moment the tide had receded enough to allow passage back onto the main island. Curtis had

111

suggested he run ahead and bring the Land Rover as close to the shore as he possibly could so as not to attract any unwanted attention as they carried a giant chest through the village. He knew there would be some locals who would be up this early, and he couldn't risk being caught, seen or worse: recognised.

"I can't wait any longer." said Curtis. "I'm wading across to get the car."

"Fine. Don't break your ankles and get back here as soon as you can. Don't beep the horn or anything when you get back, we need to be covert." said Cassidy.

"Ok Mr. Bond." said Curtis as he walked towards the water. "I'm not an idiot."

"That's debatable." said Cassidy quietly, viewing his predicament, for which he blamed Curtis entirely.

Curtis tried to look for the shallowest looking stretch of water, and swiftly began to wade across towards the priory on the far shores. As it happened, the water was only ankle deep for the majority of the crossing to the other shore, apart from the central section which went above the knee, and chilled Curtis to his core even further. His teeth were chattering as he shook the water from his boots before pushing his sodden and freezing feet back inside and hurrying off towards the car park at a brisk yet squelchy walk.

He saw his Land Rover a few minutes later and blipped the key fob to unlock the doors. He climbed inside and started the engine immediately, desperate for the warmth from the heater to permeate his bones. He revved it for a few seconds, then thought better of it as the loud exhausts barked their cold greeting, and slowly, and as quietly as his engine would allow, he moved out of the car park, along the access road to the centre of the village, and on to the priory gates. They were of course locked with a sturdy looking padlock.

Curtis noticed the road headed directly towards the beach a little further ahead so he followed it and discovered, to his relief, that it did grant access for cars such as his Land Rover: he imagined attempting this in any of his other cars would result in a severely damaged undercarriage and an almost immediate beaching.

He drove as quietly as possible along the rutted sandy tracks, used solely, he imagined, by the odd tractor, and swiftly

112

reached the sand and shingle shores, upon which he drove as close to the island as the tide would allow. He was half tempted to beep his horn, just to annoy Cassidy, but he dismissed that notion as too risky, and sat for a few seconds, hands pressed to the heaters as the very beginnings of warmth blew through onto his cold fingers.

A few moments later he saw Cassidy stood, waiting on the island, and he decided that the quicker he helped get the large and heavy chest into the back of the Land Rover, the quicker he could return to the warmth of his car heater. So he left the car, and waded once again over to the island to his friend and the exciting potentials currently locked inside an ancient chest.

The moment that the Land Rover motored up the incline onto the Northumbrian coastline from the causeway, closely followed by Cassidy's Golf, both men drew their respective breath and relaxed a little. The heater had finally blown warmth into Curtis, and there was a giant wooden chest filling the entire boot of the car that had potentially been buried in the ground for over five hundred years.

Curtis suddenly selected Cassidy's phone number and dialled it. Cassidy picked up almost immediately.

"What is it? Miss me already?" he said.

"How hasn't the chest deteriorated in the ground?" asked Curtis.

"What?" asked Cassidy wearily.

"The chest. If it was buried in the 1400s, surely the wood would have crumbled to wet mush by now." said Curtis.

"They were quite often painted with a thick resin." said Cassidy. "Similar to the embalming process in Egypt I suppose. We'll have a closer look at the museum." said Cassidy. This made Curtis feel a little better.

"God I need a coffee." said Curtis.

"Alnwick's your best bet at this time." said Cassidy. "There's a McDonalds there that does half decent coffee."

"Urgh, I might wait." said Curtis, always the coffee snob.

"We haven't discussed what the next move is." said Cassidy. "Where do we go now?"

"I'm going to bed." said Curtis. Cassidy paused.

"Can I crash on your sofa? I'm too tired to drive all the

way back to Penshaw, and I guess you'll be wanting to get straight to scanning it at the labs." said Cassidy.

"Erm, yeah, if you want." said Curtis, a little surprised. "We actually have spare rooms you know, you don't have to sleep on the sofa."

"Thank you." said Cassidy.

"Is there not a Mrs. Stuart, who will be missing you?" asked Curtis as he joined the A1 and headed south, still followed by the man he was speaking to through the car's bluetooth phone connectivity.

"Not right now, I haven't got time for all the crap that comes with women." said Stuart. "I ended my last relationship because they were too clingy. I like to be given space. I have too many hobbies."

"Fair enough." said Curtis, thinking how difficult he would be to live with. "Did you say you live in Penshaw?"

"Aye, my house looks out over the Monument and the Washington Wetlands."

"Ah beautiful. I love Penshaw Monument. Such a cool place." said Curtis.

"Ah it just gets constantly vandalised nowadays." said Cassidy.

"Little *scallys*." said Curtis. "So much history to it as well."

"Yep."

"Built by John Lambton, right?" said Curtis.

"Actually: built in memory of John Lambton." corrected Cassidy.

"Ah, and the dwelling place of the Lambton Worm." said Curtis.

"Well, sort of." said Cassidy.

"Shush lads, hold your gobs, I'll tell you's all an awful story aboot the worm." sang Curtis through the phone in his mock Geordie accent and getting both the lyrics and the tune of the local shanty fantastically wrong. Cassidy winced.

"No." he said, wearily, frustration clouding the single word he uttered.

"What?" asked Curtis.

"That was the worst rendition of that song I think I've ever heard." said Cassidy.

"Come on then, it's something like that." said Curtis, laughing. Cassidy sighed and cleared his throat.

"One sunday morn young Lambton went a-fishin' in the Wear

and catched a fish upon his hook he thought looked mighty queer

What'n a kind of fish it was young Lambton couldn't tell

But he couldn't be bothered to carry it hyem so he hoyed it doon a well, hey

Whisht, lads, had ya gobs, I'll tell you's aal an aaful story

Whisht, lads, had ya gobs, I'll tell you 'boot the worm

Curtis was smiling and trying to join in where he could, but Cassidy sang over him and kept going as both men drove in convoy down the A1 towards Morpeth.

Now Lambton felt inclined to gan and fight in foreign wars

he joined a troop of knights that cared of neither wounds nor scars

So off he went to Palestine where strange things him befel

and very soon forgot aboot the strange thing in the well, hey

"Was he a Templar too??" asked Curtis, but Cassidy was now in full swing, and continued the song without reply.

Whisht, lads, had ya gobs, I'll tell you's aal an aaful story

Whisht, lads, had ya gobs, I'll tell you 'boot the worm

Whey noo that worm it grewed and grewed, and grewed to an aaful size

with a geet big heed, and a geet big gob, and geet big goggly eyes

and when at neet he crawled aboot to pick up bits of news

if he felt dry upon the road he'd milk a dozen coo's, howey then

Whisht, lads, had ya gobs, I'll tell you's aal an aaful story

Whisht, lads, had ya gobs, I'll tell you 'boot the worm

This fearful worm would often feed on calves and lambs and sheep

and swallow little bairns alive when they lay doon to sleep

and when he'd eaten aal he could and he had had his fill

he crawled away and wrapped his tail ten times roond Penshaw Hill, yeh buggers!

115

Whisht, lads, had ya gobs, I'll tell you's aal an aaful story
Whisht, lads, had ya gobs, I'll tell you 'boot the worm.
Anyway," said Cassidy, suddenly stopping, "it goes on."

"No don't stop now!" said Curtis, smiling at the brief and intimate glimpse into a different side of Stuart Cassidy.

"I literally haven't got the mental capacity to carry on." said Cassidy.

"To be honest, I know how you feel." said Curtis, as both men yawned in unison and ended the call.

"Coffee?" asked Curtis when Stuart Cassidy finally made his way into the kitchen later that evening.

"Yes, please, lots of it." he said, stifling a yawn and looking rather groggy: eyes narrow and puffed, dishevelled and wearing an almost startled and bewildered look. "I woke up and had no idea where I was."

They both sat at the Old Rectory's kitchen table and sipped at their strong coffees in silence for a while, and once they both felt a little more human and awake, they began to discuss the plan ahead.

"Right," said Curtis, "as we did last time, we'll wait until the lab is quiet, and do our stuff then. We scan it, and then if the thing seems safe, we attempt to open it. To be honest it's nearly five o'clock now, so the building will be emptying as we speak."

"You've got the key?" asked Cassidy.

"I have."

"What *is* the significance of the burner and the bell in this story?" asked Cassidy. "I understand keeping the key and the chest separate for obvious reasons, but what the hell even is a *burner*? Are we talking about a candle? Or a flame thrower? Or some acid? And a bell? Why?"

"That was a great rant, Stuart. Well done." said Curtis, holding up his coffee mug in admiration.

"I'm assuming they are some sort of ritualistic aspect of this relic as a whole." said Cassidy, ignoring Curtis. "It's the only explanation, really."

"Well I suppose we can look for them at Hulne after we've got this current chest open and we've examined the contents."

"Let's get going then." said Cassidy, draining his coffee and getting up from the table.

Lugging the large wooden chest around the corridors of the museum was hard going, and both Curtis and Stuart felt very exposed; all illegal and wrong, and kept looking out for straggling students and cleaners who would catch them with something they really shouldn't have, at one point even diving into an empty class room to avoid someone Curtis vaguely recognised as a member of staff from the university passing the end of their corridor.

They eventually made it to the room containing the x-ray machine, and as Curtis closed the door behind him, they both relaxed and placed the large chest onto the plinth.

"Right, let's see what this thing is hiding." said Curtis.

The chest was at least four feet long and banded by metal strips all around it. The lock seemed hugely oversized and was filled with dirt, but Curtis was determined to get into it before the day was over.

"Do your thing." said Cassidy, retreating to the back of the room while Curtis tapped away on a keyboard, and few minutes later, they had their first image.

"Holy crap." said Cassidy as he looked at the screen in front of them. He placed his hand on Curtis' shoulder and began to laugh a strange, excited laugh.

"Well would you look at that." said Curtis quietly to himself.

The x-ray revealed that within the wooden chest lay something large, rectangular and very metal; a glowing beacon of white against the dark wood of the outer chest.

"That's a metal chest." said Cassidy. "A very metal chest."

"Yes." said Curtis quietly.

"We need to get this wooden chest open." said Cassidy.

"We need to x-ray it from a few different angles first to see if there is a mechanism attached to the lock." said Curtis. "It's hard to tell from this image."

They took four other angled x-rays, and once they were completely satisfied that it was just a regular fifteenth century lock, they powered down the x-ray machine, and decided to take the chest to Curtis' office, whereupon they would open it in private.

This time Curtis would take no chances, so found a wheeled trolley and a large sheet, which proved to be a much easier and smarter way of travel between the floors and down the corridors, with the chest hidden from the prying eyes of the non-existent students and members of staff who were no longer frequenting those sections of the building, until finally they made it to the museum and Curtis' office down in the basement.

He closed the door behind him and pulled the sheet away as if revealing a magic trick, finishing his flourish with an audible "ta-da!". Cassidy followed suit by removing a large crowbar from his backpack he was still wearing, and copied Curtis with an equivalent "ta-da!".

"Teamwork makes the dreamwork." he added, pointing the crowbar at his friend, and moved towards the chest.

"Wait." said Curtis. "What about the key?"

"I'd imagine that would be for the inner chest, wouldn't you?" said Cassidy.

"Probably, but I feel it's worth a try. At the end of the day, this is still a hugely valuable fifteenth century wooden chest that quite probably houses a Templar golden casket and some sort of religious artefact of significant worldly importance, and therefore is absolutely a vital part of this entire project and should really be given the same level of care and protection as the rest of the items, therefore I'd like to try to pick the lock before using brute strength and permanent damage."

"And breathe." said Cassidy. Curtis took a breath as instructed. "Yes I suppose you're right. How are you at picking ancient locks?"

"I mean, I've never tried, you?" said Curtis.

"Likewise." said Cassidy.

"Bob!" shouted Curtis suddenly. This gave Cassidy a small fright and he glanced around towards the door.

"Who?" he said, realising there was no one there.

"Bob'll do it!" said Curtis.

"Who the heck is Bob? And why are we involving him?" asked Cassidy.

"Bob is our housekeeper and mechanic." said Curtis.

"Of course he is. Of course you have a house keeper." said Cassidy, rolling his eyes.

"He's helped me pick locks before, mostly on cars, but..."

"What?"

"I have bought 'barn-finds' before to restore, which quite often come without any keys, and we therefore have to sometimes break in to get access to the thing. Bob is very handy when it comes to that sort of thing." said Curtis.

"Right, so where is Bob?" asked Cassidy.

"He lives in the village. We're going to have to head up to mine again, I'm afraid." said Curtis.

"Right," said Cassidy, "here's the plan: I'll leave my car here, we drive the chest back to yours, collecting fish and chips on the way…"

"Hang on, why are you leaving your car here?" asked Curtis.

"Because I like your beer, your whisky, and your spare room. And I think we'll be a while. Is that ok?" asked Stuart, not waiting for a reply. "Then we drag Bob over to pick the lock, and once he has, send him on his way before we open it and reveal what's inside."

"I agree with the majority of that plan." said Curtis. "But Bob is fiercely loyal and can be trusted. I don't think it's fair to exclude him from the big reveal. Also, it's not related to tractors, so he won't have much interest in what's inside anyway."

"Fine, but we get him to sign a confidentiality agreement before we start." said Cassidy.

"No, I'll just tell him it's sensitive material that we're trying to keep a secret until we've completed our research. He'll understand. It's happened before. I can vouch for him."

"Well, your career rests on it." said Cassidy. "I wouldn't like someone who works for me having access to that kind of information. This will take the total number of people who know what we've found to five. It was always supposed to be two."

"And I completely trust three of them with my life." said Curtis. "I haven't known *you* long enough to form that opinion yet."

"Well obviously I'm not going to blab, am I?" said Cassidy, defensively.

"Well we really shouldn't have anything to worry about, then, should we?" said Curtis, removing his iPhone and calling Bob Common. He waited a few seconds, and then began to speak.

"Bob, am I interrupting anything?... You sure?... Can I borrow you for a little while in about an hour's time at the Rectory?... Brilliant... If you could bring your lock picking kit... Old... Very old... No, older... Not a car, no. A wooden chest...

Probably fifteenth century... Yeah... You're a legend. There's fish and chips and a beer in it for you... Cheers. Oh, and Bob? Can we keep *schtum* on this please? At least for the moment... Thanks buddy. See you soon."

Just over an hour later they were both sat, with Bob and Naomi, around the kitchen table of the Old Rectory, enjoying a large fish supper, while the two men filled the other two in on the story so far. Even Naomi was now fully engrossed and subscribed to the potential of the discovery.

"So what's in the box then?" asked Bob in his broad Northumbrian accent.

"We don't know. They seemed to revere it as a religious artefact. And if it *is* Templar in origin, it could re-write history the world over."

"You know..." said Naomi, slowly, "the Ark of the Covenant was described as being a large golden casket with the power to destroy enemies on the field of battle."

"You've changed." said Curtis, shaking his head at his fiancee who, until very recently, pooh-poohed the idea of a Templar artefact being buried on Lindisfarne.

"Did you know, also, that the Ark was purported to be made from the wood of the Shittah Tree?" said Cassidy. Curtis snorted his pleasure at this fact.

"Seriously though," said Naomi, "could we have potentially found the Ark of the Covenant? And is it here in my kitchen? In theory at least?"

"No." said Curtis. "The Ark of the Covenant is in Ethiopia. The Queen of Sheeba's son stole it."

"That is incorrect." said Stuart. "There is a copy of the Ark of the Covenant in every Ethiopian church. That is what they do. They claim the real one is in a church there, but surprisingly no one is allowed in, ever, other than the one protector who lives there his entire life like a prisoner and is not allowed out. So clearly, they are lying and are using the ancient tale as a weapon of fear to govern. Anyway, it's in Rennes-Le-Chateaux, in France." he said with a clarity that he hoped would end the conversation.

"Oh someone's been reading a lot of Dan Brown!" said Curtis.

"Wrong again." said Stuart. "But I have read a lot of

Baigent who puts forward very convincing theories surrounding Rennes-Le-Chateaux." Said Cassidy. Curtis scoffed in retaliation.

"Well I thought it was in Rosslyn Chapel." said Naomi. This time both men scoffed their derision at Naomi's claim. "What?"

"You've definitely been reading too much Dan Brown." said Cassidy. Naomi replied with a barrage of swearing aimed at Stuart Cassidy, but using such a pleasant tone to her voice that he found it so disarming he backed down and stayed quiet.

"Look," said Curtis, "I think we've found one tiny piece of the Templar hoard that was spread around the world when they went into hiding. That's my prediction."

"Well I think the Ark is still in the flooded tunnels underneath the Temple Mount in Jerusalem." said Bob quietly as the conversation fell silent. All three looked at Bob, shocked that he, a simple man from a farming background and one who was never known to hold an opinion on anything other than tractors or livestock, was so knowledgeable about the hidden artefacts surrounding Christianity in the middle east.

"Look, there's a slim chance it could be." said Naomi, realising how uncomfortable Bob had suddenly made himself.

"Do you really want to open it?" asked Bob.

"Look, this is just the outer chest. We have a key for the inner chest." said Cassidy. "And, yes, we really want to open it. So do you think you can or not, because I've got a crow bar in my bag that will do it if you can't."

Bob held Stuart's gaze for a fraction longer than what would be considered civil. "Aye, I can do it." said Bob, despite his ageing years, still had a raging fire behind his eyes, carrying with him a certain self-confidence and courage that could be intimidating to a lesser man.

"Good, shall we get started then?" said Cassidy, breaking the tension by rising from the table and walking towards the chest, possibly feeling that little bit intimidated.

"I'll clear the plates then, shall I?" said Naomi, rather curtly. Curtis and Bob both helped her clear the detritus of their supper, and then Curtis helped lift the large wooden chest onto their kitchen table, aided by Bob.

"Thanks Bob." said Curtis. "Right, there appears to be dirt clogging the key hole, so let's try to clear that first. What do you think? Water or a pokey thing?"

"I think you should step to one side and just let me do it." said Bob with a smile. "Why don't you make us some coffee, *that* you do very well." he said with a tap to Curtis' upper arm.

"It's a good job I like you Robert Common." said Curtis.

Curtis busied himself at the other end of the large kitchen, where he was joined by Naomi, while Cassidy observed what Bob was doing.

"I *don't* like him." said Naomi quietly as Curtis fired up the coffee machine.

"Stuart's ok, I think he's just over excited and used to spending life on his own." said Curtis.

"He's rude. There's no excuse for that." she hissed.

"I know, but without him we wouldn't have found any of this, and it has to be worth putting up with a little rudeness for." said Curtis quietly.

"Just don't expect me to sit there and take anything aimed at me." she said. "I *will* call him out."

"I absolutely wouldn't." said Curtis with a wry smile.

"Right!" said Bob a few moments later.

"Are we done already?" asked Curtis.

"No, but I've got all the dirt oot the hole." said Bob.

"I'll crack on with the coffee then, shall I?" said Curtis, jumping the gun a little with his excitement.

It was proving to be a challenge, even to Bob who bragged about once breaking into a safe using only two wooden tooth picks during the war, although the others were very reluctant to accept that as actual truth, and more as romantic nostalgic alcoholic nonsense.

Bob was using various metal implements to try to open the lock, but was simply getting more and more annoyed with the situation. He eventually threw his lock picking tools on the table and sighed.

"I think the wards are stopping me picking this one." he said.

"The who?" asked Curtis.

"You know those old keys that have a nice pattern cut into 'em?" asked Bob. The others nodded. "Well, those run through the equivalent shaped runners, called wards, that allow the key to turn in the lock." he said. "So I can try two things; the first is to shove something into the hole and try to bypass the wards, which will hopefully work, but could risk damaging the lock a little, failing that, I can get a blank key and try to impress the ward shape onto it with a bout of fiddling the key from side to side until I can see the shape in the metal. Then I'll need to cut the key to shape, and hopefully that will produce a working key for the lock."

"But that would take days." said Cassidy.

"It would take *a* day." said Bob, a clear dislike upon his face.

"The first idea we could try now though." pressed Cassidy, as keen as Curtis to get the chest open.

"Well, aye, obviously we'll try that one first. I've got the correct tool here." said Bob in a dismissive tone, selecting yet another metal pick of different form from his plethora of tools, that looked more like a screwdriver than an intricate lock pick. He also selected a hammer, and after placing the tool into the hole he tapped the end with the hammer until it was firmly in place. He then twisted, and the faint sound of a lock disengaging could be heard, as the eyes of the onlookers widened with renewed anticipation. Bob gave a wink to Cassidy, before stepping away and drinking his coffee in triumph, allowing the others to approach the now unlocked chest.

CHAPTER 12

Curtis was first to put his hands on the chest, and therefore claim the opening rights, and with a slow and powerful lift, with Cassidy holding the base against the table, the lid began to part ways with the body for the first time in over five hundred years.

Whatever was inside was wrapped in a brown blanket of sorts, but as they unfolded the old fabric that covered it, they were met with the top of a dulled golden casket that took their breath away. It was far and away the most beautiful metal box any of them had ever seen, covered in ornate details, carvings, and inscriptions.

"This could be the most significant historical find of the twenty first century." said Cassidy, quietly.

"It's beautiful." said Naomi.

"Is it gold, do you think?" asked Curtis.

"I'd say so." said Cassidy.

"Bloody Nora. Let's lift it out." said Curtis, his excitement almost uncontrollable.

Both he and Cassidy took hold of the small metal handles on each end of the chest and tested their structural strength before lifting.

"Mine feels ok." said Curtis.

"Mine too." said Cassidy. "On three; one, two, three."

They both lifted and the golden casket was removed from it's wooden outer chest. Bob took the wooden chest off the table, removed some remnants of fabric that had adhered to certain parts of the casket, and it was then laid on the towel back on the kitchen table.

"Well it's certainly heavy." said Curtis.

"And remarkably dry given that it has been in the ground for hundreds of years." said Cassidy.

"Look at all the inscriptions." said Naomi quietly.

"Is it Templar?" asked Curtis.

"I don't know." said Cassidy, exhaling and shaking his head in pure awe.

As Cassidy said this, a dial tone suddenly could be heard coming from Naomi's iPad, followed shortly by an electronic beep, and Amy's voice filled the kitchen. "Hi guys!" she said.

"Hey sweetie." said Naomi, holding her iPad up as Amy's

face appeared.

"How are the tomb raiders getting on?" she asked. "Hi Bob!" she added, seeing him in the background.

"Hello." he said. "I'm going to head off." he added.

"Ok, thanks Bob, you're a legend, we owe you big time, but we'll talk later." said Curtis. Once they all said their good byes, Naomi was first to speak.

"We have something to show you." she said in an excited tone, as she turned the iPad around so Amy could see the golden casket sitting on the kitchen table. There was silence for a few seconds while Naomi zoomed the iPad around the relic.

"Guys, is this a joke?" asked Amy through the tablet.

"Absolutely not." said Curtis. "Stuart and I recovered this from St. Cuthbert's Island on Lindisfarne in the early hours of this morning."

"Oh Curtis, you're going to be in so much trouble." she replied with genuine apprehension in her voice. Naomi looked at him with a stern look on her face.

"Don't worry, we sought permission to detect along the sands of the straits, and this chest," said Curtis, pointing towards the large wooden chest now demoted to the kitchen floor, "was as near as damn it on those sands." Cassidy nodded in agreement. Amy had her hands on the side of her face that wore a troubled expression, but she seemed to ease a little at this news.

"So what do you think then Amy?" asked Cassidy. "Could it be Templar?"

"Are you *sure* this isn't a wind up?" she asked.

"Hand on heart, Amy, this was dug up from the location we predicted it would be, from the information on the old parchment." said Curtis.

"Right, well, if that's the case, it's far, far older than Templar." said Amy.

"What do you mean?" asked Curtis, confusion clouding his mind.

"This iconography is at least two thousand years old, the Templars were around, what, 800 years ago?" said Amy.

"1119 to 1312ad." said Cassidy.

"Well there you go." said Amy.

"So..." said Curtis, thinking out loud, "...this chest is two thousand years old, referred to in a fifteenth century script, as a

125

Templar relic from the thirteenth century, and buried at a priory built in the seventh century."

"It's been around a bit." said Cassidy.

"Where's it from Amy?" asked Curtis.

"Looking at the symbols, it's Christian, but this seems middle-eastern too." said Amy. "And there are stranger symbols that I haven't seen before, I'll have to look them up. Can you send me some high-res images from all sides?" Naomi nodded at the screen.

"So Christian, middle eastern, and two thousand years old?" said Curtis. "That would put it as a contemporary piece to Christ and Jerusalem and all that Bible stuff?"

"I guess it would." said Amy.

"Could this be the Ark of the Covenant?" asked Naomi. "In all seriousness, could it be?"

"I don't think so." said Amy. "That was allegedly bigger than this, had golden angels on the top, and contained the stone tablets with the ten commandments written on them. Also that was old testament stuff, and that would place it a few thousand years older than Jesus, remember. And it was supposed to have golden rings for wooden staves to be used to carry it. Does it have those?"

"No, just a handle at each end." said Cassidy.

"And no spooky tendrils of death have emanated from it as yet." said Curtis.

"Good to know." said Amy. "Have you opened it yet though?"

"We do have the key for it right here." said Cassidy, already holding it in his hand.

"Woah there, Belloq!" said Curtis. "Let's not be hasty. We're not racing the Nazis here." Cassidy looked confused. "Rene Belloq? He opened the Ark of the Covenant in Raiders of the Lost Ark... It's an Indiana Jones film?" said Curtis.

"Right. Yeah. Ok." said Cassidy, clearly not as much of a movie geek as Curtis clearly was. "So do you want to x-ray it again first?"

"Stuart, I'm exhausted. I want to go to bed." said Curtis, much to the expressions of objection from Stuart Cassidy.

"But we're so close to finding out what's inside." said Cassidy. "You can't possibly be serious about just going to bed!"

"We're also all tired, and we saw what shot out of the last chest we opened. We need to have our wits about us and we need to make sure we know what we're dealing with before we put this key anywhere near that lock." said Curtis, taking the key from Cassidy and placing it back into the small stone box it came from.

"Guys, Curtis is right, it's potentially very dangerous, especially when everyone's fired up and short of sleep. Tomorrow is another day, and I'd say the best day to have a proper look at what we've got in front of us." said Amy, still connected through the iPad held in Naomi's hand.

"Do you want me to ring you again tomorrow, before we do anything?" asked Naomi.

"Are you kidding me? I'm about to get into the car and drive up." said Amy.

"What?" asked Naomi. "Amy it's after ten o clock, it's a four hour drive!"

"I'll stay at a local hotel then, but I really want to be there when you open it. I think it's important." said Amy.

"No you won't stay at a hotel, you will obviously stay here, I just don't want you to drive through the night." said Naomi.

"Best time to travel." said Amy. "It's quiet."

"Ok." said Naomi, shocked at Amy's decision. "Well, we'd all love to see you. Ring me when you're ten minutes away, and I'll come and open up." said Naomi.

"See you soon Amy, will be good to meet you finally." said Cassidy from across the room, clearly planning on also staying at the Old Rectory. Amy shared an apprehensive and slightly wearisome look with Naomi out of the sight of Cassidy, before the call was ended.

Before they all retired to bed, Curtis and Stuart sat at the kitchen table with a large whisky each, and looked back over the translation of the parchment once more. They both had a slight unease in their stomachs about what was written, and Cassidy was the first one to broach the subject again.

"What does he mean by *darkness*?" he asked Curtis. Curtis shook his head and shrugged his shoulders in response.

"Who knows. The ancient religious orders were a little

fanciful, and relied on fear to get their own way a lot of the time." he said. "Also, it's highly likely, and suggested even, that the Templars included pagan and other strange rituals that they picked up on their travels through pre-christian places, in their own ceremonies. I think they got all kinds of weird, and if Blackwater was part of a continuation of the Templars, I bet their rituals were just as weird."

"What do *you* think is in there?" asked Cassidy. Curtis thought about this for a moment.

"The Templars liked to collect relics, I'd say more for the gold content than the religious content, but they certainly ransacked countless shrines and holy places throughout the world during their 'crusades', and who knows what they ended up with." said Curtis. "There have been many accounts of weird relics from body parts of saints, to shards of the cross, golden gem encrusted crosses and who knows what else."

"There's rumour of them worshipping Jesus' head, you know." said Cassidy.

"What, his actual head?" asked Curtis.

"Yeah, his physical head." said Cassidy. "We may be sitting here, a foot away from the head of Jesus Christ. There are rumours of them having John the Baptist's head too." Curtis wore a reluctant and slightly troubled look as he stared at the golden casket.

"Do you think there's really something as dark as that in there? I mean, given what's happened to me in the past, I can't discount anything anymore." said Curtis, taking another large gulp of his peaty Lagavullin whisky.

"What *was* your experience then?" asked Cassidy. "All I've been able to gleam from the museum exhibition, and what I've read, was that you experienced an awful lot of bad luck and a muscle spasm. What actually happened out in that jungle." he asked as he topped up Curtis' glass with another generous helping of expensive aged Islay malt to prolong this moment as best he could. Curtis took a breath before telling his story.

"So you know an old lady brought an insect into us that she'd received from her ancestor. The insect itself was rubbish, but I found a folded up letter underneath the wadding that talked of treasures in the Amazon. Anyway, to cut a very long story short, we found a blue stone inside the skull of a Baboon in a cave somewhere in the vastness of the Amazon rainforest, after following these clues. I was expecting treasure. I thought it could be a very large unpolished sapphire, so took it with me. The bad luck was all circumstantial at first and could be easily explained away, but then after one of these daily freak events, my hand clamped around the stone and literally died. Something like rigor-mortis set in and the blood drained from it. I then started to hallucinate, visions of a woman with a deathly white face and tattered black clothes. And when she spoke it was like pure evil filling my mind. She even touched me once, in my vision, and pain like I've never felt tore through my entire body like I'd been tasered." said Curtis, taking another large gulp of whisky.

"What did she say to you?" asked Cassidy, now totally engrossed in the story. Curtis shook his head.

"I don't know. It was in a language I couldn't understand." he said.

"So how did you get away from it?" asked Cassidy.

"I had to physically snap the fingers of my hand until the stone was free from my grasp." he said, as he slowly moved the fingers of his left hand. Cassidy looked at his hand. It looked normal, yet when he looked closely, there were the telltale signs of an underlying health condition, much like arthritis. "A medicine man from a tribe helped fix my fingers once we made it to their camp." Cassidy nodded at what he heard.

"So in your eyes, there's no question that there are unexplained forces in this world?" asked Cassidy.

"I guess so." said Curtis, draining his glass and looking at his watch.

"Can I ask you one more question?" said Cassidy. Curtis waited. "Do you think she's still with you?" Curtis took a while to reply.

"That's a difficult question to answer, buddy. The medicine man of that tribe performed a strange ritual on me where I fought with her in my mind. I felt like I'd won. He told me he had placed a protection on me. She seemed to leave me. I assume she's somehow connected to that stone..." Curtis paused for a moment. "...yet I feel like there's still something. I could have sworn I've seen her in my periphery on occasions. Just disappearing, you know? Out of sight. And she's made her way into my dreams the odd time..." again Curtis paused, staring into the middle distance, before mentally snapping himself out of his trance. "...but as you said the other day, none of it can be proved, none of it could be used as evidence of anything other than psychosis."

"I don't think you're psychotic." said Cassidy.

"No, neither do I to be honest." said Curtis. "But I *am* tired." he said. Cassidy nodded, looking at his watch. "I'm going to bed."

"Sweet dreams." said Cassidy, immediately regretting his choice of words. "You know what I mean."

The following morning, Curtis was up first, and making himself a coffee when Amy wandered into the kitchen.

"Hey!" said Curtis, hurrying over and hugging her.

"Curtis!" said Amy giving him a kiss on the cheek. "How are you?"

"I'm good thanks, really good!" he said.

"How's the hand?" she asked, taking it in hers, as she always did when they met, and giving it a good study. "All still normal?"

"Almost! What about you?" he asked.

"All the better for being back here." said Amy.

Once Naomi, and eventually Stuart, had joined them and they had enjoyed their toast and morning coffees, they all sat around the kitchen table, upon which the golden casket still stood, unopened.

"This is the stuff dreams are made of." said Amy, examining the minute details of the carvings and inscriptions.

"So what do you think, now you've actually seen it in the flesh?" asked Curtis.

"It's exquisite." she said, more to herself than the others around the table. "Utterly amazing."

"You think it's older than Templar?" asked Cassidy.

"As I said yesterday, it's far older. *Far* older. And intriguing." she said, as she ran her finger over a series of symbols, studying it closely.

"So it's early Christian? Yes?" asked Curtis.

"I think so, but there are anomalies that are making me question that. You see this symbol here?" she said, pointing to a large figure holding something in each hand, "I'm pretty sure that is the Godself. It's an ancient symbol found all over the world. Not Christian, but something that was believed to unite the ancient worlds. But it was also a symbol used by the Masons, who obviously have a link to the Templars." said Amy.

"So... this could be Templar then?" asked Cassidy.

"No." said Amy, as confused as the rest of them. "Because it's far too old."

"Sorry, unite the ancient worlds?" asked Curtis. "What do you mean?"

"I'm not exactly an expert on the Godself." said Amy. "But I know that it's a symbol that has been found on ancient carvings in Egypt, Iraq, North America, Peru, Nigeria, China, India, Spain. It's amazing really, when you think about it, that this symbol has stretched throughout the world, thousands of years before people supposedly began to travel."

"Why have I never seen it before?" asked Curtis.

"Oh you have." said Amy.

"What do you mean?" he asked.

"Well, it's the symbol of Starbucks for starters." said Amy. "A forward facing figure, holding a long object in each hand. Some places it's animals, some places weapons, some places drapes of fabric. In this case, a horned figure holding two... what are they? Snakes? Sticks?"

"So what does that mean?" asked Cassidy.

"I don't know. That's a Pagan symbol there," she said, pointing to a circle with a crescent moon resting on the top, "And I'm pretty sure that's Norse!" she said, pointing to another intricate icon. "And then you have christian symbols too, middle-eastern symbolism. And none of it makes sense." she said, sitting back in her chair.

"Well I guess it matches with the nonsense on the stone box that held the key too then." said Curtis. "At least there's a link there."

"The Anunnaki!" said Cassidy suddenly. All three looked at him.

"Come again?" said Curtis.

"Perhaps it's Anunnaki in origin." said Stuart, this time far more sheepishly than his previous outburst.

"You think it's alien in origin?" asked Amy.

"There is overwhelming evidence for their existence." said

Stuart.

"Stuart it's nonsense invented by Americans on the Discovery Channel." said Curtis.

"No. History as we know it is a nonsense." said Cassidy. "A fabrication to explain away the inexplicable: just taking the path of least resistance, or to justify an atrocity. There *were* ancient advanced civilisations. What we are taught in history; *that's* the fake news." he said.

"Christ you sound like Donald Trump!" said Curtis.

"Look at the pyramids!" said Cassidy.

"Oh god." said Amy under her breath. She'd had more than her fair share of conspiracy theorists peddling their ideas on her in the past. "You think they were built by Aliens?"

"Actually no." said Cassidy. "But I think they were built by an advanced civilisation who channelled some sort of energy through them. You admit they're not burial chambers, right?" he asked Amy.

"Well, yes, but..."

"And you admit that we don't actually know what they are." he pressed.

"Correct, but it's quite a leap to the Anunnaki philosophies." said Amy.

"I think we should try and open it." said Naomi, suddenly.

"Really?" asked Curtis.

"Yes. I mean, we don't think it was originally Templar, so we don't think it's booby-trapped, it could contain proper treasure, a significant religious artefact." said Naomi. "It could make world news. The golden box alone should make world news, even if it's empty."

"I've got the key." said Cassidy, waggling it in front of his face, looking towards Curtis.

"But have you got the secret?" asked Curtis.

"Which secret?" asked Cassidy.

"It doesn't matter, I'm quoting from a nineties dance song, Stuart, but do you have any secrets you'd like to divulge before we start?" said Curtis.

"No." said Cassidy.

"Right, if we are doing this, we need to take precautions." said Curtis, shifting his attention back to the chest. "We unlock it, we stand behind it, and we open it slowly, facing it away from us, and towards a wall."

"Ok." said Stuart, jumping up and making his way straight to the lock, key in hand. He lined it up, and it slipped straight into the hole, almost clicking into place. "Well it fits." he said.

"Slowly and carefully." said Curtis, already bracing himself; the two girls standing even further behind him.

Stuart Cassidy began to turn the key, however it refused to move. His trepidation turned to frustration and he waggled the key side to side in the lock that refused to budge.

"It's the wrong key." said Cassidy. "It's the wrong bloody key!"

"It's not the wrong bloody key, give it here." said Curtis, taking over in the attempts to unlock the chest. But he too was unable, and sat back, frowning.

"Well that was the biggest anticlimax of my life!" said Amy. Naomi tried to unlock the chest as well, but to no avail.

"I think it is the wrong key." She said.

"It can't be the wrong key." said Curtis. "It literally can't be." he said, rubbing his hair hard with both hands, leaving his hair style all wild and unkempt.

"Well it's not working though, mate." said Cassidy.

"I know that." he said, through gritted teeth. "What are we missing?" he said, looking at the casket again. "Could it just be a rusted mechanism?"

"Well, we know what we're missing." said Amy suddenly. The others looked at her. "The burner and the bell." They all thought for a moment, and all seemed to come to the same question at the same time. It was Cassidy who spoke first.

"How can they help, though?" he asked. "Unless they are key shaped."

"Perhaps they come with another parchment, giving instructions." said Amy. "Or they are specifically shaped to fit into another section to act as a lock release, like the key box and the arrow head?"

"Oh I thought we were there!" said Cassidy, a little like a petulant child. "I thought the secrets were about to be revealed."

"Me too, buddy, me too." said Curtis.

"Ok, so we can't get into it yet." said Naomi. "But we've got it, and we've also got the key." she added. "Both those items were expected to be found in specific places. The parchment speaks of a burner and a bell in Hulne Priory, right?" The others nodded. "So let's, all four of us, go to Hulne Priory, and find these two items."

"Now?" asked Cassidy.

"Right now." said Naomi.

"I'll go and get ready." beamed Amy as she turned and left. Cassidy shared an excitable look with Curtis, and he followed Amy out of the room.

"Stuart and I have both been very naughty up until now, and Hulne is on private property, albeit with public access, but if the Duke or one of his alarmingly vigilant game keepers spots us digging up his thirteenth century Carmelite abbey, I think we'll probably be shot, despite he and I being aware of each other. Are you sure you and Amy want to be involved?" asked Curtis.

"We'll both be angry if you exclude us." said Naomi. "Besides, he won't shoot you. Shop you to the rozzers, maybe, but I think the days of the landed gentry shooting common folk such as ourselves are probably behind us."

"He has a *lot* of guns." said Curtis.

"To shoot pheasants with, not peasants." said Naomi.

"Magnificent pun, as always, my darling." said Curtis, acknowledging her quick-witted prowess. "Right, let's get sorted then."

CHAPTER 13

Half an hour after they had left the Old Rectory, and still only mid-morning, they had parked on the road leading to the gates of Hulne Park; the Duke of Northumberland's sprawling private estate, at the centre of which, stood the ruins of the Priory.

"Now the public have been granted access by the Duke to walk the grounds of this park, so we're fine to just wander." said Curtis. "But there is someone who lives in a small dwelling inside the priory ruins, and the Duke uses the main tower that still stands as his hunting lodge, so does often entertain in there, so we will have to be careful and really try not to attract any attention to ourselves."

They entered through the large arched gates and made their way along the wooded paths, over landscaped bridges and streams, winding through fields of sheep and cows, past cottages, lodges and wood-cutter's yards nestled within the parklands, until eventually they came upon the priory.

"Oh wow." said Amy, as she cast her eyes for the first time upon the ruins, after entering through the small wooden gate.

"Idyllic, isn't it?" replied Naomi.

"I can't believe I didn't know about this place." she said.

They wandered the interior of the priory walls for a while, looking at the various statues and sections of wall, before converging in the very centre of the structure, and sitting down on the grass in the warmth of the summer sun.

"Well it's totally deserted, which is a help." said Cassidy.

"So what do we know? Tell me everything you have gleamed about this place." said Amy.

"Well, we know that this priory was built by the Carmelite Monks who settled here from the middle east in the thirteenth century. Apparently they chose this spot because, from the river, it resembles Mount Carmel in Israel, although I think that's stretching it slightly." said Cassidy.

"And were the Carmelites linked with the Templars do we think?" asked Amy.

"I've done a bit of research on this." said Cassidy. "There are rumours that the founder of the Carmelite order was in fact a crusader who suddenly decided to live a life of reflection and peace, as supposed to pillage and persecution, so set up his own

Christian religious order. This was around the time of the Templar order too, so there is definitely an overlap of timelines, they were all involved in the crusades, but no one really knows who founded it." he said. "What we also don't know is who the Northern Carmelites were, who are referenced by Friar Blackwater of Lindisfarne, and names the Friar here at Hulne as John Croy. They claim to be the last surviving members of the Order of the Northern Carmelites, who are the secretive protectors of a Templar relic that appears to be inside that golden casket, but there is no documented evidence of their existence in history other than the parchment that I found and the tapestry that was in the archives of your museum. Also, and here is the exciting part, I found a link where Friar John Croy, Grand Master of the Northern Carmelites is named on another parchment as Johannes Croyus, Grand Master of the continuation of the Templars on matching dates."

"Well to me that's a long shot." said Amy. The two men looked back at her, Cassidy wearing a look one should reserve for finding an unidentifiable chunk of matter in a drain. This clearly riled Amy. "Doesn't that strike you as remarkably coincidental and lucky?" asked Amy. "No mention of Templar artefacts anywhere in history other than something *you* found," she said, pointing at Cassidy, "and something that just happened to be sat in a box in *your* museum?" she added, this time pointing at Curtis.

"Hang on!" said Cassidy, clearly irritated by the subtext of Amy's line of questioning. "Not really if you actually think about it, Amy. I am a detectorist and found the parchment buried in centuries of subsoil right next to one of three priories mentioned in it; I have been metal detecting for over ten years in this area of the world. Curtis owns the local museum that stores the majority of the local artefacts found throughout history, so no, this is actually *not* anything other than remarkable luck, coupled with the hard work and problem solving by the two of us who have already dedicated over a hundred man hours of research both at home and in the field. I didn't see *you* scrabbling around in the dirt at three o clock in the morning discovering the most exciting piece of history the world has ever seen, only found thanks to *our* dedication and problem solving!"

"You wouldn't have seen me scrabbling around in the dirt

Stuart, as what you've just done is highly illegal and punishable by a spell in jail, and *you,*" said Amy, turning to Curtis with an anger kindling behind her bubbly personality, "should know better given that the entire future of your family business hinges on *this man* not blabbing to the authorities about how it was recovered."

"Amy, shut up." said Stuart, curtly. "Why would I 'blab'?" he said, punctuating the air in front of him. "I would be shopping myself too. It would make no sense. Stop trying to cause trouble. If you don't want to be part of this then piss off back to wherever you came from."

"Woah!" interjected Naomi and Curtis both together. "Stuart that is uncalled for." said Naomi.

"No one else is calling me a fraud and a criminal. Maybe she's just jealous that she didn't find it!" said Cassidy.

"Ah, you're a child." said Amy.

"Let's all just take a breather, ok?" said Curtis. "This isn't helping us solve this problem, is it?"

"*This* is causing more problems." said Cassidy, pointing at Amy. Who returned an incredulous look, and laughed at the rudeness.

"Stuart, you really don't know when to shut up do you?" said Naomi, jumping to the defence of her best friend.

"I'll tell you what, I'm going to go and actually do what we're here to do, yeah? Why don't you go and do the same somewhere else." said Cassidy.

"I actually think that's a good idea." said Curtis, as both women turned with a now burning fury in their eyes and looked straight at Curtis, making him visibly shrink a little. "I simply mean to diffuse the situation." he added.

"Gladly." said Amy, who actually wanted nothing better than to leave the area and return home, but wasn't going to give Stuart Cassidy the satisfaction of honouring his rude request.

As she and Naomi headed one way and Cassidy headed the other, Curtis found himself on his own in the middle of the ruins, pondering what just happened. Eventually, he shook his head, took a deep breath, and headed over to his own section of the priory to once again look for clues to a hidden artefact, while all the others stewed in their own antagonism and umbrage.

Despite the priory being in ruins, it was not simply a

series of low walls, but an overgrown labyrinth of crumbling structures, some still two and three stories high. There were doorways and buildings through which one could walk, there were clear rooms and fortified walls, large gates and gate houses. It was still a large sprawling collection of beautiful buildings, only recently opened to the public after being in the private grounds of the Percy family for countless generations. Despite its dilapidated state, it was still a place of profound peace and tranquility, and quickly all four of them were calm and relaxed once again, provided they couldn't see each other.

Naomi and Amy were walking through some of the central rooms of the building, talking about the plights of having to live in a world with men and their over inflated egos, and not really paying attention to anything they saw as they went, whilst Stuart was stood, staring at the same section of wall that he had been looking at for the past five minutes, staring into his own middle distance, playing out the conversation that had just happened earlier, but embellishing it with the fantasy of out arguing them all, discovering the missing relic, keeping it for himself, and eventually seducing Amy, and taking her home. His mind had wandered into the realms of current impossibilities, so he brought himself back to the slightly more depressing present, and refocussed on the matter at hand; examining the walls in detail.

Meanwhile, Curtis was stood, very much in the present, staring at a small watchtower built at the furthest corner of the priory walls, where an external stone staircase hugged the wall and climbed to a door half way up the walls of the tower, allowing for access, via an internal stone spiralling staircase, to a viewing platform at the top. His eyes moved from the top section, down to the overgrown foundations; to the tangles of huge mature Rhododendron bushes that were thriving in the damp and sheltered environments of the priory. As he surveyed the fauna, a sudden jolt of realisation hit him. He saw, through the intertwined branches of the evergreen shrubs, a wooden section at the base of the walls.

"Is that a *door*?" he said to himself as he moved forward towards the bushes. As he said that, Naomi and Amy appeared from behind another part of the building and sauntered over to Curtis.

"Well we haven't found a bloody thing." said Amy.

"I think I have." said Curtis, slowly.

"Where's Bear Grylls' dickhead brother?" asked Amy.

"I dunno, Stuart!" shouted Curtis.

"No, ssshh!" said Amy. "Can't we just do this ourselves?"

"Come on, you've all said your bit, it's out there, now can we just focus on the matter in hand?" he said as Cassidy came into view. "I think I've found a doorway." he said, so all could hear.

They looked through the foliage and sure enough, there was a small doorway at ground level.

"That is probably a store room under the turret for munitions." said Cassidy.

"It's a priory." said Amy quietly without looking away from the doorway, shaking her head so he knew exactly how she felt, as his eyes bore into the back of her head.

"Alright, a storeroom for Bibles then." said Cassidy, clearly still ready for confrontation.

"Can we get to it?" asked Naomi, trying to diffuse the situation by ignoring it.

"Yeah." said Curtis, already trying to negotiate the web of thick twisting branches. After a minute or so, he was fairly close to the doorway, and scratched all over from the bushes. "It's locked with a big old padlock." he said.

"Do you think we could prize it?" asked Cassidy.

"This is so illegal." said Amy, stepping back and looking into the other reaches of the priory for any signs of other people.

"I think it would just pop off." said Curtis. "Have you got a screw driver?"

Cassidy removed his small tactical backpack that he took everywhere with him, and took out a canvas roll that included a screwdriver. He tossed it over the Rhododendron bush and Curtis caught it. He bent back down as easily as he could, and inserted the shaft of the screwdriver into the loop of the old lock. He then yanked the screwdriver upwards to try to free the rusted metal, but the lock held fast. He tried again, but once more, all he got was a worsening pain in his shoulder. One more try, this time putting as much strength into it as he could in the tight confines, and this time the lock popped and fell to the ground. A surge of excitement gripped all four of them, even Amy who was very reluctant to be involved in this illegal unauthorised access of a

Duke's private property.

Curtis pulled at the door which only moved two or three inches and then stuck in place, caught in the dirty collection of ancient mud and roots at the base of the thirteenth century tower.

"How about a trowel Stuart?" asked Curtis, his head bobbing up from behind the bush once again. Cassidy fished around in his bag and brought out a small black trowel, and this time passed it through the branches to Curtis, who knelt back down and began to dig out the area the door would arc into. Meanwhile, Cassidy ventured back into his pack once more and pulled out a handful of head torches. He put one on himself, handed one to Naomi, and then held one out for Amy.

"I'm sorry about before." he said quickly as he offered her the torch.

"Ok." said Amy, who took the torch a little aggressively. Cassidy would let that one slide as he was starting to like this sassy blonde from the internet. He never usually got to actually meet any of the other ones he interacted with.

"How are you getting on?" asked Naomi after a minute had passed.

"Almost there." came the muffled reply.

"I've got a head torch for you." said Cassidy, venturing into the undergrowth to try to get to his friend.

With a final hard pull, Curtis managed to wrench the door open and create enough of a gap for them to pass through. The others had made their way as close to the door as possible. Amy gave a last look around the deserted area to make sure they weren't being watched or overlooked, as they were alarmingly close to the private cottage that sat in the grounds of the priory, but as far as she could tell, there was no one home.

"Coast clear?" asked Cassidy, flicking on his torch.

"As far as I can see." said Amy.

"Do we all need to go in?" asked Naomi. "It looks very small."

"We'll check it out and then let you two know if we find anything." said Cassidy, proceeded by a tut from Amy.

Curtis was the first to ungracefully crawl through the doorway, and his torch didn't illuminate much in the gloom. Once Cassidy had joined him, they both surveyed their surroundings. It was just tall enough to stand in, and the outer walls were so thick;

the interior space was cramped at best. The detritus of the centuries littered the floor, from matting to old rusted gardening implements, from what they could see. The room itself was thick with ancient cobwebs, and as the two men looked around it quickly dawned on them that this was not the hiding place of associated Templar artefacts.

"Hmmmmm..." was all Curtis could manage as he looked around.

"I thought we were on to something here." said Cassidy. The girls entered next, unable to contain their excitement and intrigue at the possibilities lying within.

"Well?" asked Amy as she followed Naomi in, and stood up, realising how cramped it was and ended up almost nose to nose with Stuart Cassidy.

"Well isn't this cosy." he said.

"No relics then?" she asked, "other than you two?"

"Doesn't look like it." said Stuart, still unintentionally far too far within Amy's personal space and shining his head torch directly into her eyes.

"What's that?" said Naomi suddenly, causing everyone to rotate within the claustrophobic confines around one hundred and eighty degrees, so she could pick up whatever she was looking at. It turned out to be a relatively modern wooden box, containing a few rusted gardening tools and some twine. She threw it back down.

"Lets go." said Cassidy, who was now nearest the door, and he stooped to make his way out and back into a face full of Rhododendron. Curtis followed. And then Naomi. Amy was left in the small room, frustrated with the entire day and the people contained within it.

"This is so stupid." she said to herself, kicking the box with her large walking boot. It hardly moved, caught on some of the ancient matting that covered the floor of the room. This seemed to enrage her even more; a personal antagonistic move towards her from the box itself, so she kicked it again, this time with even more venom and hostility, and sent not only the box, but the matting that was now attached to it, into a dark corner. "Arsehole." she said, and she turned to leave. Yet something made her stop dead in her tracks and refocus. There, under the matting that had been kicked away in rage, was a trap door.

"Guys." she said. There were muffled voices outside the dark room. "Guys!" she repeated, but once again got no response. She poked her head out of the door and could hear the three others talking about whether to try another spot or head off to the Dirty Bottles Smokehouse for some food. It seemed the latter was the suggestion of choice for Curtis and Stuart.

"What's that you're talking about?" asked Amy.

"It's a great restaurant." said Cassidy. "I'll buy you a cocktail to make up for earlier." he said with a wink.

"Yeah. Yeah we could do that I suppose." said Amy. "Or, we could go through the trap door I've just found." she said, beaming a big smile, even towards Stuart Cassidy, who was clearly trying his best to make up for his outburst earlier. They all stared back at Amy.

"Are *you* joking now?" asked Cassidy, still not sure how to take Amy.

"Come and see for yourself, big lad." she replied. This made Curtis laugh out loud, and hurry towards the doorway once again, reattaching his head torch as he went, and slapping Cassidy on the back as he passed him.

Once inside, they all looked down at the square wooden trap door with it's large metal ring to grant access to whatever was below. Amy tried to pull it open, but given centuries of non-use, it was proving hard work, but with help from Stuart, they managed to haul it open.

"As above, so below." said Naomi as she looked on into the abyss below.

"This has to be it." said Stuart. "It has to be in there. What can you see?"

Amy was on her hands and knees, looking into the hole. "Only darkness really. Have you got a better torch in that bag, Mary Poppins?" she asked. Even Cassidy sniggered as he removed his backpack.

"Yeah, I've got an LED light bank in here somewhere." he said. "Hang on."

"Of course you have." said Amy.

He pulled out a padded case, unzipped it, and removed a small black object about the size of a slice of bread, with a yellow metal stand attached to it. He turned it on, the small room filled with light, and he passed it to Amy who lowered it into the

142

darkness.

"What can you see Amy? Talk to us." said Curtis. Amy was now lying on the floor with her head through the trap door.

"There's a set of stairs and a tunnel. It seems to go on for a while." she said from within the hole. She brought her head up and looked at the others. "I think it's tall enough to stand in. Shall we?"

"Oh we shall!" said Curtis.

"I think I'll stay up here." said Naomi. "Keep an eye on things. Make sure the Duke doesn't ride in with his ten thousand men."

"Scared in case there are spiders?" asked Curtis.

"Yeah." she replied instantly.

Amy was first down the steep and narrow wooden stairs and illuminated the way in front of her with the high powered torch. Cassidy was next, followed by Curtis. The walls seemed to have been painted white once in the distant past, although now they resembled a dirtier return to nature.

When they accustomed to the gloom, Amy seemed to take charge and move slowly forward, into the darkness beyond, illuminating her way with the powerful light bank, leaving the two men in relative darkness with their rather weak head torches. After roughly ten meters, she stopped abruptly.

"What is it?" asked Cassidy.

"A fork in the road." said Amy, a little too dramatically.

"A toad? Down here?" hissed a frustrated Curtis at the back of the pack, unable to really hear what was going on. "I suppose there could be a water course or a natural spring."

"There's a side tunnel, Curtis." said Cassidy over his shoulder, spelling it out for his friend behind him. "No toads as of yet."

"Well let's have a look down there first, make sure there isn't anything noteworthy, and then carry on down the main tunnel until we find something." said Amy. "We need to be systematic."

"Even if we don't find the items we're looking for," said Curtis, "we still might find something of serious historical importance down here. I don't think anyone's been down here for centuries. I bet the Duke doesn't even know about it."

"Let's focus on finding whatever we can, and then get out." said Amy.

"Scared of the spiders too?" asked Curtis. "I haven't seen any yet by the way."

"No, scared of the authorities, if we get caught." she said. "We are trespassing on private property, not only that, we are trespassing on property owned by a Duke, and we're trying to essentially steal his possessions, whether he knows about them or not."

"I know. And as soon as we've found everything, and realise it's place in world history, I *will* inform all the landowners and try to calm the situation should it escalate." said Curtis, the knot of guilt tightening his organs as he scuttled behind his friends. But the yearning for discovery drove him, and the other two, onwards into the darkness. None of them were prepared to leave empty handed. They had come too far.

Curtis knew he was a great negotiator; he always had been, which was why his museum's archives were growing by the month with amazing items from all over the world. That was down to him; vying with far bigger names in the museum and research world, all clamouring for certain items. He was as fierce as he was charismatic in his negotiations, fighting off the might of the British Museum and the Smithsonian at times. There were items locked away in the vaults of The Craxford Museum that were priceless and really shouldn't be in such a small back water establishment, despite its ties with a respected university, but thanks to the smooth talking and beguiling charm of Curtis Craxford, or even sometimes his intense and intimidating business brain, he was able to secure such items. And he was quietly confident that he could talk round not only the Duke and Duchess, who he knew from the countless local and charitable functions he attended as often as he could, but also English Heritage, and probably end up with all the items on view at his museum.

Amy disappeared around the corner and plunged her two followers into relative darkness once again. Cassidy quickly followed, but saw that the side tunnel ended fairly abruptly, so backed up, back towards Curtis.

"Anything down there Amy?" asked Cassidy, in a low tone.

"Nothing of note." said Amy.

"Let's press on then." said Cassidy, suddenly finding

himself in the lead and holding his hand out for the LED torch. Amy handed it on to him, and then shared a look with Curtis that silently spoke of her lack of trust in their new friend.

He continued down the main tunnel, looking down various tributaries, seeing nothing but stone and rubble. Their adventure was turning out to be frustratingly fruitless in this barren labyrinth. And the air was so thin and old, they were struggling to keep their breath as they went.

"These tunnels must go under the whole priory." said Amy. "It's like a maze."

"Let's hope we can find our way back out." said Curtis.

Cassidy eventually found himself at the end of the main tunnel, and the tunnel split to the left and the right at 90 degrees. He stopped and began to think.

"Left," said Amy, "always left."

"Why?" asked Cassidy, expecting some unwritten rule regarding the exploration of ancient Egyptian burial sites.

"It just feels right." she said.

"That literally makes no sense whatsoever." added Curtis. But Cassidy was just laughing.

"Genius logic!" he said. "Left is right."

They turned left, along another chokingly tight and low tunnel of painted stone, the air growing thinner with each step; the smell of foist growing in their nostrils the deeper they went; the dust stirred up by their feet choking their airways. It was an oppressive environment, and one they were not particularly enjoying.

Again the tunnel split, and again Cassidy chose the left fork, this time, when it ended, it ended, with nothing to see but a wall of rock. This meant that Curtis suddenly found himself at the front of the party as they all turned 180 degrees, and once the LED light bank had been handed through to him, he set off, this time taking the right fork and searching along that tunnel.

The stuffiness of the very air around them, the clinging ancient spiders webs that hung from the low ceilings, and the claustrophobic darkness was beginning to take its toll on the three explorers as they inched their way back along the tunnel, heads bowed against the roof, retracing their steps, before exploring the new arm of possibility.

Again, this tunnel came to an abrupt end with a wall of

145

stone. "Dead end again folks." said Curtis, turning to meet Amy behind him.

"Wait." she said, looking over Curtis' shoulder. "This dead end looks different to the other one. This looks like it's been built as supposed to just bare rock."

Curtis looked again, and realised she was correct. This was a bricked up wall, meaning the potential of a void behind it. He stepped back and tried to kick one of the central stones to see if it would move.

"Start at the top Curtis, remember how gravity works?" said Amy. Curtis shot her a sideways glance and began to tap the top brick with the heel of his hand, slowly increasing in pressure until an ache made its way up his forearm, yet no movements could be felt through the rock. Curtis then reverted to a full shoulder charge, yet was simply met with a solid opponent, and a painful upper arm to go with his aching forearm. "Oww." he said as he stepped back, almost into Amy.

He then gingerly kicked at the bottom stones, until the final one, in the far bottom left hand corner of the wall, moved very slightly. Curtis' eyes widened as he met the stares of his expectant comrades, and almost immediately fell to his knees. He stood the LED bank on it's plastic stand, facing the wall, and began to scrabble in the dirt at the bottom of the course of ancient stones.

"What is it?" asked Cassidy, frustratingly stuck at the back of the pack with a poor view of what was happening in front of him, and craning his neck for a better view. "What's happening?"

"I think *Crackers* has found a loose brick." said Amy.

Curtis had managed to scrape away all the dust and detritus that had gathered in the millennia of these tunnels, and then pushed the stone gradually away from him, and into the void behind the wall. The stone was roughly the size of a shoebox, and as it slid away from Curtis, puffs of dust made their way back out towards his face, which he blew away with a silent whistle. After pushing through way past his elbow, he pulled back and grabbed the light.

"I'm going to put my head in." he said, thrusting the light through the small hole, and following it closely by poking his head through at ground level. The dust and the air were choking as he found himself inhaling the stirred up, bone dry flotsam of the tunnel floor. But all of a sudden, that no longer mattered, as the light revealed a wooden chest sitting in the three feet of void space behind the man made wall and the natural wall, for hundreds of years, untouched and undetected.

Curtis grabbed it, extracted his head from the hole, and then pulled the chest through to the whoops of encouragement from the others in the dim subterranean passageways.

"Now can we please get the hell out of here? I feel like I haven't breathed fresh air in months." said Curtis, stifling a cough and handing the torch to Cassidy, whilst tucking the small wooden chest under his arm.

The three explorers made it back out into the cool fresh Northumbrian air a few minutes later and gulped it down into their dusty lungs. Naomi was waiting for them, and breathed a sigh of relief as she saw Amy emerge first. Her grin gave away their triumph almost instantly, and Naomi rushed in to get a better look as the other two followed her out into the open space of the priory interior.

"You found it?" she asked, in an excitable tone.

"We've found *something*." said Cassidy.

"Look, can we not open it here? Can we put it in the rucksack and head off home?" said Curtis. "I'm feeling all wrong. Like a thief."

"What is the difference between taking this, and taking that stone you found? That was on land belonging to the native tribes, this is land belonging to a native Duke." said Cassidy.

"I mean, where do you want me to start with that one, Stuart?" stated Amy. "Laws are very different here."

"Yeah, here you get a slap on the wrist and a stern telling off, there you get your head eaten off by a man with a painted face and a club, whilst what remains of you cooks slowly in a pot." said Cassidy.

"Well, that's offensive on a number of levels." said Amy.

Whilst this conversation was happening, Curtis and Naomi had stored the small chest in Curtis' rucksack and he had hoisted it onto his shoulders.

"Let's go." he said, and waited for no response before heading for the exit.

CHAPTER 14

At the Dirty Bottles in Alnwick, after an unnecessarily large lunch of various barbecued meats, the four of them sat around a small table with Naomi's iPad, viewing the pictures of the wooden chest that was sitting in the boot of the Land Rover parked outside.

Suspicion, and previous experience meant that they were all reluctant to jump right in and open it when they got home, given that there could quite possibly be another Templar booby trap just waiting to catch out the uninformed or the greedy.

"What do we think then?" asked Curtis, eyeing the images of the inconspicuous looking wooden box as if it were a coiled Taipan ready to strike through the screen.

"Well, we need to scan it, before we can do anything else." said Cassidy.

"Experience tells us that if the box containing the key was booby trapped, odds are so is this one." said Naomi.

"Ok, so from here we head to the museum. We may need to hang around for a bit until we know the scanning wing is free of students and lecturers, but that is where we must start." said Curtis.

"The Templars were a bunch of shits, weren't they!" said Amy, sipping on a fruit based cocktail bought for her by Stuart Cassidy as a peace offering: one she gladly accepted, yet her feelings towards him hadn't changed.

"They were hero knights of their time and were incredible crafters to make these intricate defence mechanisms." said Curtis.

"No they weren't!" said Naomi. "They were blood thirsty raping and pillaging terrorists. They were corrupt treasure hunters who committed unknown atrocities in the name of god!" she said. Cassidy opened his mouth to respond, no doubt with evidence to the contrary, however Naomi hadn't finished. "They *were* masters of finance, but trained up like Royal Marine Commandos. They are essentially what we would now recognise as a world power like Goldman Sachs, then militarised, and given literal global free reign. It's a terrifying combination, and they were accountable to no one. They could do what they wanted, which just happened to be theft of property and treasures the world over." she said sitting back in her chair.

"Much like the Americans." said Curtis.

"And they guarded their treasures with these horrible rigged chests designed to kill or maim some poor unsuspecting person who tried to open it." said Naomi, finally finishing her statement and taking a large drink.

"Look," said Cassidy, "For what it's worth, I agree with you all, especially you Curtis." he said, as the two girls' eyes met across the table. "America is the new crusader state. They take what they want and tell the world they're being saved from terrorists. They caused 9/11. They claim that bombing the third world is to rid them of nuclear weapons when it's really all about money and oil. And they claim they don't have dealings with extra-terrestrials when there is clear evidence to the contrary."

"Oh god, Stuart, that was such a good point until the last sentence." said Curtis. "Come on, let's finish up here and head off to the museum."

"Ok," said Curtis, addressing his friends within the scanning room of the university complex that evening, "it's pretty clear cut that this particular chest has an identical defence mechanism built into it as the other one. This looks like it also fires a metal dart from within it. Now Stuart found a way to disengage the previous one, so I suggest we do the same thing with this one."

Cassidy stepped up and didn't take too long to find the hidden button that gave an audible click to signify the spring had been disabled, however, they took no risks and very carefully opened the lid facing it directly towards the far wall. But it opened without any drama, and Cassidy lifted out a small bell, and an equally uninteresting incense burner.

"Is that it?" said Amy, a visible disappointment on her face.

"So it would seem." said Curtis.

"Are they gold?" asked Cassidy.

"Bronze I' say." said Amy.

"They must have a significance. Come on, let's get them back home and try to get this thing nailed." said Curtis.

"Why won't it open?" said Cassidy in another child-like

bout of frustration.

"What are we missing?" asked Naomi, trying to rationalise her way into the chest. "We have the key and the chest. We also have what looks like a prayer bell and a small incense burner."

"My bet is both those bronze items fit into some of the sections of the carvings and act as extra release mechanisms or secondary keys, to then allow the master key to turn." suggested Amy.

They all looked closely at the intricate carvings of the chest, in it's dulled, aged state. The very potential of the chest on its own, especially when returned to it's former shining glory was enough for Naomi, but the other three were hell-bent on opening the chest to reveal it's contents and answer the question of what potential 'darkness' St. Cuthbert was protecting them all from.

"Try there." said Curtis, eventually, looking at a small depression in the metal, where a horned being stood beside a tree-lined path that allowed perspective to give it a never-ending look as it trailed away to a pin-point on the chest. Cassidy pressed the base of the small brass incense burner into the depression, realising quite quickly that it was a slightly different shape, and therefore wouldn't sit flush. Curtis meanwhile tried again to turn the key but to no avail.

"How about lighting the incense and ringing the bell?" suggested Naomi.

"How can that help?" asked Cassidy, exasperation prevalent in his tone. "It'll be something blindingly obvious to do with a failsafe for the mechanism. Look at the shape of the bell, it's squat and doesn't really look like its shape would help it actually ring, if anything its strange squat shape would hinder its sole purpose of ringing, *unless* that wasn't its sole purpose, and it was also made to perform another task, such as disable a locking mechanism somehow."

"I hate to admit it, Nom," said Amy, "but I agree with Stuart."

"And an incense burner? How would that help?" asked Naomi, frustrated with Cassidy's air of arrogance when it came to talking over people, especially women, and a little irked by her friend taking his side over hers.

"I'd imagine the same kind of thing. It must act as a

further disabling key. Somewhere." said Cassidy.

The four of them poured over every inch of the metallic casket, suggesting possibilities and coming up against dead ends. Eventually, Curtis was the first to loose his enthusiasm and leave the arena of discovery that was his kitchen table; wandering off to the toilet, swearing under his breath as he went.

When he came back, Cassidy and the two girls were whispering yet they stopped and looked straight at Curtis as he entered the room.

"What, what is it?" he asked. Cassidy pushed his chair back and each girl presented the chest to him. "What? You've put the incense burner on top of the chest? Why?" he asked.

"Because it twisted and clicked into place." said Amy. "We actually heard a click!"

"Can we get it open?" he asked.

"Nope." said Cassidy.

Later that evening, once they had all enjoyed a pasta dish cooked by Curtis; all garlic, herbs and cured meats, washed down with wines plucked from his father's still plentiful wine cellar under the Old Rectory's pantry, the girls had both retired to bed, exhausted from the day's shenanigans, and a little worse for wear from the alcohol.

Curtis and Stuart sat at the kitchen table in relative silence, enjoying a large whisky and a fat but stubby cigar each. Curtis had opened the top section of the wide stable door that granted access from the kitchen to the gardens at the side of the house to avoid a chastising from Naomi the following morning for 'stinking the place out', allowing a cooling freshness to mix with the lingering heat and aromas of the kitchen.

"You know when you've come so far and feel like you've fallen at the last hurdle?" said Cassidy on a long exhale of sweet smelling smoke.

"Oh, I don't know." said Curtis, taking another few puffs on his cigar, and another sip of whisky before continuing. "I consider it just another hurdle in this long race. We haven't fallen, we're just eyeing up this particular jump and adjusting our pace accordingly, choosing when to leap and how high. Perhaps tonight was just a stumble."

Cassidy looked at Curtis for a moment, before both men sniggered at Curtis' attempts at such a poetic description of that day's events mixed with the alcohol of the evening. "Christ, I think I'd better get to bed before I start trying to sound like William Wordsworth."

"*Before* you sound like him? I think that particular boat has sailed, mate." said Cassidy, placing the smouldering butt of his cigar in the brass incense burner that was now clicked in place atop the chest, and absent-mindedly fiddling with the key in the lock as they spoke.

"Well in that case I will now sail aboard that boat. Bed ahoy, starboard side!" he said, drunkenly ringing the little prayer bell, as if they were heading toward an iceberg.

But as he rang the bell, he and Cassidy both heard an audible clunk, and the key Cassidy was toying with suddenly turned in the lock. Both men froze and glanced at each other.

"What the actual f...." started Cassidy.

"Girls!!!" shouted Curtis, cutting off Cassidy's sentence.

A few minutes later both girls came rushing into the kitchen looking bamboozled and worried, until they were told what had just happened.

"I bloody told you!" shouted Naomi at Cassidy, possibly a little more aggressively than she ought.

"To be fair Naomi, when have you ever heard of a little bell opening a locked golden casket?" asked Cassidy.

"Well... fair point." she conceded, keen to keep the mood of her kitchen light, after all, Cassidy was a guest in her home, and the reason they had just made the greatest discovery the museum could ever hope for. At least this time, if Curtis could use his extensive contacts, the artefacts were to be displayed in the museum, pride of place, and hopefully bring in a tidal wave of new visitors.

"So, what, you just rang the bell and it magically opened?" asked Amy, her voice clouded with suspicion.

"Pretty much... I mean, I put my cigar into the incense burner, Curtis was being weird and ringing the bell, I fiddled around with the key and it opened." Said Cassidy.

"How can a ringing bell open a lock?" asked Curtis.

"I've heard of these." Said Amy, her eyes narrowed as she tried to recall something from the vaults of her memory. "Egypt, 1998, I was working with a guy on a dig, Rick, and he had once found a box that was locked with what he called a resonance lock.

Apparently, when a bell, or in his case a gold rod was hit with another gold rod, the resonance of that particular note managed to vibrate something inside a mechanism that then allowed a simple latch to drop. This must be similar."

"Resonance locks?" asked Cassidy. "This is all a bit 'advanced civilisation' stuff, isn't it? I mean, I'm a *big* believer in all that. Aren't you?" he asked Amy.

"I mean, kind of. There is plenty of evidence for advanced tooling for cutting stone, but nothing can really be proven." said Amy.

"Yeah, but you all *know*. You know that the official line for ancient Egypt's history is a load of bollocks." said Cassidy.

"Well, I'll give you that one, yes, I'd say so." said Amy.

"And the burner?" asked Naomi, trying to steer the conversation away from conspiracy theories again..

"I don't know, perhaps heat from the ashes travels down and into the lid of the casket, allowing another piece to move? I don't know." Said Amy.

"We haven't opened it yet." said Cassidy. "We thought we'd wait for you two for the big reveal." This caught both girls off guard, and they both gave a little thanks to Cassidy before slowly huddling around the golden chest.

"I'm going to set up my phone to record what happens next, ok?" said Curtis. "This needs to be documented, like all the other stages." Curtis hurried off and propped his iPhone up against some books, making sure as much of what was happening was in the frame. He hit record.

"Right, firstly, given what happened back at the museum when we opened a Templar box, can we all head over to the back door again and one of us needs to open it very carefully." suggested Cassidy, looking this time at Curtis. "Mate, I'm pretty sure it's your turn."

Curtis nodded slowly. "I think Amy should do it."

"Why?" asked Amy, already standing in the kitchen doorway.

"Curtis!" exclaimed Naomi.

"Right!" he conceded, immediately. He walked over to the log burning stove that was fitted into an inglenook fireplace at the far end of the kitchen, and took up the fire tongs that were hanging on one of three hooks containing different fireside tools.

He then walked slowly up to the dull chest, and positioned the tongs so that they clasped the top and bottom of a section of the lid. He stood as far away as his own arms would allow, and positioned himself so he faced one of the corners of the chest, and began to slowly lift the lid.

"Mate, you look like you're going to literally poo yourself, take it easy." said Cassidy, stifling a laugh at Curtis' strained facial expression.

"My flat mate at university once poo'd himself, and I maintain to this day that the smell set off the upstairs flat's burglar alarm." said Curtis.

"Can we focus, please?" asked Amy.

Curtis continued to use the fire irons to lift the lid, a millimeter at a time, and sure enough, when the lid lifted around a centimetre there was an audible click followed by a loud swooshing, and Curtis' fire irons were ripped from his grip and flung across the room toward where the other three were now cowering. Curtis watched as they clattered to the stone floor a few feet from where his fiancee was standing, now on one foot, the other lifted as high as she could; a futile attempt to make herself as small a target as possible.

Curtis refocussed his attention on what could have ripped the heavy fire irons from his grasp and thrown them directly toward his companions. And what he saw made him feel a little nauseous: two curved blades, like scimitars, each almost half a meter long, were now sticking from the lid of the still closed chest. Had he been sat at the table and lifted the lid, or indeed crouched down in front of it, he would have simply lost his head, or currently be trying to gather up the majority of his internal organs from the floor.

"Bloody hell." was all he could manage in a breathy and indistinct tiny voice.

"Jesus Curtis!" said Naomi, rushing over and placing a calming hand on the small of his back whilst diverting all of her attention to the chest and the curved blades now sitting at right angles from the chest like a pair of sharpened metallic arms.

"This is amazing." said Stuart, joining the others. "Look how sharp they are after all of these years."

"I could have died." said Curtis, rather matter-of-factly, more to himself than anyone else in the room.

"But you didn't. You took precautions. And it saved your life." said Stuart.

"That is designed to decapitate the opener, should he open it in the wrong way." said Amy. "Or at least remove their hands for trying. Or even chop off an on-looker's legs."

"I could have died." said Curtis.

"They were a nasty bunch." said Naomi.

"Or they were protecting something very valuable." said Stuart, and all four of the inhabitants of the Old Rectory looked at the chest once again, all silently wondering what was within.

"I could have *died*!" repeated Curtis, this time with more anger.

"Oh shut up Curtis." said Naomi.

Curtis finally retrieved the fire irons from the other side of the room, and once again tried to open the lid. "I'd take cover again." he said. "I wouldn't put it past them to have built in a secondary device."

But they needn't have worried, for Curtis managed to lift the lid, which hinged back with the two curved blades attached, sending Stuart's cigar butt bouncing away across the floor, and showing the intricate mechanisms and cogs built into the inside of the lid, able to deliver such a devastating blow.

"Regardless of what is inside," said Curtis, "we have a priceless golden booby-trapped casket belonging to the Knights Templar. Today is a good day, boys and girls."

They all bustled forward to see what was inside, expecting a golden religious artefact or indeed a small chalice. At a glance, it appeared to be a bundle of old oily, stained cloth which instantly cast confused looks across the faces of the four observers of history being made.

"Ok," said Cassidy, "Unexpected."

"What of this whole bizarre situation *has* been expected?" asked Curtis.

"I totally thought we were going to see some stone tablets." said Naomi.

"It's not the bloody ark of the bloody covenant!" said Curtis as he took his iPhone from its book-based rest, and now held it in his hand, recording what was being seen in real time. "I'm going to try to uncover whatever is wrapped in this cloth." he said.

"Please be careful." said Amy, leaning in closer to get a better look.

Curtis lifted a piece of the cloth and managed to find an end to the fabric. "There could be anything inside this." he said. "Literally anything. A golden sword... a horses head... a baby... a nuclear bomb."

"The head of Jesus Christ." said Cassidy. "There are rumours they had it." He added to Naomi and Amy, who returned slightly disgusted looks.

"The holy grail." said Naomi. Curtis looked at her. "It's equally plausible to Christ's head!" she said, defensively.

Curtis took another breath, handed his phone to Naomi, and began to unwrap something hard, roughly two feet in length, slowly removing the soiled cloth it was wrapped in. *Why*, thought Curtis, *would something so religiously significant and valuable, and so fiercely fought for and hidden from history, be wrapped in such disgusting rags?*

But soon his question was answered, as he pulled away the final layer of rag that adhered to the thing below with the viscosity of treacle, he uncovered something grotesque and unnatural. At first, he thought it was an oiled goat's skull; blackened and still glistening with unknown sticky matter, but the closer he looked, the quicker he realised that this was no goat.

CHAPTER 15

"What is it?" asked Naomi.

"Not what we were expecting." said Cassidy.

"It's not... anything." said Curtis.

"What do you mean?" asked Amy.

"I mean I've studied and seen every type of skull in existence, including ones that no longer in existence, and this is... nothing." he said. "It's an amalgamation of creatures made into something else."

"Is it..." started Cassidy.

"I don't know what it is!" said Curtis in a frustrated tone, cutting off his friend.

Cassidy reached into the casket slowly and ran his fingers along the oddly shaped horns that protruded from the forehead of the blackened skull. When he withdrew them, they were stained with a deep, dark crimson brown substance.

"Ok." said Curtis. "Ok. Right. What are we looking at here?"

"Well it's not the head of Jesus Christ." said Amy.

"Let's lift it up so we can get a good look at it." said Curtis. "Stuart, give me a hand, we need to be very careful, I don't want it damaged."

Naomi placed another one of their large towels down beside the casket, and the two men lifted the large dark skull onto it, before they both stood back.

"Ok, this isn't a goat, it's far too big." said Curtis. "It's not a horse, because as we all know, horses don't have massive horns. It's not an Eland or a Kudu. It's not a moose. It's not a stag..."

"Could it be a Giant Sable?" asked Naomi, whose knowledge of natural history was impressively vast.

"That's a good shout, the horns look a bit Sable-ish, but no." said Curtis.

"What about some of the prehistoric mammals?" asked Naomi. "You know, things like the Giant Bison?"

"Again, it turns me on a little that you even know about *Bison latifrons,* but with that the horns come out the side of the skull, like cows, whereas these start just above the brow yet the rest of the skull is all wrong. It's incredibly thick, like that of a musk oxen, the teeth are carnivorous, and the brow and eye sockets are distinctly simian. This is like a fusion of musk ox, panther and... human." he said, visibly not wishing to even mention the latter, for the futility that came with it was verging on embarrassment.

"But *why?*" asked Amy, glancing back into the chest and lifting the material that was used as packing to see if they had missed anything.

"It's Baphomet." said Stuart Cassidy, who had remained quiet since he'd touched the horns, and now speaking in a strange tone the others hadn't heard him use before; all low and worrisome. He sank into one of the kitchen chairs, and stared at the skull before him.

"It's a what?" asked Naomi. Curtis and Amy were also looking at Cassidy.

"Baphomet." he repeated. "The Goat-headed deity... The Devil. I know enough about the rumours surrounding the Templar Order to know what that is." he said, quietly.

"You're saying we have the head of the Devil in our kitchen?" asked Curtis.

"Yes." said Cassidy.

"*Yes?*" replied Curtis, amazed at the response from Cassidy.

"I'm telling you, it's Baphomet." repeated Stuart Cassidy.

"Stuart, what are you talking about? I was expecting a religious artefact, but come on, Satan's head?" said Naomi.

"No. Not Satan. Baphomet." said Cassidy.

"I didn't think you bought into all that religious claptrap." said Curtis. "In fact, that's not even Christian, thats the Occult."

"Look," said Cassidy, standing up and putting distance between himself and the strange skull on the table, "I've done an awful lot of research on the Templars, right? And when they were brought to trial, they were accused of an awful lot of things: amongst other things, devil worship, dabbling in Pagan black magic and odd rituals, and worshipping *that*." he said, all the time his eyes fixed upon the blackened skull.

"But..." tried Naomi, but was talked over immediately.

"Most historians believe that it was a ploy of King Philip of France to try to denounce the Templars by making up these wild accusations; that they worship Baphomet, that they spit upon the cross, that they kept the severed heads of either John the Baptist, Jesus Christ himself or Baphomet and used it in ceremonies throughout the lands. But many of the Templars admitted to these claims, albeit under severe torture, but by the looks of things... it was true." said Cassidy.

"But they were appointed by the Pope, weren't they?" asked Curtis. "They protected pilgrims who travelled to the holy lands seeking enlightenment. Was there really any devil worship required?"

"At first, yes, but eventually even the Pope turned them over to the king. He shopped them, screwed them over, and put distance between them and the church." said Cassidy. "Because, after granting them free reign essentially, they soon became very powerful, both in a military sense, and in a monetary sense. As Naomi said earlier, they were the people who basically started the banking system. They were the people who were feared by rulers throughout the world, becoming so powerful, they could do whatever they wanted. And, of course, they were the people who started what is now the Freemasons, which is itself wrapped in mystery."

"But the majority of those particular mysteries have been debunked." said Curtis.

"Debunked by the same people who have debunked other things that have turned out to be true. By the people who claimed that it was a weather balloon that crashed at Roswell, that Bin Laden was killed and dumped at sea, that the governments aren't listening in through your smart phones and computers, and that 9/11 was a terrorist attack. And guess what, the Illuminati and the New World Order exist and control *everything*." said Cassidy, his voice breaking with a new fear that the others were beginning to buy into. Curtis shared the briefest of looks with Naomi that spoke a thousands words to each other.

"Stuart, are you controlled opposition." asked Curtis.

"You're sounding like a nut-job." said Amy, shaking her head, but not taking her fearful gaze from the skull sat in front of her.

"Yeah, probably, but having spent time looking at all this, I can say that there is so much lying and covering up going on in the world by the people in power, that we don't know about, and has been since the time of the Romans, if not earlier."

160

"Can we refocus on the fact that we have an unidentifiable skull from the time of the Templars sitting on our table that may or may not be the skull of the Devil." said Naomi, in a voice verging on hysteria.

"The Templars," said Cassidy, who was now in a panicked state and not to be quelled, pacing the kitchen in front of the other three, "often worshipped false-idols to make it easier to cope when captured and tortured by the enemy. That's *fact*. We've said already that it is believed that they dabbled in occult and pagan ceremonies as they travelled the world, and inserted some of these into their own ceremonies. They famously used strange religious artefacts in their initiations, and as I said before, some have suggested it is the head of Christ, some have said the head of Baphomet, amongst other things. Isn't it now coincidence that we have an unidentifiable skull that very closely resembles the description of Baphomet that has been recovered through a series of clues left to us by a descendent of the Templars?"

"This is freaking me out." said Amy.

"I'm going to go and get my eye glass to inspect this thing." said Curtis. "I'll be able to tell if it's for real or a hoax."

"I'm telling you, it's Baphomet." said Cassidy.

"So you keep saying buddy, but I just can't believe you. I *can* believe that the Templars may have created a hoax skull to intimidate their young initiates. I just want to inspect it to see if its another 'Jackalope'." said Curtis.

"Jackalope?" asked Amy.

"Those weird little animals that looked like a rabbit but had deer's antlers." said Curtis. "It was an American taxidermist hoax. Or the Fiji Mermaid, that turned out to be a mummified monkey sewn onto a big fishes arse. It's far more likely that this skull here is a combination of different skulls expertly combined and then covered in this oozy oil that looks like old congealed blood, to hide the joins. I'd put money on that being the case."

Cassidy shook his head, but stepped aside to let Curtis pass, on his way up to his office to fetch his favourite magnifying glass: one with a twisted horn handle of considerable age, that seemed fitting for the task ahead of him. As he walked through the corridors of his house he relaxed a little; partly due to the familiar surroundings and smells of his beloved home, and partly because, the more he thought about it, the more ridiculous the notion of an otherworldly deity's head was.

Yet, there was a diminutive knot tightening in his stomach as his thoughts strayed from the possibility of an exciting and elaborate 12th Century hoax to the horrifying and eerie incident in the jungles of the Amazon that engulfed him a few years earlier, where he was entirely convinced that an evil spirit that inhabited a strange blue stone had wholly taken him and caused untold misery while he and his friends only just managed to escape with their lives. And, again, he had been sent on a similar wild chase of ancient puzzle solving and treasure hunting that abruptly delivered an unwanted and chilling reward.

He stopped in his upstairs office, *the insect room*, and looked down at his hand. The hand that grasped the blue stone and would not let go. The hand that died upon his wrist. And yet, the hand that made a recovery, thanks to a jungle shaman somewhere deep in the rainforests of South America, who managed to free Curtis from the grip of an evil spirit within him. And had he now potentially placed himself and his friends in a similar situation due to his inability to turn away from danger? He really didn't know the answer until he took a closer look at what they had just discovered.

He picked up the Victorian magnifying glass and made his way back to the kitchen at the other end of the house. When he entered the room he noticed the exhausted and slightly wretched looks on the faces of his companions. It was the early hours of the morning, they had all had a lot to drink, and had all had to sober up very quickly after the chest was opened. *This should be a moment of celebration and excitement,* he thought. But even he didn't believe his own thoughts.

Armed with a Maglite torch in one hand and the magnifying glass in the other, he began to inspect the skull for signs of foul play, or at least human intervention. But the closer he looked, and the more he concentrated on the areas where joins *should* be found, he saw nothing but bone. His brow was now so furrowed he was giving himself a headache. His breathing had become a little erratic, and a panic was starting to take hold. He needed to discredit this as a Templar hoax, for the other would be beyond comprehension.

"What do you think?" asked Naomi through a yawn.

Curtis sighed and shook his head. He looked up at his fiancee.

"I... can't find any hint of a hoax." he said in a quiet voice.

"What? You're saying it's real?" asked Amy wearing a disgusted look. Curtis only managed a shrug of his weary shoulders.

Naomi headed over to the large coffee machine and turned it on, causing various modern bleeps and noises that brought everyone out of their intense situation and back into the present.

"What are you doing?" asked Curtis.

"What, you really think any of us are going to get any sleep with *that* in our house?" she said, stabbing her finger towards the skull as she spoke.

"She's right," said Cassidy, "I'm not sleeping, this is too much."

"Ok, look, it's the skull of some weird mutation of an animal, can we all agree on that? It's a natural abomination of genetics, surely?" suggested Amy. "You've seen weird things all the time Curtis. Pigs that look a bit like humans? Two headed ducks? Genetic abnormalities. That cyclops goat from India, and cyclops babies, the Zika virus! Weird mutations. Cows born with legs growing out of their bloody heads! There are entire museums dedicated to that kind of thing, hell, you've probably got some crazy shit in the vaults of your museum!"

"I've seen some weird stuff, granted, but nothing like this." said Curtis, eyeing the skull with unease.

"But none of those things are worshipped as deities, are they? They are donated to science. Maybe back in the tenth century or biblical times they were revered, maybe even in rural India still, but now there are scientific explanations – as there are with *all* things." Amy added, with a tone that held much more gravitas with Curtis and Naomi, than Cassidy. She was of course referring to the incident in the jungle, that she was part of, but which she has fought to find a scientific explanation for ever since, for her own sanity: natural group-suffered hallucinogens was her choice. And her explanation was based on science, but with more holes than Swiss cheese.

"It's definitely organic. This is a creature's skull, I can say that much, and I can add that it is a creature's skull that grew into adulthood and most probably old age." said Curtis. "There is no hoax here. No foul play that I can see. It's no animal that I can recognise, and it's not a dinosaur that I've ever seen recorded to science. I'm going to show it to Bernie at the uni, and see what he says." he added.

"Woah!" interjected Stuart. "Who is Bernie?"

"He is the university's Professor of Archaezoology." said Curtis. "He lectures in, and studies bones, essentially."

"I really don't want to involve anyone else in this, folks." said Cassidy. "This needs to remain top secret."

"I mean, this is about to be world news, Stuart." said Curtis in a wearied voice. "I'd rather go into this announcement with all the facts than sound like another lunatic spouting false claims."

"Can we just calm down." said Cassidy, holding up both hands. "That's all I'm asking. Can we at least try to solve as much of this ourselves, here, before we go public? Or tell anyone else?"

"Well we are. And we have kind of solved it, haven't we?" said Amy.

"We've solved the clues to find the item they were protecting, but we don't really know what the item is, what it was used for, or what *powers* it possesses." said Cassidy, putting a sharp emphasis on the word 'powers'.

"And with some help, we can answer those questions far quicker than we would if we lock ourselves in here for the next few months." said Curtis. "Bernard Johnson will be able to help me out with the 'what', John Featherstone, our Professor of Medieval History would be able to hopefully shed more light on the 'why', and as for the 'powers', I'm not entirely sure, to be honest. Perhaps Mystic Meg could pop over for a chat."

"I don't want them involved yet, Curtis." said Cassidy, sternly. "I came to you with this. This is *my* baby. I asked for your help and your secrecy, but didn't ask for you to take over. So far, it hasn't cost you much, and I've let you be involved 'in the field', like you asked. But please don't start bringing more and more people in. Our group is already twice the size it should have been, no offence to you girls, I like you both and have grown to trust you." added Cassidy. Naomi and Amy shared a look that said *aren't we honoured.*

"Ok, Stuart, this is your baby, I get that, although the Craxford Museum is financing it and will exhibit all these findings, so I'm not sure why other people affiliated to the museum can't help us in getting this right?" said Curtis.

"It's just not the time for that *yet*." he said, a desperation and hysteria to his voice.

"Well I have to respectfully disagree with you," said Curtis, "but right now, I'm going to bed."

"You're going to sleep, knowing that it's here on our table?" said Naomi.

"If it makes you feel better, I can put it back in the box." said Curtis.

"No!" said Cassidy. "What if we can't open it again?"

"We can leave the big giant knives hanging out each side!" said Curtis, now a little irritable at his lack of sleep and constantly argumentative friend. "And tomorrow, we *will* discuss what our next move will be."

Curtis woke early, despite only having a few hours broken and disturbed sleep. His dreams were filled with images of the skull, and more alarmingly to him, the white faced woman from the Amazon jungle made the briefest flash of an appearance before he was jolted awake in terror. He felt a little nauseous as he unwrapped himself and rose from Naomi, and slowly pulled on some joggers and a t-shirt, before deciding that he would go downstairs and have another look at the strange skull sitting on his kitchen table, maybe even take some images on his phone and send them to his colleague without Stuart's knowledge.

He padded along the corridor as quietly as he could, past the rooms Amy, and further down the corridor, Stuart was shown to last night on their way to bed, outside which they bid each other a slightly awkward goodnight. As he walked he listened for any sounds, but heard none. They must both have still been asleep. This was good, it meant he could work undisturbed for a while.

Once he had negotiated the staircase and crept down, avoiding the squeaky sections of the stairs as he had done so many times before, he made his way to the kitchen.

It took him a moment to realise what the problem was, but it hit him like the bullet of a high-powered rifle. The chest was gone.

He instinctively hurried back upstairs and slowly opened the door to Stuart's room. As he poked his head around the corner, he saw that the bed was still made, and had not been slept in. He rushed back down stairs and, in a blind panic, looked into all the other rooms of the house, before running back into the kitchen, looking around wildly. *He's taken it.*

He ran upstairs again and woke Naomi up. "Nom, Nom, wake up." he said, shaking her shoulder lightly.

"What, what is it?" she said, bleary eyed, and in a panic.

"Stuart's gone, and he's taken the chest." said Curtis.

"What? Why?" she asked.

"I don't know. I can't find him, and the chest isn't where we left it." he said.

"How could he have gone? His car isn't even here." said Naomi. "It's still in the museum car park isn't it?" Curtis' eyes widened as he leapt from the bed and raced back along the corridor, down the stairs, through the side door and out into an empty courtyard where his Land Rover had been parked the day before.

"Bastard!" shouted Curtis, loud enough to alert the residents of the neighbouring villages for miles around. He ran back inside, by which time Naomi was hurrying into the kitchen tying her dressing gown around her waist.

"What's he done?" she asked.

"The lunatic has nicked the Landy and the chest!" shouted Curtis. "What the hell is going on?" he said in a hysterical voice.

"Right, calm down." said Naomi. "Let's just take a breather."

"Naomi, some guy we hardly know has played me like a flute, stolen a hugely significant artefact and pissed off in my Land Rover!" shouted Curtis.

"Ring him." said Naomi. "Ring him and ask him what he's doing. He might have an explanation."

"Oh I'd like to see how he's going to talk himself out of this one!" he shouted as he took out his mobile phone, swiping and punching the screen in anger. He then sat in silence as the phone rang. "He won't answer." he said. "He's too much of a c... Stuart? Stuart? Where the hell are you?... Where?... Driving? I know you're driving! You're driving my bloody Land Rover!... But why Stuart?... What?... No I'm not!... Where are you going?... Yes, but where?... Why won't you tell me!... I thought we were in this together?... You're acting really weird buddy... It what?...

166

Spoke to you?... Stu, mate, you're not making any sense. Come back here, and we'll sort this all out, just me and you... Stuart?... He's hung up on me!"

"What did he say?" asked Naomi. Amy entered the room with a troubled expression on her face as she put on her glasses.

"What's going on?" she asked, sitting on one of the chairs, her expression changed to concern when she saw Curtis.

"Stuarts nicked the chest and my bloody car and driven off sometime in the night." said Curtis.

"Driven off? Where?" she asked.

"I don't bloody know! But he's taken the chest with the skull in it." he said. "And stole my bloody car!"

"Curtis!" shouted Naomi, which made him physically jump. "What did he say?"

"He said that I was pushing my agenda too hard, taking over the project, blah blah blah, he's going off *for a bit...*" said Curtis, quoting with his fingers, "...to try to solve this on his own... and here's the mental part... because it spoke to him and told him not to trust me." he said, shaking his head wearing a wild-eyed expression.

"Ok, well he can't do that." said Naomi. "Did you draw up a contract?"

Curtis' eyes narrowed as he realised he didn't want to answer that question. There was no contract, only what he would refer to as a 'gentleman's agreement'.

"We had an agreement." he said. Naomi shook her head and threw up her hands in desperation. "We had a gentleman's agreement, but it appears only one of us is a gentleman." he said.

"Yes, and also an enormous idiot." she replied. Curtis sighed in frustration.

"Did he give any indication as to where he was going?" asked Amy.

"No, he was annoyingly vague." said Curtis.

"How vague? Anything is something!" said Amy.

"Vague to the point of not telling me anything." said Curtis.

"Christ. Any idea where he might go?" asked Naomi.

"I've only known the guy a few weeks!" said Curtis. "He could go anywhere! I mean, I'll try his home first, but after that I'm pretty much out of ideas!" he said.

"Right, well, can we track his phone?" asked Amy.

"Oh!" shouted Curtis, looking at Amy with a sudden change of mood. "Why didn't I think!"

"What?" she replied.

"Amy, you beautiful genius. I can't track his phone, but I can track the car! It's got a tracker! And one that works off an app too!" he said, removing his phone and swiping across the screens to find the relevant icon. "All our cars are fitted with these trackers. I usually only use this to see how far away from home you are to see if I can sneak in a quick bag of crisps before you arrive." he said. All Naomi could do was to look blankly at him.

"Right," he said, "just select the Land Rover from the list... and it's triangulating its position on the map now... and... oh for god's sake! He's in Inver-bloody-ness!" shouted Curtis, slamming his phone onto the kitchen table.

"Inverness?" asked Amy. "What the hell is he doing there?"

"Buggered if I know." said Curtis. "He must have driven right through the night. Pissed as well! We drank a lot! I let him smoke one of my Monte Cristos! Never again!"

"What are we going to do?" asked Naomi, trying to be the voice of reason in this conversation.

"*We* are not going to do anything. *I* am going to drive to Inverness." said Curtis.

"Curtis, I don't think you should." said Naomi.

"It's fine, I just think I need to talk to him face to face, on our own, and assure his fragile ego that it's still the Stuart Cassidy Show." said Curtis.

"What if he's a lunatic?" asked Amy. "I never liked him! What if he has a gun?"

"He's not got a gun, unless he's bought one from a service station on the drive up." said Curtis. "Honestly, it's fine. I'll be careful. I just want to talk to him. I think he's just a bit panicky."

Both girls tried to convince Curtis otherwise, and that this was a matter for the Police, for a few more frustrating minutes until they both backed down and accepted that he would be careful and not too confrontational. They knew Curtis was good at diffusing difficult situations and also could be charismatic with the most hardened businessmen and win them over, so they reluctantly allowed him to go.

CHAPTER 16

Twenty minutes later, he was in the car, after a rapid breakfast, and was now motoring as quickly as he dared in his Alfa Romeo, ever northwards towards the border and on to Scotland. He was incensed at the effrontery of the man who had come to him for help, and then when Curtis had indeed helped, and offered even more help for the final few pieces to this bizarre puzzle that was constructing before them, he snatched it all away from him and even stole his car.

Curtis gradually calmed the further he drove, partly because he loved Scotland as a country, and partly because a drive out in his Alfa Spider was his version of deep spiritual meditation.

But right at that moment he was still uneasy as he passed Edinburgh and crossed the huge and looming Forth Road Bridge; unsure what to make of the discoveries that he and Cassidy had made in the wilds of Northumberland. He hadn't really had a chance to inspect the skull properly. Ideally he would have been under lab conditions, deep within the university, hidden from any eyes that he didn't trust, as he looked at every square millimetre of the strange artefact, with the help of scans and experts he could have hand picked from the universities extensive list of distinguished masters in their relevant fields. But instead he was playing a ridiculous game of cat and mouse around the countryside, crossing borders, and chasing priceless historical artefacts unnecessarily, against a man he hardly knew, who had an extremely fragile ego and a propensity for panic.

He pulled off the A5 somewhere near Pitlochry and brimmed the fuel tank of the thirsty car as he fuelled himself with a beige sandwich and a bottle of caffeine enriched sugary drink. A cold breeze blew through the service station as he stood by his car, and he pulled his coat around him, turning up his collar to protect his neck from the biting Scottish winds, as he checked the location of his Land Rover on his app once again. Right at that very moment, the car was moving again, heading into Inverness city centre. That meant that Cassidy hadn't abandoned the car.

He still had a good two hours of driving ahead of him before he reached Inverness, and had the might of the Cairngorm National Park to circumnavigate. He stopped again in Aviemore, just to check on Cassidy's location, and it appeared that the Land Rover was now heading in the opposite direction, away from the centre of Inverness. Curtis, with a concoction of nerves and anger bubbling in the pit of his stomach, pressed north, along the A9, cleaving through a dramatic medieval landscape in his red cacophonous missile.

As he reached the outskirts of Inverness, he pulled the car to the side of the road, stretched his aching back, and once again fired up his tracker app on his phone, waiting for what seemed like an age for the triangulation of his stolen car. A minute or so later, he saw that the car appeared to be stationary at a remote location not far from Loch Ness, and still a good distance away from where he was currently parked up. The road along Loch Ness was one well know to Curtis, and he couldn't help but be slightly excited about taking the Alfa along the twisty roads with their epic backdrop of the famous monster loch.

But more important matters were ahead of him, and he programmed the location into his iPhone's sat nav, and set off again, with a predicted 59 minutes to his destination, a place called Knockie Lodge, at the south end of the loch, along the military road running along the southern shores.

The Scottish lochs always had a calming effect on his psyche. He used to love driving the roads that hugged the various lochs, from Ness down to Fyne and all in between. There was something about the very landscape; the sounds and smells, that always drew him back: the romance, the drama, the fishing and the whisky. But at that moment, he was struggling to even acknowledge the scenery or the memories that were attached to the places he passed. The knot in his stomach was tightening with every mile he covered: the closer he came to his destination, the more uneasy he felt. He wasn't sure what to expect, but his instincts told him, that whatever lay ahead of him in the forests of Scotland, wasn't going to be a stroll in the park. Cassidy appeared to be an unpredictable individual, with paranoia playing a large part in their current situation.

A little less than 59 minutes later, Curtis turned off General Wade's Military Road, and onto a single track lane that looked like it ran off into the dark wilds of the Scottish highlands, away from civilisation, for miles and miles to some unknown Laird's mansion. He eased the Alfa slowly along the loose gravel, as the lane cut through fields of heather and fern, woodland and boulder-studded forest with an increasing lack of ground clearance. He had given up on the sat nav now, and was relying purely on the tracker app. He was less than a mile away from his Land rover, and, as the lane split, and turned into a dirt track in the direction he needed to go, he decided that it was too rugged for his low-slung sports car, so pulled the Alfa out of sight onto an open section of mudded gravel near a farm gate, and decided to make the rest of the journey on foot.

Not sure what to take with him, he ended up armed only with a small pair of binoculars, three Mars Bars, two cigars, and a hip flask of whisky as he trudged along a track lined by thick pine forest that blocked out most of the light. He had decided that kid gloves were preferable to boxing gloves in this situation, so he was going to massage the ego, and calm the flighty animal that had become of Stuart Cassidy. This was too important a discovery for individual squabbles to interfere with, so Curtis was well prepared to apologise, charm, bribe, and beg Cassidy in order to get the relic back safely into the hands of Craxford Museum.

He rounded a corner, and saw further up the track what looked like a tumble down cottage, more like a glorified wood store than a dwelling, with a thin line of smoke rising from the tiny chimney. And there was Curtis' Land Rover Defender Twisted V8 that he enjoyed so much, still looking unscathed from the unauthorised jaunt from his home, if only a lot dirtier than usual.

Curtis was less than one hundred yards from the cottage when the front door opened and Cassidy came out with an axe in his hand. Immediately, their eyes met and both men stopped dead in their tracks, each as shocked as the other.

"Hi Stuart!" said Curtis, as friendly as he could, but wearing a slightly manic grin. Cassidy's eyes narrowed.

"How the hell did you find me?" he asked, incredulously. Curtis pointed to his Land Rover.

"Tracker." he said, with a weak laugh. Cassidy replied with a tut and a sigh, shaking his head.

"I just needed to get away, Curtis." he said, placing the axe down against the wall of the cottage, much to Curtis' relief, and walking over to a pile of logs. "It was all getting a little bit intense, you know?" he said, picking up a large piece of wood and carrying it over to his makeshift chopping block. "In your kitchen," he continued, "when you had all just gone to bed, I couldn't sleep so I went back down to the skull, to look at it a bit more." he said. Curtis approached him slowly, reducing the distance to no more than ten yards.

"Look..." he started, but Cassidy kept on talking.

"Well the skull kind of spoke to me, I know that sounds ridiculous but you're going to have to trust me – you of all people should." he said, collecting the axe from its resting place and pointing it towards Curtis as he spoke, making him stop dead once more. "It *told* me to get away. It was quite persuasive." he added, as he brought the axe up in a high arc and brought it hard down on the log, cleaving it in two.

"Where is it?" asked Curtis. Cassidy nodded towards the small cabin. "Look, Stuart, I'm not here for a fight. I'm not here to take anything *away* from you, yeah? I'm here to make things right. I'm here to assure you that I'm not taking over, ok, I'm not. We can play this your way, I was only trying to help, which was what you came to me for in the first place."

"It doesn't want to go to a museum, Curtis. It doesn't want to be studied. It doesn't want to be displayed like a trinket." said Cassidy.

Curtis was now leaning against his Land Rover, trying desperately to look calm and collected, like this whole situation was *no big deal*, and he decided to take out the two cigars, and silently offer one to Cassidy. He felt like this would be a deciding factor to gauge how pliable Cassidy would really be during this fragile negotiation. Cassidy wearily accepted, and they both enjoyed a moment of calm.

"You know, for what it's worth, I believe you." said Curtis, after lighting Cassidy's and then his cigar, flicking his zippo closed and blowing out a long exhale of smoke.

"Well I was hoping you might." said Cassidy, now also leaning up against the car he stole 24 hours earlier.

"How did it speak to you? Was it a voice inside your head? A vision? Just thoughts?" asked Curtis. It took a while for Cassidy to reply.

"Honestly, I can't really remember, but I know that it did, and that I had to get it away from...well from you." said Cassidy. Curtis didn't rise to the challenge of confrontation, just stared at

173

the view across the tree tops of the forest, waiting for Cassidy to elaborate a little more. Right at that moment, his hunch was that Stuart Cassidy was inventing this story as he went along. He was waiting for him to trip himself up. "I remember sitting, looking at the skull in the chest, and suddenly began to feel weird. My eyes felt...cloudy, like a thick mist was inside your kitchen. I woke up lying on the floor, knowing exactly what I had to do." he said. "I knew that I wasn't to trust you, like you somehow aren't the right person to be in possession of it. So I had to do something drastic."

"And that was to steal my car and drive to Scotland?" asked Curtis.

"Well, not exactly." said Cassidy. "For what it's worth, that is a ridiculous Land Rover. Physics shouldn't allow it to be that fast."

"It's got a six litre Corvette engine in it." said Curtis. "And five hundred horse power."

Cassidy leaned in a little closer, as if he were sharing a secret and not wishing to be overheard. "I'm sorry I borrowed your car without asking, but I treated it well. I even put some fuel in for you. I would have brought it back."

"Look, Stuart, that was a bit of a breach of trust there, you know, dashing off in the middle of the night with no message or anything, on a whim." said Curtis eventually. "We need to be able to trust each other, don't we? If we're going to work as a team. We've been a good team so far. We've solved all the clues in an amazingly short space of time; these things usually take years, decades even, or people just hit dead ends. We've been very lucky, and we've managed to keep it all under wraps."

"But that's my concern now." said Cassidy. "Keeping it under wraps. Secret. We can't let anyone else know what we're doing, until the time is right."

"And that's fine." said Curtis. "I totally agree. But when is the right time?" Cassidy stayed silent, uneasy, staring into the distance. "There is going to be a point, Stuart, soon, when we will have to start telling people what we've found." said Curtis, like a psychologist talking to his most volatile patient, desperately trying to avoid trigger words or create an episode, yet also try to make them understand. "Now, I'm happy to be guided by you up to a point, ok, I don't want to step on your toes here, but at the same time, I'm a little bit excited about telling the world what you

174

and I have found. If we cover this up, we're no better than those tossers with the Dead Sea Scrolls."

"It's not time yet." said Cassidy, throwing the remainder of his cigar to the floor, stamping it out, and walking back to his chopping post. "And you're not the man to help. I realise that now."

Curtis remained where he was, internally at boiling point; his anxiety screaming and thrashing within his mind, but externally a sea of calm as he smoked more of his cigar and enjoyed the view of the Scottish Highlands. He really had felt like he was making progress, yet also felt like he was suddenly back at square one. Cassidy didn't seem to mind that he had turned up unannounced, yet the moment he pressed the subject of publicity or even continuing as a team, he was shut down in an instant. Cassidy seemed to be holding all the cards, and Curtis desperately needed to tip the balance somehow, back into his favour. He needed to regain control of the situation, yet he was struggling to find an angle he could pursue.

He thought for a while longer; his mind a high-powered computer searching a vast database of possibilities and struggling, as Cassidy chopped wood nearby. Eventually he broke the silence. "Ok, so, what are we going to do then?" he asked Cassidy, who stopped chopping the logs and turned slowly to Curtis. "How are we going to work out what the hell this thing is?"

Cassidy looked towards the tiny cottage, but said nothing. It looked to Curtis like he was having an internal struggle between protecting the artefact, and exploring it further.

"It's why I'm here mate. It's just you and me, like at the beginning. We've found it, we now need to see what in God's name it is." said Curtis, realising the poignancy of his choice of words, as he carefully laid his smouldering cuban cigar atop a wooden post, and motioned for them both to enter the cottage.

He saw Cassidy give the briefest of nods in agreement before walking back inside, still gripping the woodcutter's axe, much to Curtis' unease.

Once inside, Curtis realised just how basic the structure was; with bare stone walls and a concrete floor, a cast iron stove, beside which a primitive camp bed was set up. There was a tiny round wooden pedestal table, and two ancient-looking pine chairs beside a grubby, spider web encrusted window across the other side. And atop the table, overhanging on both ends, was the chest, with the ancient curved blades still protruding menacingly from each side.

"Well this is cosy." said Curtis.

"Yeah, well, it's off-grid." said Cassidy.

"That it is." said Curtis, still surveying the interior of the shack.

"Fat lot of good that did me." said Cassidy.

"Don't underestimate a man who treats his cars like children." said Curtis.

"Well, now that you're here, you can make yourself useful." said Cassidy, handing Curtis two chunks of freshly chopped wood and pointing towards the stove. Curtis obliged, and stocked the wood burner with the fresh, fragrant and slightly damp wood. He turned back to Cassidy, who was now sat at one of the old wooden chairs.

"Have you found out anything new, then?" he asked, nodding towards the chest. Cassidy shook his head.

"I haven't opened it since I left." he said.

"I need to have another look at it, if I may?" asked Curtis, pulling out the other chair that was even older and dirtier looking than Cassidy's. It was of the wood that became grey over time, as it gradually absorbed the detritus of life that amassed around it over the many years, and the seat had a distinct elm grain that was still visible through the grunge as he sat down upon it.

"Help me lift it onto the floor then, and you can put the skull on the table." said Cassidy, standing up the moment Curtis sat down. Curtis couldn't help but feel that Cassidy was still trying to play a game of power and control, yet he was prepared to overlook it all, if it meant that the skull, the chest and the associated artefacts made it all back to the museum unharmed. The two men hauled the heavy chest onto the floor, taking the utmost care to avoid the protruding razor-sharp scimitar blades, and Curtis lifted the oversized and unidentifiable skull onto the table where it sat, still darkened with the oily viscous liquid that covered it for millennia.

"What are you?" asked Curtis as he looked closely once again at the bizarre item in front of him. "You're a very thick skull, with pointed canines and significant simian features, and

176

two horns protruding from the forehead that I've never seen on a mammal. Only you're not a mammal, are you? You're a cryptid." he said. "You're not real, yet here you are."

"I've been looking into the legend of Baphomet." said Cassidy, quietly. "This morning, when I went into Inverness, I thought I'd do some research. And there is a solid link between the Templars and Baphomet. In fact, a French Crusader, called Anselm, he wrote about his enemies 'calling on Baphomet' prior to battle. Those enemies were then defeated. Perhaps, this relic came into the Templars possession after that battle. It fits the description too, a goat-headed deity. And, get this, there are carvings not only on this casket, but on Templar church walls in Brittany and Paris of figures resembling Baphomet; horned beast men, all matching.

Yes, they were accused of worshiping Baphomet by a crazed French king hell-bent on wiping out the Templars, but what if he was right?" he asked. "There were certainly many Templars who admitted to such under the inquisition, and it kind of makes sense, when you think about it; the Templar Knights worshipping idols to brainwash themselves into an easier situation, should they ever be captured or even just accused of following Christianity in the far corners of the Templar reach." said Cassidy. "At least that was their reasoning, but what if it does have some kind of power? Perhaps even the most powerful of all powers: the power of persuasion. Mind control."

"Stuart, I don't think..." started Curtis, but once again he was spoken over as Cassidy continued.

"This thing," he said, pointing at the skull, "made me take him hundreds of miles away from you. It made me not think twice about stealing a car and running, regardless of any risks. I knew I *had* to. I was so certain that I had no choice, I did it all without hesitation." said Cassidy.

"So you're pretty sure this is the skull of Baphomet." said Curtis, sitting back and folding his arms. "A goat-headed God from mythology and legend...Satan, essentially?"

"Not Satan, no, he wasn't even linked to Satan and the occult until the 1800s, but he was a deity who wielded great power; we're talking baptisms of fire and enlightening of the minds, with a bit of Pagan witchcraft thrown in there for good measure." said Cassidy.

177

"And this *great power* that this thing is purporting to wield, you think that's..." asked Curtis.

"Persuasion." said Cassidy. "Total mind control. Think about it, what is more powerful than getting other people to do your bidding? What ever you need? Need someone killed? Get a town of people to hunt them down. Need money? Persuade people to bring it to your feet. Want someone's army? Persuade them to had control over to you. Want to control the world? Enlighten the world's minds."

"Stuart..." said Curtis, slowly shaking his head.

"It told me you're the wrong person for it to be around. It brought me here." said Cassidy.

"No." said Curtis. "My Land Rover brought *you* here, and the tracker on my Land Rover brought *me* here. Your paranoia made you get into the Land Rover. My inquisitive nature woke me up early and made me discover your midnight flit." said Curtis.

"Why are you so against this being real?" asked Cassidy. "After everything you went through a couple of years ago?"

"Because the law of averages won't allow it!" said Curtis, raising his voice in the tiny building. "There is simply no way that this kind of thing can happen twice to the same person in the space of two years, when there is zero documented evidence of an item being possessed by an evil spirit, other than the ramblings of mad people!"

Cassidy smiled at Curtis which caught him off guard. It was a strange smile; equal parts warming, excitable, and unhinged, and his brow was set too high. In contrast, Curtis was frowning hard.

"And this brings us almost full circle." said Cassidy, calmly. "Where's your evidence of a possessed stone in the jungle? How can you prove that the woman you saw inside your head was anything other than the *ramblings of a mad person*?" he asked, punctuating the air as he spoke. "I *believe* you, but where's your proof? What makes your story any more believable than those spoke about on an obscure facebook page or a podcast about conspiracy theories?"

Curtis' breathing was heavy as he sat, stewing in his own anger at what was being levelled at him across the table. But the truth was; he had no proof. Cassidy was right. There was no hard evidence to prove his account of what went on in the jungles of the Amazon, other than a few photographs of a withered looking hand holding a dull blue stone. In fact, there is more evidence proving the existence of the Loch Ness Monster, than there is of his white faced woman.

"Look," said Cassidy, seeing he had proven his point, "humour me then, while you're here. Can you at least do that? Open your mind to the possibility that your jungle stone is just one of many things that are unexplained in this world, yet also very very real." Curtis remained silent, but seemed to deflate a little on his chair, allowing Cassidy to continue.

"When I was sat in your kitchen, once you'd all gone to bed, that thing," he said, pointing a finger at the skull, "communicated with me in a way that I have never experienced before. It was like a clear voice inside my head, as real as you are, telling me that you weren't the right person to decide what to do next... something about you not being right, telling me that it was not to be experimented upon, telling me to run, to take it somewhere safe; hidden. It needed rescuing and I was lucky enough to be chosen as the man for the job. The voice was loud, and firmly in control." said Cassidy, who could now see that Curtis' hand was visibly trembling as he sat at the table. Curtis was beginning to believe him.

"But what does it want?" asked Curtis in a tiny voice. Cassidy shrugged.

"Hasn't told me that bit yet."

"Did you not gleam anything about what it wanted?"

"Not really. I mean it was all over quite quickly and I woke up on the bloody floor." said Cassidy. "But I knew I had to get away that very minute. It was desperation, panic, like I had never experienced. And I didn't have my car. Your Land Rover keys were sitting there in front of me, and I'm sorry to say I acted on impulse and just got the hell out of there. I stay here from time to time, the owner of the house lets me use it whenever I want. It's totally off-grid, and I like coming up here. It was the obvious choice."

Curtis nodded, but said nothing for a while. Their attentions both turned back to the skull on the table. The uneasy feeling Curtis had experienced on the drive up was now an oozing sludge of dread within him, and he was struggling to maintain his calm exterior. Cassidy's account of how the skull managed to put a voice inside his head was worryingly accurate to how the woman of the jungle managed to communicate with him. But Curtis had to take control of this situation, and soon.

"Right," said Curtis after a while, springing up from the table and walking out through the open door into the fresh air of the Scottish forest. Cassidy visibly jumped as Curtis broke the intense silence that had descended on the shack, but slowly followed him out. "I have a plan: It's getting late, and I don't particularly want to be here for the night, so I am going to go and book into a B&B somewhere. Tomorrow, we spend the day looking at this bloody thing to try to work out what the hell it is."

"There's a tent in the back of your Land Rover, why don't you just camp out here?" said Cassidy.

"I'm not camping. I haven't camped since I was in Brazil, and a tree landed on me." said Curtis. "Besides, there's no phone signal here, and the girls will be worried sick, so I'm going to head off and make a phone call while I find somewhere near by."

"You can get signal up there." said Cassidy after a brief pause, pointing to a jagged Scottish hill towering over their encampment. "But do me a favour, don't tell them where we are. Keep it between us, please? It's up to you where you sleep mate. I'll not do another runner, I promise."

"Well, no that's true, because I have the keys to the Land Rover, and they're coming with me." said Curtis, patting the pocket of his jacket.

"Ok, whatever, but you're coming back here tonight, and you're going to bring fish and chips, and I will provide the beers, of which I have many. We'll light the fire pit, and we'll enjoy a night sitting out in the forests of Scotland. What do you think?" asked Cassidy.

This annoyed Curtis, partly because Cassidy was still giving out orders and wrestling with the control of the situation, and partly because it sounded like a delightful way to spend an evening, in any other situation but this particular one. But he accepted and headed back down the track to his Alfa Romeo, knowing full well that he needed to put all his efforts into getting that skull back to the museum at all costs.

CHAPTER 17

"Curtis! We've been worried sick! Why has it taken you so long to get in touch? You could have been dead!" shouted Naomi down the phone before Curtis had even managed a *hello*.

"There has been no signal out here, I'm sorry, but I'm trying to sort the situation." he said once Naomi had run out of breath.

"What's that idiot playing at?" she asked.

"He's just having a bit of a freak out. He's claiming that the skull spoke to him and told him not to trust me and to get it out of our house." said Curtis. "Apparently Baphomet thinks I'm a 'wrong-un'."

"Oh god, we've got involved with a mental patient." said Naomi. "This could be dangerous, Curtis."

"Can I just play devil's advocate here and say that a few years back it was I who was sounding like the mental patient, out in the jungle, remember? I claimed the exact same thing, and you believed me." said Curtis. There was silence on the other end of the phone. Eventually she spoke again.

"So you believe him?" she asked.

"I don't know yet, but his description of the voice in his head was scarily similar to my own experiences, and I cannot simply dismiss it as a lie: that would make me a hypocrite, and an arse hole." said Curtis as he looked out over the waters of Loch Ness, from the grounds of The Highland Club, situated at the very southern tip of the loch, looking north east up the length of deep, dark water as the light was beginning to fade from the sky.

"So what are you going to do?" she asked him.

"I'm working on getting the skull back, but that involves getting Stuart to drive the skull, and my Land Rover, back to us. Right now, he's still a bit jumpy and I'm treating him as gently as my tolerances will allow. It's an unstable situation right now, so I'm taking it very slowly." said Curtis.

"So what are you going to *do*?" asked Naomi, again. Curtis sighed.

"I've booked into a hotel, and I'm going to take the guy some fish and chips later on, and we're going to just have a blokes night sitting out around a fire, drinking some beers, hopefully alleviating his concerns, and then tomorrow we're going to try to get to the bottom of this; work out what the hell it is, and try to then get him to agree to bring it, and my car, back home." said Curtis.

"And if that fails?" asked Naomi.

"Then I am going to steal it back, and my car, and I'll have to leave the Alfa somewhere he can't get to, and then come back and get it at a later date." said Curtis.

"Please be careful, Curtis. You're not Indiana Jones, you're not Jason Statham, sadly, don't do anything stupid, and make sure you bring yourself back in one piece, that's the only important thing." said Naomi.

"I'll text you tonight, when I get back to the hotel, and then I'll let you know how tomorrow goes. It may be that I'll need you to get Amy to drive you up here, so you can pick up the Alfa if this all goes pear shaped." said Curtis.

"Amy's going home tomorrow morning. She's got work." said Naomi.

"Bugger."

"Which hotel are you staying in?" asked Naomi.

"Oh, just a little hotel on Loch Ness, called The Highland Club." said Curtis, quickly, masking the name with a cough.

"Curtis, I know that hotel! I've been to a wedding there before! It's anything but little! And hundreds of pounds a night!" said Naomi.

"Naomi, it's the closest one to where Cassidy is holed up, and the only place for miles with availability. I don't care if it's the bloody Balmoral, I'm not sleeping in a tent." said Curtis.

"Who said anything about sleeping in a tent?" said Naomi.

"I'm not sleeping in a tent, Naomi!" said Curtis, raising his voice.

"Ok! I didn't ask you to sleep in a bloody tent." she said. "There is a middle ground you know."

"Look, I've got to go and get fish and chips, I love you, and I'll speak to you tomorrow." said Curtis.

Curtis rolled the Alfa slowly to a stop on the gravelled area beside the dirt track that led to the hovel Cassidy was currently occupying, and walked the rest of the way on foot, carrying a bag containing some very large battered fish and

183

enough chips to feed a family of ten. On top of that, Curtis had decided to order some battered haggis and smoked sausage to accompany the feast. He had borrowed plates and cutlery from the Highland Club to assist them in engulfing the huge amounts of food that were now weighing down the bags that were beginning to cut into his fingers as he walked.

By the time he reached the door of the shack, in front of which Cassidy was sitting and grinning at Curtis, he was out of breath and red in the face.

"You took your time." said Cassidy.

"Sorry, I had to wait for the Monster Fish and Chip Company to farm more potatoes to create enough for two portions of large chips." said Curtis, marching past Cassidy and placing the heavy bag onto the unoccupied chair beside the table that was still supporting the odd skull. He gave the skull a quick glance and found himself grimacing at it involuntarily before refocussing on the food.

They ate well, yet although the conversation was flowing and light, there was still the awkwardness at the end of every dialogue when both their thoughts strayed straight back to the events of the last twenty-four hours the moment silence fell.

Once both their chip papers, and the remaining detritus of the nights carousal of comestible debauchery were cast onto the fire, they both sat on their respective wooden chairs in the open air, and sipped at a couple of beers while the dusk took hold of the forest surrounding them, the temperature began to slowly drop, and the day-time animals bid their good-nights to the replacement nocturnes.

They were talking about places they had visited, and Curtis had happened to mention Paramaribo, the capital city of Suriname in South America, and the starting point of the journey that led them to discover the famous blue stone.

"Tell me," said Cassidy, "when you had your visions, how did it *feel?*"

"Like she was in control of *everything*. It felt like she was a part of me, yet very foreign, and I don't mean in an ethnic sense, but a foreign body within me; a cancer, that made me feel utterly defenceless against her raw power. I was merely a puppet; a vessel for her to inhabit. And the tinnitus that accompanied her was like my head was being split in two." said Curtis, almost

184

blurting it out as he spoke as if he were in one of his many therapy sessions.

"Mate, I couldn't have put it better myself. That is exactly how I felt in your kitchen. That's the reason I just left without a word. I had to. It told me to, and, once I woke up, I couldn't *not*." said Cassidy.

"Because at the end, you're so exhausted, you pass out." said Curtis quietly, as the truth dawned on him that he and Cassidy had somehow experienced almost the same thing, yet years apart and on opposite sides of the world, with two very different objects, but connected through one commonality, it seemed: Curtis Craxford.

It hit him hard as the realisation kindled that perhaps it was he who attracted these odd artefacts, and not mere coincidence. And as an atheist, he struggled with the idea of good and evil forces being something very real, yet he knew from his own experiences that the stone and its bizarre powers were something that could not be explained away as natural hallucinations, or the side effects of unknown exotic poisons. And it was happening all over again, only thankfully not to him personally.

But why not *him?* Why Cassidy? Surely if he was susceptible to this kind of thing, the skull of Baphomet, or whatever it indeed was, would have picked him, however it appeared to be quite the opposite: the skull didn't like him. Or was he a spent vessel? Once marred by an evil force was he hence forth sullied? Or had that jungle shaman given him a life-long protection against these evil spirits? These were big questions, none of which he could answer.

While they had been talking, the light had all but been purged from the sky, and what had been a peaceful dusk, was now an oppressive and intimidating void beyond and above the tree line. It was getting late, and Curtis' eyes were growing heavy as he began to nod in his chair as they both stared at the fire, lost in their own reflective contemplation.

He jerked himself awake after what felt like only a fraction of a second, but when he looked he saw Cassidy sitting close to the fire, upon the ground, cradling the dark skull in his lap.

"Stuart?" said Curtis, quietly. No response. "Stuart, what

you up to?" he asked, but again got no reply. A thick mist was orbiting the periphery of the clearing from the surrounding dense forest, and with it a chill that penetrated Curtis' body within seconds. "Stuart, mate, I don't like it. What's happening? Stuart!" he shouted at the end, and Cassidy turned with a smile on his face, as if Curtis were the butt of a rather twisted practical joke.

"He's coming." said Stuart, in a strange and excited hush.

"Stuart, shut the hell up mate, what are you playing at? Who's coming?" asked Curtis, an anger rising within him as his body temperature drastically fell. The mists were now more like wood smoke as they rolled over them and swirled around the two men: unnaturally thick and dense. Stuart seemed to momentarily snap out of whatever trance he had been gripped by and began to look around the clearing at the encroaching mists, and he suddenly realised what he was holding on to. When he saw the skull in his cradled arms, he dropped it into the dirt at his feet and scrabbled away on hands and feet back to where Curtis was sitting.

"What's happening?" he asked Curtis, grabbing his wooden chair, pulling it close, and sitting next to where Curtis appeared to be frozen in fear.

"I dunno mate, just sit tight." he said, watching the billowing mists engulf the entire clearing as the breeze seemed to pick up suddenly and whip around them, causing the mists to swirl as if the two men were sat in the eye of a tornado. The fire in front of them was the only source of light, causing the mists to appear even more menacing in the flickering flames.

"What the hell..." said Curtis, but was cut short as a low growling laugh echoed around the trees all about them; guttural and thick, as the mists continued to wildly writhe and heave in and out of the darkness in all directions.

"What was that?" whispered Cassidy, barely audible now above the winds that caused the flames of the fire to roar and rage, sending curious shadows through the mists. And there it was again; that low gloating crow, only this time, before their very eyes, a shadow began to materialise in the far reaches of the light from the flame, already unnaturally large, growing in stature and beginning to take the form of a heavy creature with impossibly broad shoulders and an odd, elongated head. And then both men saw the horns. Huge thick horns, sprouting from the forehead of

186

the shadowy form, together with long protruding ears that were unmistakably hircine.

The guttural snicker turned to a long, low baritone growl and the shadow seemed to reach its full stature. Curtis welcomed the disorientating and blinding mists now, as he wasn't sure he would survive seeing this cryptid creature in all its glory.

"Are you seeing this?" asked Cassidy to Curtis, not breaking his stare from the shadow.

"I'm not sure what I'm seeing." said Curtis, also transfixed on the shadow.

But another noise was beginning to form in the periphery of the clearing; a rhythmic low tapping noise that was slowly building in volume. The noise grew into what felt like footsteps; the metallic marching footsteps of a group of men, and as the two friends sat in pure disbelief, shadows of armour clad and helmeted warriors passed into the clearing, projected onto the walls of mist from the light of the flames, yet no solid figures could be seen. They were all around the two men now, and, in unison, the marching suddenly stopped, and all the shadows came to an abrupt standstill in a perfect ring within the fog surrounding Curtis and Stuart.

And then, again, the rumbling mirth of Baphomet echoed around the trees from a huge throat heavy with secretions as the croaking laughs continued.

"What do you want?" shouted Cassidy, his voice trailing away into the mists where it dissipated and lost its force. Curtis immediately shushed him, but too late. The laugh abated.

"Come forth... he who disturbed my... mortal... remains...?" spoke the voice; loud, slow and powerful in the darkness, terrifying the two men to their cores.

Cassidy stood up and walked a few steps forward, whilst Curtis visibly shrank back into his chair, whispering Cassidy's name but to no avail.

"Come..." spoke Baphomet, his large and formidable shadow opening its arms wide. Cassidy began to walk forward, past the open fire, and directly towards the shadow of the horned giant. As he walked the shadow knights surrounding them began to stamp their shaded pikes on the ground with every footstep that Stuart took, in unison, emphasising his terrified journey.

Curtis managed to stagger to his feet; acutely aware of the

187

moment, but fear pushed down with all its might onto his shoulders as the ground came up to meet him, roots of horror fusing him as one with the earth. He looked on, paralysed, as Cassidy slowly headed through the edge of the mists and turned into just another shadow as his tiny stature was dwarfed by the larger shadow that stood before him.

When Cassidy stopped, along with the lance and halberd banging knights, Curtis saw the shadow of Baphomet bring his giant clawed hands down slowly and appear to clasp Cassidy's head. The thunder rolled above them, and the wind whipped the mists even harder around their clearing, but as Curtis' anxiety was reaching fever pitch and his terror had his heart beating out of his chest, the mists blew away on the high winds, taking the shadows with them, and as quick as it arrived, it was returned to a quiet, calm and secure woodland clearing.

Curtis took a long-needed breath as he glanced, wide-eyed, all around him, collapsing back onto his wooden chair, terrified that the shadow figures were still hiding in the darkness. As he looked, he could have sworn he saw a figure dart behind a tree: a figure in tattered black – a woman. One he'd seen before, and one he never wanted to see again. Yet she was returning with more of a regularity to his dreams; but not since the jungle had he seen her when he was awake. *It couldn't have been her.* It must have been his anxiety playing tricks. She was gone; rid by the Shaman using old magic. He kept his eyes fixed on the tree at the very edge of the light cast by the fire, and began to walk towards it, but between himself and that tree, he saw Cassidy, lying on the ground. Unmoving. *Was he dead?*

"Stuart?" he asked, the small child-like voice returning. Nothing. He looked back to the dark trees and couldn't see any movement, then back at Cassidy. He was sprawled uncomfortably upon the dirty ground, with his back to the heavens, and his face turned away from where Curtis was slowly approaching. One arm was by his side, the other stretched out towards the flames of the fire, and his legs were at awkward angles; bent with his feet turned in upon themselves.

"Stu mate?" asked Curtis, this time stopping on unsteady legs and leaning against a fence post. "Come on buddy, get up."

To his relief he began to move, slowly at first, but with accompanying groans that eventually led to him turning himself over and lifting up onto his own elbows. He wore a confused look on his weary face.

"You ok?" asked Curtis, noticing internally that he felt genuine concern for the man he considered a friend, despite what had happened in the last day.

"Er..." was all Cassidy could manage, as Curtis dragged his wooden chair over to him, and helped him up into a sitting position upon the chair. "What happened?"

"What can you remember?" asked Curtis.

"Erm, did we have fish and chips?" asked Cassidy, frowning at Curtis.

"Yes, what about after that? The mists? The wind? The... shadows?" asked Curtis. Cassidy shook his head.

"Just, give me a minute." he said, raising his hand and leaning forward as a wave of nausea hit him hard and he vomited onto the grass to one side.

"Please tell me you remember what just happened Stuart! I'm going to go mad otherwise." said Curtis, an insistence in his tone.

"I had a strange dream, I think." he said.

"Tell me." said Curtis, crouching down next to him, avoiding what had just been deposited nearby.

"Ghosts were all around me. Monsters. And knights. All up in smoke. One grabbed me." he said, managing a weak laugh.

Curtis breathed a sigh of relief and placed a hand on Cassidy's shoulder. "It wasn't a dream Stuart. It happened. We got surrounded by a thick mist, then shadows of bloody Templar Knights. And Baphomet was *here*. They were all around us, we both saw it. Baphomet spoke to you, and you went to him. He seemed to grab your head, I couldn't see properly through the mists, then it all faded away." said Curtis, babbling in a distressed and jittery tirade.

"Bloody hell." said Cassidy. "Were we hallucinating, do you think?" Curtis tried to slow his breathing as he sat back on the ground.

"I mean, it's possible that the Scottish slipped some mescaline into our fish and chips, but I'm fairly sure it was somehow real." said Curtis, relaxing a little as the world slowly returned to normal and the threats seemed to disperse. Despite the darkness surrounding them, the scourge and the terror were not

189

present. It was a different kind of darkness: a comfortable one. Cassidy managed a snigger at Curtis' words as he hauled himself up onto his feet.

"So, I was touched by Baphomet?" asked Cassidy. "In real life?"

"You kind of offered yourself to him." said Curtis. "Willingly."

"Right." said Cassidy, clearly confused about what he was hearing. Curtis pulled the wooden chair back next to his, and they both sat down again.

"For the record, Stuart, I think I believe you now." said Curtis eventually.

"Good." he replied in a weak voice. "I think I need to go to bed."

"Yeah I'm going to do the same." said Curtis.

"Ok."

"I'm going to go back to the hotel. We can pick this up tomorrow, in the daylight, and work out what the hell we're going to do." said Curtis.

"Ok." said Cassidy, a heavy reluctance in his voice.

"Right." said Curtis, not moving from his chair. He noticed Cassidy was also rooted to his own chair, staring into the fire. They remained at the fireside together for nearly an hour.

CHAPTER 18

"Morning sweetie." said Curtis wearily through the hands-free kit of the Alfa as he exited the grounds of The Highland Club. It was a cold and crisp Scottish morning, but the clouds were sporadic and distant, allowing the sun to slowly warm the ground as it rose into the sky.

"How did last night go?" asked Naomi. "I got your 3am text, and it didn't give much away as it was one word."

"It was quite eventful." said Curtis, chirpily. "We both saw a load of ghosts in the forest, and then Stuart appeared to gift his soul to a goat-headed giant." Naomi remained quiet. "Hello?"

"What were you smoking?" she asked eventually.

"Nothing." he replied.

"Did Stuart, by any chance, prepare some mushrooms to have with your tea?" asked Naomi.

"There was no drug abuse. There was no mass alcohol consumption. And as far as I know there was no hallucinogen-infused foods." said Curtis. "It was a very strange experience, and one that reminded me a little of what happened in the jungle, then I could have sworn *She* manifested."

"So, what happened?" asked Naomi, concern rising in her voice.

"Well, there was a strange mist, the wind got up, shadows of knights were all around us, then a very large goat-headed shadow began to speak to us. Stuart offered himself to it, clearly in a weak mental state as he couldn't remember doing it, the shadow grasped his head, the mists faded, and I found him lying on the ground." said Curtis.

"Curtis, this is all getting a bit *occulty*." said Naomi. "I don't like where it's going. I think you should grab the casket, leave the flipping skull, and get the hell out of Dodge. The trunks alone are priceless." she added. "They're our prize in this, not whatever unnatural Satanist stuff you found inside. There could be poisons and god knows what oozing out of that thing."

"Yeah, I think you're right." said Curtis.

"You know I'm right, darling; I'm always right." said Naomi.

"Well, apart from the fact that you still think Black Friday is to do with racism." said Curtis.

"What are you going to do now?" asked Naomi, ignoring the jibe.

"I'm going to negotiate like I've never negotiated before." said Curtis. "I need some, if not all of the Templar relics to come back to the museum. Even the skull, Naomi. If it's locked away in a museum vault, it's not going to wreak untold revenge on mankind. This isn't The Mummy. We need it."

"Well, I still don't trust Cassidy as far as I could throw him, which isn't very far because he's a hefty chap, so I just want you to be careful, ok?" said Naomi.

"I'm always careful." said Curtis.

"Just don't do anything reckless." she said.

"It's fine, I'm going to charm my way through this." said Curtis.

"Oh, and could you give Bob a call? He's found a couple of issues with your Mercedes he wants to talk through with you... says it's urgent." said Naomi.

"Yeah I'll call him after this. I hope it's nothing serious... Naomi?..." the call ended with a beep and drop in signal in the wilds of the Scottish Highlands. Curtis decided that climbing the hill near where Cassidy was staying was the best place to get signal, and he was only a few minutes away from the turning.

From the top of the hill, Curtis sat and caught his breath on a boulder whilst having a momentary scan of the horizon for wildlife through his field binoculars he'd brought with him. This was prime Golden Eagle territory, but at that moment the skies and surrounding relief appeared bereft of life.

As he scanned the landscape, his binoculars made their way to a gap through the trees, beyond which he could see the tiny shack that Cassidy was using as his home, complete with the smouldering remains of last night's fire. He levelled his powerful binoculars at the tiny dwelling and settled in to see what was happening.

The door to the shack was open, which meant Cassidy was awake, and after a few minutes he saw him exit the cabin. He was acting strangely; rushing around and seemingly preoccupied with something Curtis couldn't quite place. As he observed from his lofty position, he could see Cassidy talking, yet couldn't see anyone else in the vicinity. He was animated as he spoke, and as Curtis looked on, he saw Stuart obscurely conversing with the air around him, gesticulating with his arms as he went.

What also struck Curtis as strange, was that Cassidy was barefoot. He was walking around on gravelled dirt on a cold Scottish morning wearing nothing on his feet, and Curtis was growing increasingly worried for his friend's mental state. *And who was he talking to?*

Curtis stayed rooted to the spot, sat atop the boulder, high up on the hillside, binoculars glued to his face as he watched the strange happenings in the clearing below. Cassidy was now building what looked to be a large fire, laying armfuls of branches upon the unlit pyre, all the time chattering away to the ether. Once he finished his construction, he disappeared back inside the cabin. Curtis stayed where he was and continued to watch for any more movement.

A few minutes later, Cassidy appeared once again, only this time he was bare-chested, as well as bare foot. His white skin was reddened in the coldness of the morning, yet he seemed numb to it as he carried something in his hand. It looked like a large stick with something wrapped around the end, and to Curtis' increasing unease, he saw, hanging from Cassidy's other arm, the horned skull.

"What the hell are you doing?" whispered Curtis as he followed the proceedings through his binoculars. Cassidy propped the stick against the chair he was stood next to, then slowly and ceremoniously placed the skull onto his own head so he wore it like a hat. He then collected up the stick once again, held his lighter to the wrappings at the end of it, and suddenly found himself holding a flaming torch.

Cassidy slowly walked towards the pile of sticks he had created, skull still perched atop his head, and he slowly pushed the torch into the base of the sticks. As smoke began to billow from the pyre, he let go of the torch, leaving it to burn with its brethren in the flames, and he began to walk slowly backwards from the fire, arms slowly making their way into an outstretched gesture of conclusive fulfilment.

Watching on from his voyeuristic vantage point, Curtis saw Cassidy now swaying slightly in a trance-like state, and he appeared to be chanting; saying the same thing over and over, though Curtis was not accomplished enough of a lip reader to translate what he was seeing. He was now concentrating hard on Cassidy's mouth, trying desperately to translate the chant, when suddenly he saw him stop, open his eyes, and look directly at Curtis. It was a look that penetrated Curtis' psyche and made him feel very uneasy, but he held Cassidy's gaze through his large binoculars. Curtis felt like he was surely too far away to be seen by Cassidy with the naked eye, camouflaged against the rocky hillside with his green Barbour coat and grey trousers, yet Cassidy was indeed looking directly at him, and his fears were soon confirmed when he grinned a menacing grin, and waved slowly at Curtis, before taking hold of the large skull still perched atop his head, and placed it over his face like a grotesque mask.

An unnerving uneasiness oozed inside Curtis' stomach as he watched the strangeness for a few moments longer before tearing himself away and heading back down the hill to confront Cassidy and find out what he was up to.

Hurrying up the dirt road, potted with mud puddles and loose gravel, he saw Cassidy still standing outside the shack, still shirtless, and still wearing the mask upon his face as he danced in front of the burning pyre.

"Stuart? Stuart!" snapped Curtis in a stern voice. There was no reply from his friend, who continued to slowly dance with his arms outstretched. "Stuart, what are you doing?" he asked as he neared his friend. He seemed to be chanting a quiet, mumbled chant that Curtis couldn't quite hear or decipher. "Stuart man!" he shouted. The chanting stopped, and he turned and looked towards Curtis; his face masked by the strange skull staring back at Curtis like something out of one of the budget horror movies he and Naomi loved to watch of an evening with a glass of good wine and a tasty takeaway. But that currently felt like a world away to Curtis who was currently face-to-face with the skull of a deity that appeared to have taken full control of his friend. Curtis took a deep breath and approached Cassidy.

"What's happening Stuart?" he asked, stepping to within two feet of him. "What are you doing?" Cassidy offered no response. Curtis fingered the keys to the Land Rover that were nestling in his coat pocket. Half of him wanted to bolt into the shack, take the Templar chests, and run away back to the museum leaving whatever abomination was currently being worn by

Cassidy, yet the other half screamed concern for his friend, and made him stay rooted to the spot as if his feet were set in concrete.

"Take the mask off, for God's sake!" shouted Curtis through gritted teeth, now angry at the situation before him, and the fact he was getting nowhere with his friend. Again, no response. There was nothing for it, he was going to have to resort to physically trying to remove it. If nothing else, it should provoke a response.

Curtis stepped forward and went to take hold of the skull. Cassidy instinctively swatted Curtis' hand away, but Curtis pressed on, and with Cassidy's reduced vision, soon grabbed the horns of the skull with both hands, whilst Cassidy took hold of Curtis' forearms in an attempt to stop him removing it from his face. The scuffle lasted far longer than Curtis would have liked, and Cassidy showed great strength in resisting the unmasking. As they tussled, Curtis managed to knock Cassidy off balance by tripping him with his leg, and as Cassidy fell backwards, Curtis managed to wrench the skull from the falling man and loose his grip of his arms in the process.

When Cassidy landed on the ground and the wind was knocked out of him, a moment of sudden realisation and terror crossed his face as he locked eyes with Curtis, holding the skull of Baphomet in his hands.

"Help me." wheezed Cassidy, yet as soon as the words had crossed his lips his expression changed like a switch had been flicked inside his head and returned to a far more threatening melancholy. "You think you can compete with me, pathetic little man?" he said. Even his voice had grown deeper and thick with malice, as if uttered from another mouth.

"Stuart? Snap out of it." said Curtis, carrying the skull a small distance away and resting it upon the bonnet of his Land Rover. "Come on. Enough."

"I have watched empires fall. I've seen blood flow like rivulets upon the field of battle." said Cassidy.

"How romantic." said Curtis. "Now get up!"

Upon this command, Cassidy rose not by bending at the waist and heaving himself up, but simply rising from prone upon the floor to a standing position without using muscles; some other force was working for him, pulling as supposed to pushing. This made Curtis take a step back and suddenly focus on what was happening in front of him. His eyes narrowed on Cassidy's glassy expression of hatred.

"I have returned." spoke Cassidy, and another spine-chilling grin spread across his face.

"Congratulations." said Curtis. "But what is your next move exactly? Why is my friend unable to control himself?" Another low and bass-rich snigger could be heard coming from Cassidy's mouth.

"He is weak. He is now my vessel." said Stuart, or more accurately, Baphomet.

"Why him? Why not me?" asked Curtis.

"You are different. You are unwanted. You belong to another."

"What does that even mean, Stuart?" asked Curtis, keen not to get dragged into Cassidy's psychotic episode.

"She owns you. I will not come between Matinta and her prey." he said, as another unnaturally low laugh came forth.

Curtis didn't give him the chance to speak again, instead he punched him as hard as he possibly could on the side of his jaw, knocking him once again to the ground, this time unconscious. This surprised Curtis as much as it presumably caught Stuart, or Baphomet, unawares, and he wasted no more time in beginning to collect up the chests from inside the shack and placing whatever he could find that was at all related to their discovery in the boot of his Land Rover, while Cassidy lay unmoving on the ground.

Curtis was shaking uncontrollably; from equal parts adrenaline and terror, but he had to get out of there, quick, and once he was sure that all the items, including the skull, were stashed in the boot of the four by four, he jumped in the driver's seat and sparked the powerful engine into life.

He instinctively checked his mirror and was about to grab his seatbelt when the driver's door flew open as a large hand grabbed him, and with great strength, Curtis was ripped from the Land Rover and thrown several feet towards the flaming pyre that was now roaring with intense heat.

When he landed, the air was knocked out of him momentarily, and he watched the bulk of Stuart Cassidy jump into the Land Rover as he tried to haul himself back up as quick

196

as he could. Once back on his feet, he ran at his own car, and reached it just as Cassidy floored the accelerator and spun the tyres on the loose gravel, sending Curtis spinning as he just missed the door handle and ricocheted off the side of the car as it sped away, crashing over the burning pyre in Cassidy's haste to leave, sending embers and burning sticks in all directions.

Curtis acted quickly and sprinted after his Land Rover as it disappeared in a cloud of dust down the track. He had one aim, and that was to get to his Alfa Romeo as quickly as he possibly could: he was not going to let Cassidy escape again.

Before Curtis had even made it out of the clearing on foot, the Land Rover was nowhere to be seen, and all that was left was a slow-settling dust cloud and a roaring engine note growing more distant by the second. Still brimming with adrenaline, anger and fear, Curtis was now sprinting the few hundred metres down the slope to where he had parked his Alfa out of view, and when he reached it he had already unlocked it and had the key in his hand. He virtually threw himself into the low sports car, and he fired it into life and was immediately moving away at speed as he joined the hard tarmac of the main driveway.

He employed all his driving skill as he accelerated hard up the paddle-controlled gearbox, and down as he braked for each corner. Where the Alfa was nimble and light, the Land Rover made up for in sheer torque and grunt, and Curtis knew that once they got onto the main road, the Land Rover would be hard to catch, even for the Alfa Romeo, so Curtis knew he had to get him in view before they reached the end of this private road to Knockie Lodge.

"Come on, come on, come on, come on." said Curtis to himself as he thundered along the access road, and as he rounded the final corner before the road reached the T-junction at the end of the track, he saw his Land Rover in the distance turn right and roar off along the B-road. He followed a few seconds later and accelerated hard in pursuit.

"Matinta?" said Curtis aloud to himself as he drove, keen to keep that word at the forefront of his mind that had been uttered by Cassidy in his deranged state. "Matinta... Matinta... Matinta." He'd never heard that name before.

The Land Rover was being driven erratically and quickly by Cassidy, who seemed totally overwhelmed by whatever was in control of his psyche and his physical body as he ran from Curtis. He kept his distance, wanting to observe as supposed to attack. *Just what was Cassidy's next move going to be? Where was he going to go?*

They both motored quickly down the B-road that ran to the southern tip of Loch Ness, and once Cassidy reached Fort Augustus and the turning to The Highland Club, where Curtis had stayed the night before, he turned onto the A82 and blasted northwards up the other side of the Loch. The traffic was heavier on this larger road and Cassidy was once again driving beyond his capabilities, weaving through the traffic and taking what Curtis would describe as unnecessary risks in a big heavy tank-like vehicle.

"Call Stuart Cassidy!" shouted Curtis to his hands-free phone software that was installed in the Alfa, and he immediately heard a ringing tone through the speakers of the car. It was a long shot that Cassidy would pick up as he drove so erratically, but to his surprise, Cassidy connected to the call but remained quiet; "Stuart, you're being a dick, and you're about to crash my Land Rover. Please, mate, pull over and we'll talk about whatever issues you're currently going through. None of this is worth dying for buddy... Stuart?"

"I have to take him away from you." said Cassidy in a fearful voice. "He wants to be free, and you are causing him harm."

"Stuart you're not making any sense." said Curtis. "I'm not causing anyone harm, I'm trying to understand the situation, and I'm trying to protect a relic."

"You're trying to destroy him!" shouted Cassidy. "I have given myself to him. I am helping him. Leave us alone."

"Yeah that's not going to happen." said Curtis. "Not while you're driving my car. Not while you have priceless Templar artefacts in the boot, and not while you're acting like you're possessed."

"Just go home." said Cassidy. "I'll return your car later. We have to go into hiding until we can gather enough strength to make our mark."

"What does that even mean, Stuart?" asked Curtis, keeping Cassidy in his sights.

"I have been chosen to do his bidding. I am his warrior

now." said Cassidy. "I will bring him back to power."

"Stuart, bloody hell man! Listen to what you're saying!" said Curtis, overtaking another slow-moving vehicle that Cassidy had dangerously overtaken a few seconds earlier causing an oncoming car to brake hard and sound his horn in anger.

"I can't let you come in the way of such raw power. I will take the skull of Baphomet and we will regenerate his powers so that he may rule over us all." said Cassidy. "All will bow before him. And I will be there, by his side, but before that, I will be him and he will be me."

"What are you saying, Stuart? That you're going to take over the world?" asked Curtis. "That you're going to lay waste to entire armies? Governments?"

"We won't need to." said Cassidy.

"So, are we talking pure evil here?" asked Curtis. "Is that the route you're choosing?"

"We will make the world a better place. There are too many people, who take too much without a moment's thought. We will rid the world of such mindless *taking*." said Cassidy. "We will destroy the destroyers, and the weak will cower at our feet."

"You're going to kill people? Is that what you're saying?" asked Curtis.

"Only the damned." said Cassidy, and the line went dead.

"Stuart? Stuart? Bloody hell." said Curtis.

CHAPTER 19

They were more than half way up Loch Ness before Cassidy made any signs of slowing down, and Curtis was hot on his tail as Cassidy weaved in and out of traffic in the overpowered Land Rover he was driving, closely followed by Curtis in his Alfa Romeo, yet the gap was constantly changing as Curtis waited for safe opportunities to overtake.

They had just passed the famous Castle Urquhart and Cassidy, with no hesitation, made the sudden move of turning off the main road at speed. He had seemingly spotted a dirt track that seemed to wind its way up the hills behind the castle and at the last possible moment, swerved towards it, but Cassidy had misjudged the turning angle, and failed to scrub off enough speed. Curtis watched as his expensive Land Rover skidded on the loose surface and slid off the road, nosing into a deep ditch at speed, the back of the car lifting up as the bonnet dug into the soft mossy embankment and came to a sudden and abrupt stop.

Curtis pulled the Alfa to a swift stop just off the road, before running over to the steaming car that was now half buried in mud and grass. There was no movement from inside the car, and as Curtis looked, he saw Cassidy was unconscious in the drivers seat; blood trickling from his nose and forehead as he leaned awkwardly on the deployed air bag. The front of his beloved off roader was buckled and twisted and was certainly not capable of being driven any further.

Curtis looked wildly around him. *What was happening?* He took out his phone to instinctively call the emergency services, but the iPhone was struggling to find any bars of signal in the mountainous terrain. There was now no traffic on this stretch of road, and by the looks of it, no witnesses to the crash. He began to panic. He was less than a hundred feet from the shores of the Loch, and as he looked about him, he suddenly spotted something that caused him to make a snap decision: a moment of clarity in all the absurdity.

He opened the back door of the Land Rover as it sat angled into the ditch, and jumped into the boot, pulling out the horned skull. He dashed over the main road, carrying the skull by one of its huge horns towards the large body of water gently lapping at the shores. *This was it.*

He stopped at a small rowing boat that was tied by a rope to a large rock further up the shoreline, and he placed the skull into the small fibreglass hull. He untied the heavy rope from the rock, gathered it up, and bundled it into the boat alongside the demonic head. He also picked up another rock; one that was roughly the size of a bowling ball and almost as round, and manhandled that into the boat where it landed with a dull thud upon the coil of rope.

He pushed off from where the little rowing boat was beached, and jumped inside, icy cold water now saturating his shoes and bringing the reality of what he was about to do crashing down on him, a sickness building within his larynx.

Once inside the boat, he took the plastic oars and fitted them into the rowlocks, and began to row himself away from the shores and out into the Ness. He kept one eye on the shoreline for any signs of movement, but it appeared deserted. He kept on rowing until he was exhausted, and finally collected in his oars and sat while he caught his breath. It was a fantastic view from where he was: views of the Castle and of just how big the loch was; the water was calm and his motion sickness was just about being kept at bay. It was quiet on the water that day, and he felt like he had the whole loch to himself.

He stared into the dark water. *Was he really about to do this?* He shook his head, took a few snaps of the weird skull with his iPhone, which then began to vibrate with an incoming call.

"Naomi?" he answered.

"Tell me good news." she said. "Tell me you're on your way home with the chest."

There was a long pause from Curtis. "Not exactly." he said with a sigh.

"Oh Christ. What's happened?" said Naomi, her voice coloured with concern. Curtis managed a weak laugh as he thought about how he was going to summarise the events of the last few hours. "Well..." started Curtis, "After our phone call this morning I went to see Stuart. When I got there, I thought I'd better give Bob a call, so I climbed a hill where he told me I could get a phone signal. Anyway, when I got up there I could see Stuart down in the clearing acting weirdly."

"How weirdly?" asked Naomi.

"Well he was dancing around a big fire with no shirt or

socks on." said Curtis.

"Oh-kay..." said Naomi slowly.

"Anyway, I never did get to ring Bob, but that's the least of my car troubles, but I'll get to that later." said Curtis. "I went down to see what the hell Stuart was doing, and he was weird: like, really weird. He was almost speaking in tongues, talking like he was somehow the *chosen one,* and to cut a long story short, I punched him in the face and tried to steal the skull and the other bits and drive off with them in the Land Rover." said Curtis, and waited for a response from his fiancee.

"From your tone there, I'm guessing it didn't go to plan?" she asked.

"Erm...not totally to plan, no." said Curtis. "I got dragged out of the Land Rover, took part in a high-speed car chase, witnessed my Landy pile into a ditch and disintegrate, and I'm currently sat on a rowing boat in the middle of Loch Ness with the skull of Baphomet and a large stone sitting between my legs."

"Hang on, he dragged you out of the car? Then he crashed it?" asked Naomi. "And where did the boat come from? Actually I don't care, are you ok?"

"Yes I'm fine." said Curtis.

"Is Stuart ok?" asked Naomi, albeit with less concern in the tone of her questioning.

"I'm not sure he is." said Curtis.

"Well perhaps that's not such a bad thing." said Naomi.

"I'm afraid I left him in the wreckage. I tried to call an ambulance, but I had no signal. And once I did get signal, out here in the middle of the lake, you called. So I decided that the last time we encountered something *evil,*" he said, almost as if he didn't really want to say the word at all but had to under duress, "we had to get rid of it. So I'm going to send it over the edge. It's going to the bottom."

"Ok, just take a moment." said Naomi. "Think about what we have discovered. Think about it's historical significance. Send the skull down, but not the golden casket, please." she added.

"The casket is still in the car, I'll get that later. I'll call you when it's done." said Curtis, ending the call, using his foot to move the grotesque skull that had caused so much unrest in a relatively short space of time. He took the heavy stone he was going to use as a weight, placed it underneath the hollowed out skull, and began to wrap the anchor rope around the two items, weaving it in and out of the horns and making sure there was no chance of it untangling itself in the depths.

It was a long rope, and he untied the end that was currently still attached to the bow of the boat, but this made Curtis take note of his location upon the loch: just north of Castle Urquhart was where the deepest section of the loch was, at 227 metres, and he was floating directly over it in his tiny rowing boat. He remembered this statistic from something he had read not that long ago; how the deepest section had been re-registered in this very location after more accurate measurements had been taken.

"Well, it's now or never." he said as he neared the end of the long rope, with only ten feet or so of loose rope left over, and realistically no further need to continue the wrapping of the item, and it was almost totally invisible under the thick nautical rope as it wound around, in and out of the skull like a long snake.

Curtis tied it off in a sturdy hitch knot, and began to position himself ready to throw the very heavy item into the water. But sudden movement and sound around the boat made his heart almost stop as something grabbed at his leg. He gave a small and rather embarrassing shriek in pure terror, as a large creature hauled itself into the boat behind him, and as he jumped and turned, to his half relief, he recognised it as a wet and bloodied Stuart Cassidy and not the Loch Ness Monster.

"What the f..." shouted Curtis.

"Don't! I can't let you do it! Please!" gasped Cassidy.

"Jesus! Are you ok, Stuart? That's a canny gash on your head, mate, it's bleeding quite a lot. You need to go to hospital." said Curtis, who found himself sitting between Cassidy and the bound skull.

"Please, Curtis, I'm fine," he said, holding his hands palms forward showing his apparent lack of aggression. "It's been a bit of a weird time for me."

"That's a bit of an understatement." said Curtis.

"Give me the skull." said Cassidy, his full body shaking from the coldness of the water he had submerged himself within to reach the boat.

"No mate. It's not a healthy thing for us to have around. It needs to be lost. This project should never have happened." said

Curtis. Cassidy began to laugh strangely as he shook his head.

"*You* don't get to make that decision. *I* found the parchment, *I* brought you on board with this project, and *I* get to decide what happens to *that*." said Cassidy, jabbing his finger at the skull, and clearly growing more angry with each passing second that Curtis obstructed his goal. "I *am* this project."

"Stuart, you've gone full Roger Waters. It's making you hysterical and mentally ill. I think it would be better for everyone, you especially, if you and *it* parted ways." said Curtis.

"You don't get to decide!" shouted Cassidy, rocking the tiny boat as he shouted with his whole body as he frantically wiped more blood from his forehead, looking at his claret hands.

"Ok, look, take a moment, ok? Don't forget, I've had previous experience with a cursed object. It took hold of me, and I had to let it go." said Curtis. "Stuart, mate, if we go back with the golden casket and the booby-trapped chests, even the burner, and the bell, and the key, we can show the world that we've made a significant discovery. The casket alone is priceless, its solid gold, and the closest to the lost Templar hoard we are ever going to get. Let's go with that! We don't need the problems that are clearly linked to whatever *this* is." he said, pointing behind him to the bound skull. "Let's live to fight another day, buddy."

"But this skull is the most powerful item the world will ever see. This skull proves that Baphomet is real. That the accusations levelled at the Templar Knights were actually true. *That* re-writes history." and his expression changed again as he looked at Curtis from below a furrowed brow. "I'll kill you before I let you destroy it." He said with so much venom it changed him beyond recognition, and as he said those last words he lunged at Curtis and knocked him backwards, onto the large skull.

They looked at each other for the briefest of moments, before both men began trying to grab the skull that was now securely tied to the very heavy rock. Cassidy was making better progress as he was using most of his body weight to pin Curtis, who had managed to turn himself over, face down to the floor of the rowing boat, and a heavy punch to the back of the head from Cassidy dazed Curtis as he went limp from the violent impact.

"It'll be a shame for those two girls to hear how their rich friend died." said Cassidy quietly into Curtis' ear, in the now familiar eerie baritone voice that he had been using since his encounter with the shadow of Baphomet. "After crashing his expensive jeep on the shores of the loch, and with severe head-injuries, you accidentally fell into the water and drowned; body never found. I can see the headlines already. They may not mention the fact that I staved your head in with a rock."

Curtis could hear everything Cassidy was saying, and as he pushed his way over him to the skull, Curtis acted on impulse and, staying still and feigning unconsciousness, quietly took the slack end of the rope and began to knot it around the ankle of Stuart Cassidy, making sure he moved as little as possible as Cassidy was distracted with struggling with his own ice cold hands to undo Curtis' steadfast hitch knot he had tied around the horns of the skull earlier; as tightly as his strength would allow.

"No one can save you now little man. Not even your bitch from the Jungle." said Cassidy, who was still trying to undo Curtis' tight knots he had secured around the skull and the rock. "You have caused me more trouble than you deserve."

In one swift move, Curtis pulled his new knot tight around Cassidy's ankle, sat up, and as Cassidy turned around, unsure as to what was happening, he looked at the knot, and then back at Curtis, who grabbed the side of the small boat and thrust all of his body weight over the right hand side, easily capsizing the tiny fibreglass tender, and sending himself and Cassidy into the icy waters of Loch Ness.

The sudden shock of his body being subjected to such a severe cold made Curtis flail around in the icy waters, opening his eyes in shock and inhaling a lung-full of Loch Ness, as he saw Cassidy only a couple of feet away looking directly at him through the murk, before the slack of the rope tied to his ankle suddenly went taught with the weight of the plummeting stone and skull, and with a brief look of horror, he accelerated downwards into the nebulous depths below and quickly out of sight in the murky waters.

When Curtis broke the surface he coughed lungfuls of freezing water out and took in a life-saving gulp of cold air before the weight of his saturated clothes almost dragged him under again just as he grabbed at the hull of the capsized boat and clung on while his body burned in agony with the drastic temperatures inflicted from the unforgiving waters.

Given the size of the boat, it didn't look too big a task to right it in the water, and he summoned all of his strength to heave the boat over and back onto it's hull once again. There was a brief moment of relief as the boat bobbed in the water once more as his shivering body felt like it was going to shut down at any moment, and as he dunked his face into the water and opened his eyes once more to try to see if he could locate Cassidy, there was no sign of him from the dark depths. By now, at the rate he was being dragged downwards, he would be nearing the bottom. There was nothing Curtis could do now, other than try to save himself. Cassidy had to be dead.

It took five attempts to drag and kick himself into the tiny boat, and when he did finally make it out of the water and land with a damp thud on the deck of the boat, he was tiring from the cold so much, all he wanted to do was close his eyes and go to sleep. But a voice in the back of his head, that sounded remarkably like Naomi, told him that that move would be suicide, and instead he raised himself back to a sitting position, fished out one of the oars that was floating nearby, rowed himself to where the other oar was floating, and began the arduous journey back to shore.

Two months later...

CHAPTER 20

"So with mixed emotions, ladies and gentlemen, I give you the Reliquary of Northumbria." said Naomi into her microphone, and with the press of a button on her podium, some curtains were drawn back for reveal the exhibition space, to polite applause, from the newest and most exciting exhibit in the Craxford Museum: the golden casket, the wooden chests, the stone box, the projectile, the key, the incense burner, and the prayer bell; alongside which the original manuscript, and its holder, beside the tapestry and a replica of the Larmenius Charter, together with a plethora of information boards and even projected footage of the moments these items were opened and revealed.

"As you can see, the items are of a stunning condition, given their age, and the significance they play in re-writing the history of not only Northumbria, but the Templars and Christianity the world over, cannot be overstated. I'm here for questions, ladies and gentlemen, but for now, please enjoy." said Naomi, as she turned the microphone off and stepped down from the small podium on this VIP and press evening.

She was immediately swamped with reporters who all wanted to ask the same question, and it was a lady from the Northumberland Gazette who managed to grab her attention first: "Miss Ashcroft, have the police made any more progress with the disappearance of Mr. Cassidy?"

"To be honest Nicola, I think you may find that out before we do, so as far as I'm concerned he is still at large somewhere." said Naomi.

"Can you shed any more light on what happened that day with Mr. Craxford? Anything you haven't mentioned to us before?" asked the reporter.

"Why don't you ask him?" said Naomi, nodding towards the entrance, through which Curtis had just attempted to sneak; late as usual. And with that, the hustle of press made their way directly to him, so Curtis, instead of blending in without being noticed by all, including his fiancee, managed to make as big an entrance as possible.

"Mr. Craxford! Mr. Craxford!" shouted the throng. Curtis stopped and looked decidedly uncomfortable, much to Naomi's delight, as the two made eye contact and Curtis mouthed the word 'sorry'. Naomi simply looked at her watch, shook her head, and offered her husband-to-be a pack of hungry reporters, whilst blowing him a kiss.

"What is it you delightful bunch want to know, exactly?" asked Curtis, instantly animating himself into what he always was when he was at work; a wealth of enthusiasm, excitement, sparkle, and knowledge. Of course; below the surface, he was a crumbling man: his anxiety spiking through the roof the moment his thoughts strayed back to the scene in the waters, which it had done every hour of every day since the incident. The mental image of his friend disappearing into the depths; the look they shared, submerged, as the realisation of an impending death hit his friends face, would haunt Curtis for the rest of his life. And the awful truth; the secret that Curtis hadn't been able to share with anyone, not even the woman he was so madly and deeply in love with for fear of risking their engagement, their relationship, their burning desires for one another, was a weight he was struggling to support on a daily basis. He'd taken to inventing meetings to allow him to get away and spend time on his own, often simply sitting in his car away from the museum, away from Naomi, and away from reality.

The account he had given to the police was that Stuart Cassidy had stolen the artefacts, and his car, and then crashed, escaping with the contents of the golden casket: an ancient goat skull, but nothing else, while Naomi and Amy thought they knew the real story, which was that Curtis sent the skull to the bottom of the loch, and Cassidy had somehow fled, avoiding capture. Only Curtis held the secret of what really happened that day.

All this flashed across his mind once again as the reporters fired questions and camera flashes at the man himself, Curtis Craxford: Curator, explorer, local celebrity, murderer.

"What do you know about Stuart Cassidy's disappearance?" shouted the first reporter, a man who was wearing a t-shirt to an invite-only night of wine and canapés, which instantly made Curtis hate him.

"Look, I've told you lot, and the police, everything that happened from the moment we met here at the museum, to the moment Stuart stole and crashed my car and did a runner while I went to get help." said Curtis, who had practiced his invented version of events hundreds of times in his head, and in various police and press interviews over the weeks following the fateful day Stuart Cassidy was dragged to the bottom of the loch.

"Come on, mate, you've summoned us all here to look at an empty box, while the interesting part was stolen by some guy who has gone completely off grid. Give me an angle. The people are more interested in Stuart Cassidy being found than an old metal box, that's the truth of it." said the reporter. Curtis held his gaze for a moment longer than he should, turning it into a far more aggressive atmosphere; he was annoyed that this reporter was belittling the Templar artefacts to his face in his own museum without a shred of remorse or shame. *If only he knew the truth,* thought Curtis, *then he'd have a story.* So, instead, Curtis smiled at him.

"What angle would you like then? Hmm? Would you like me to tell you that he became possessed by the devil? Would you like me to tell you that he slipped the skull over his head and disappeared like Frodo Baggins? That he ran away to the Caiman Islands and worships the skull like that guy in castaway with his football? What?" asked Curtis to sniggers from the onlookers. "The facts are, and I realise you're a journalist and don't really like to stick to those sorts of things, but, alas, they remain that he stole the skull from our house, then stole my Land Rover and fled to Scotland like Charles the First. I tracked him using my car's tracker, I thought I'd talked him round, yet when we went to go home he attacked me and stole both the skull and the Land Rover for a second time. Then when I chased him in my car, he crashed said Land Rover into a ditch. I had no phone signal, so walked off to try to get help or indeed some signal, as he appeared badly injured, then when I returned to the crashed car ten minutes later, he and the skull were nowhere to be seen. The Police helicopter did the rounds, there was a bit of a manhunt, but he has eluded police ever since. And here we are." said Curtis. "There's really nothing else to tell, but if you can bare to take a closer look at what we do still have in the form of our unimaginably valuable Templar artefacts, including a *golden casket with in-built blades that can deliver death in one swoosh,* you will be able to wow the world, whether a strange skull is there or not."

"Are you not angry that he has stolen the actual relic?" asked another reporter. Curtis thought for a split second how best to answer this question.

"Yes of course we are." he said. "But we are also happy about what we do have. If the weird skull, which we still believe is a 15th Century hoax by the way, somehow is reunited with the casket, then that finishes off what is a stunning little exhibit for such a small museum such as ours, don't you think?"

"This all bears a remarkable similarity to your stone exhibit you have here too, doesn't it?" asked yet another reporter, and one Curtis didn't recognise.

"Sorry, and you are?" asked Curtis.

"John Howard Caine, Paratimes Magazine." said the man.

"Paratimes?" asked Curtis.

"So we reported on your last significant discovery of a stone with alleged paranormal properties found in the Amazon." said the man. "The one you weren't able to recover for scientific study." Curtis remained quiet, to allow the man to continue, as he wasn't sure which way this conversation was going to head. "It seems like this new discovery is taking a similar route in terms of both the paranormal and the lack of the actual item." continued the man. There was now a silent excitement building amongst the throng of journalists, in the background began a muttering of conversation, all with Curtis as the subject.

"Ok." managed Curtis. "Sorry, was there a question in there somewhere?"

"Well, firstly, is there a link?" he asked. Curtis thought for a moment. This question caught him a little by surprise, but he remained guarded with his answer.

"Well I suppose I'm the link, really." he said.

"What, in that you found them both? Or is there more to it?" asked the journalist.

"I don't know, you're the paranormalist, or whatever you want to call yourself, you tell me. Is there a link?" asked Curtis, turning the question around to try to gauge what the man knew.

"There could be. You could have the gift." said the man. Curtis laughed.

"Well some would say I'm very gifted, yes, however there are others close to me who would indeed argue that fact." he said, and began to walk away in an attempt to end the conversation.

"Mr. Craxford," pressed the journalist, "There are some people in this world who can channel energies that allow passage

211

to and from other plains of existence; other realms, the spirit realm being one of them."

"Ok, John, this is a little tangential for tonight. Would you like to book a meeting?" said Curtis, removing his mobile phone from his suit pocket.

"Yes, I think that would benefit both of us." said the journalist.

"Great, well if you could pop over and book a meeting with Miss Ashcroft, my press guru, then we can meet in the next couple of weeks." said Curtis, placing his phone back into his pocket and heading off to the temporary bar area where he helped himself to a glass of white wine, which he winced at the moment he took a large gulp, although it didn't stop him finishing it quickly and taking another.

He leaned his elbow onto the bar, willing the bout of anxiety-infused nausea to pass, whilst outwardly enjoying the evening as he watched the guests marvel at the beauty of the golden casket and the other items. He watched the short loop of videos, mainly shot on his phone, showing himself, Naomi, Amy and Stuart Cassidy in the various situations they found themselves in over the period of a couple of months as they gradually solved the cryptic clues they were presented with. Another jolt of anxiety hit him as he saw Cassidy's face on the screens, which he attempted to stifle with more wine.

"How's my Crackers?" asked a familiar voice behind him, causing him to jump as he turned to see Amy in a shockingly bright and revealing red dress.

"Christ!" he said, taken by surprise.

"No, Amy." she said, smiling and leaning across him to take a glass of wine for herself. "How are you doing?"

"Ah I'm ok." he said, trying to sound as enthusiastic as he could as another mental recap of the events of Loch Ness flashed in his mind's eye and he physically winced for a moment.

"The exhibition looks great." she said. "Although, I wish I'd spent more time on my hair on some of your videos, had I known they were to be projected onto cinema screens on a loop at a press night." Curtis managed a weak laugh in response. "Look, Curtis, don't beat yourself up about... doing what you did, ok?" said Amy. Curtis met her gaze. "You did what you had to do." she added with an intensity that reminded him of his early meetings with Cassidy. And there it was; another pang of emotions flooded his cerebrum as he looked at his dear friend. *You don't know the half of it.*

"If only it was the skull of Bacchus, eh?" said Curtis. "Then we would have had some fun." He added, referring to the god of wine and debauchery, trying to keep the conversation light.

"Look, Curtis, we know the skull is gone." Said Amy in hushed tones. "But if they ever do find Stuart, surely his narrative will be dismissed as the ramblings of a madman!" she added. "He comes across as someone with poor mental health, but he's not a bad person."

"We're all bad in someone's story." Said Curtis. "It just depends who you talk to."

"Oh god, Curtis, *glass-half-full* mate!" said Amy, looking around herself and chuckling, unaware of the true turn of events. "Are you a digeridoo or a digeridon't?" Curtis frowned at her and opened his mouth to unload a lung full of sarcasm at Amy's terrible pun-infused pep talk, but she hadn't finished. "Do you dance the can-can or the can't-can't?"

He simply sighed and managed a nod in reply, and then some people meandering nearby caught his attention. "Sorry, Amy, I'm going to have to go schmooze." he said, and left her at the bar.

He welcomed the individuals, who were all high up in English Heritage that he had spent the last two months sweet-talking after the locations of the various finds made it out into the public domain, who he approached as they stood watching the screens. After a significant donation to the Heritage and a few items traded and loaned to their properties from the Craxford Vaults, they finally agreed to allow the display of the exhibition to be at Craxford Museum, as long as their name was also included, and that Lindisfarne and Brinkburn Priory were both well publicised throughout.

The Duke and Duchess of Northumberland, who were not in attendance that night, however representatives of the estate were most certainly present, had also taken an awful lot of persuading and a significant bout of what Curtis had called *brown-nosing* before they was satiated from the 'robbery at Hulne'.

Yet here they all were at his little museum, this time placed firmly on the international map due to their most exciting acquisitions, and all the other patrons dressed in their finery, enthusing and clamouring in their feverish deference of apparent appreciation of something a significant number of them could care very little about: but to be seen was their lasting intent, as these VIP nights always were. This didn't bother Curtis as much as it used to. They were here, the museum was thriving, and he and his fiancee were healthy and alive, which is more than could be said for Stuart Cassidy. Another bout of crippling anxiety hit.

The following day...

Curtis was driving the newest addition to his car collection, and the replacement for his four wheel drive work-horse that was destroyed two months earlier: a less rugged, but much faster, Audi RS6. To the casual onlooker it was a large Audi estate, but to a car enthusiast it was a supercar in practical clothing. And Curtis was happy with his choice.

His anxiety had eased a little after the success of the launch of their newest exhibit, and he began to believe that Cassidy, and the skull, were realistically unlikely to ever be found. The bouts of all-encompassing panic and guilt were becoming less frequent; perhaps once an hour as supposed to every few minutes, and he was beginning to feel slightly more at ease.

Of course, having to walk past the exhibits and re-live the stories over and over and over again on a daily basis was going to feel a little like extreme exposure therapy to him, and having to answer the barrage of questions surrounding the entire story gradually became easier with each rehearsed answer he gave, whether it was to friends, family, patrons or the press.

Curtis was brought back to the present as his telephone rang through his in-car hands free system as he drove home from the museum; telling him that it was an unknown number, and he answered it with a click of a steering wheel button.

"Hello you're speaking to Curtis." he said, already answering their first usual question.

"Mr. Craxford, hello, this is Detective Sergeant Connelly, MIT." said the heavily Scottish voice loudly projected through

214

the car's speakers. Curtis' blood ran cold in an instant as an electrically charged jolt of utter terror consumed him. He rolled the car to a stop at the side of the road, unable to continue.

"Oh. Hello." he said. "How can I help?"

"As you are aware, I am in charge of the case investigating your missing business partner, Stuart Cassidy." said the detective. There was a brief pause from Curtis before he spoke.

"Have you found him?" he asked.

"I have a few questions for you regarding Mr. Cassidy." He continued, not answering Curtis' question.

"Right. Go ahead." Said Curtis, his hands now physically shaking as he rubbed the back of his head. *This is it, they know. I'm going to prison for the rest of my life.*

"Can you tell me how long you have known Mr. Cassidy?" asked the detective.

"Not long at all, I'd only met him for the first time at the start of July." Said Curtis, desperately trying to flatten the tremor in his voice. "When he approached me at the museum with the parchment he'd found from..."

"So you hadn't had any dealings with him before then?" interrupted the policeman.

"No, none, why?" asked Curtis. *What is this? I've already answered all these questions.*

"And you've had absolutely no contact from him whatsoever since the day of his disappearance?" Continued the policeman, refusing to answer any of Curtis' counter questions.

"No." said Curtis. "What's this about detective?" he added, trying to remain calm.

"I have one last question for you Mr. Craxford." Said the detective, who Curtis had already taken an instant dislike to the moment he met him up by the shores of Loch Ness not long after the incident. Curtis had telephoned the police just before he had reached the shores of the loch, and hastily changed into dry clothes before they had arrived, yet when this Connelly chap had rocked up at the scene, plain clothed and carrying an over-inflated opinion of himself, Curtis hated him almost immediately.

"Ok." He replied.

"Why would we have found a carrier bag of sodden clothes in the wooded area not far from the site of the accident?" asked the detective. At this question another jolt of panic surged through Curtis once again as he felt light-headed with angst, knowing full well they were his clothes that he had quickly changed out of once he returned to shore, discarding them before any of the authorities turned up in case they asked questions. Questions such as the one he had just been asked.

"Sorry a bag of wet clothes? I have no idea." Said Curtis.

"They were expensive, designer clothes. Not the sort someone would idly throw away." Said the detective. "Can you shed any light on that?"

"No, sorry, I'm not sure…"

"We found a receipt in the bottom of the bag, you see, that was from the night before the accident, from the Monster Fish and Chip Company. You know that one?" asked DS Connelly.

"Erm…I think that's…"

"That's a fish and chip shop in Fort Augustus, about 300 yards from the Highland Club? Now I remember you telling us that you stayed there that night, and also that you took fish and chips to Mr Cassidy that evening. Did you purchase them from the Monster Fish and Chip Company Mr. Craxford?"

Shit, shit, shit, shit.

"I…" began Curtis, desperately thinking of a way out, whilst his mind raced with distractions. "...did, yes." He said. "I believe it *was* from the Monster Fish and Chip Company."

"Ok, Mr. Craxford, thank you for your time." Said the detective. "Do me a favour, don't leave the country please, we may need you to help us further with our investigations."

"Sorry, can I just…" started Curtis, but the line went dead before he could finish his question. "Oh Christ." said Curtis to himself, sitting in his car at the entrance to a farmer's field not far from his home.

The next few days were some of the darkest that Curtis had experienced. He had faked a flu virus, and remained at home, unable to leave due to his agoraphobic anxiety. He was convinced, every time his telephone rang, that he was about to be called up to Scotland to be imprisoned for murder. His thinking was not rational; he wouldn't talk to Naomi, who was struggling to balance her work, his work, and the housework, while Curtis stewed in his own disquietude.

But Naomi was no fool. She knew there was something

going on. She knew that it was not flu that was keeping him housebound, but something far greater, and quite possibly far worse. She'd never seen her fiancee like this, but her mother had been prone to bouts of depression, and she could spot the signs a mile off. She had tried to help, but Curtis had shut her out, much to her utter heartbreak.

"Please Curtis, tell me what's going on." said Naomi quietly one evening, as Curtis sat staring into space while the television blared a documentary that would normally have enthralled him. "I can help. Whatever this is, we can work through it."

"Naomi, it's nothing, I'm just tired and frustrated with the situation." he said dismissively.

"Do you remember, back when we first got together, and I was still struggling to come to terms with the fact that my parents had split?" she asked, trying a different approach.

"Yep." said Curtis.

"Remember when I couldn't go out? And I wouldn't return your calls? And you thought I didn't love you?" she said, her voice quivering with emotion. "Well that's how I feel right now, Curtis. I feel like you don't love me. And the thought of you not loving me breaks my heart."

Suddenly, Curtis broke down, as a huge wave of emotions flowed out of him like a dam blown apart by explosive charges. Two months of despair, passion, shame and grief tumbled from him so violently as his walls finally broke and a noise somewhere between a scream and a wail issued forth from him as he allowed himself to finally be naked and ashamed in the arms of the woman he loved so tightly.

"Oh Christ, Curtis, what is it darling?" said Naomi, cradling him almost like an infant. "Come on, nothing can be this bad."

"I killed him." said Curtis, quietly, almost a whisper once he regained enough composure to form a word. "I killed Stuart, out on the loch." Naomi looked him in the eye; hers narrow and searching, his puffy, red and wet with pain. "Say something." said Curtis.

"Good." she said, suddenly.

"Good?" asked Curtis, suddenly confused. His fiancee's unorthodox reaction brought him sharply into the present. "What do you mean good?"

"I mean *good*." she said, this time with more feeling. Curtis looked at her, confused.

"Naomi, this is anything but good." he said. "I'm a murderer."

"Tell me what happened." she said, her face more serious than he had seen for a long time.

Curtis recounted the true turn of events, how not long after his phone call with Naomi, Cassidy had somehow swum the waters and made it onto the boat, the threats, the fight, his opportunist knot tying, and the eventual capsizing of the boat causing the resultant death of Stuart Cassidy. By the end of the story, Curtis was sobbing again.

"You're not a murderer, Curtis." she said, cupping his head and willing the words into his mind where they would hopefully germinate.

"I am." he said.

"You're not. You acted in self defence if anything." she said.

"Naomi I tied a rope around his ankle with a heavy weight on it and then capsized the boat. That's *not* self defence." he said.

"Look, no one knows, ok? No one has to know. The guy was unhinged; he was mentally ill." she said. "Schizophrenia: he was exhibiting classic symptoms of schizophrenia; hearing voices and seeing apparitions. He was becoming dangerous, and if he threatened you, me and Amy, you did the right thing." Curtis shook his head in disagreement. "Curtis, no one needs to know." she reiterated.

"The Scottish police called me a few days back, asking some strange questions." he said. "Naomi, I think they know." he added.

"What did they ask?"

"Once I got back to shore, I was soaked and freezing. I ran to the Alfa and took my spare clothes into the woods. I got changed, bagged up my wet ones, which I left there in the woods. I didn't realise there was a bloody receipt in the carrier bag for the fish and chips I'd bought the night before." said Curtis. "The police found the clothes."

"Well that's not going to tie you to murder, is it Curtis." she said. "It ties you to buying fish and chips, but not to murder.

What did they get, your card details from the receipt?" she asked.

"I paid in cash, so there's no evidence it's mine." he said. "I've already denied that the clothes are mine."

"That was probably a wrong move." said Naomi. "What if there is CCTV somewhere?"

"I thought about that, but I was wearing my other clothes, the ones that were dry that night. I only changed into the other ones the following morning, and then essentially went off grid. I didn't go into any shops. I just went straight to Cassidy's." he said. "I suppose the Highland club may have CCTV though, shit!"

"Look, let's hope the coppers don't go down that route then." said Naomi.

"I was wearing my waterproof!" said Curtis, suddenly. "I kept that! They wouldn't have been able to see what I had on underneath!" he said.

"Good. Probably not worthy of celebration though darling." she said, diagnosing his flighty behaviour as most probably exhaustion.

"What are we going to do Nom?" asked Curtis, placing his hand on her knee as she sat opposite him on the sofa. She leaned forward, wiped away another tear that was slowly rolling its way towards his stubble, and she kissed him.

"Absolutely nothing."

Printed in Great Britain
by Amazon